# THE GREAT LEVEL

Also by Stella Tillyard

# THE GREAT LEVEL

Stella Tillyard

Chatto & Windus
LONDON

1 3 5 7 9 10 8 6 4 2

Chatto & Windus, an imprint of Vintage,
20 Vauxhall Bridge Road,
London SW1V 2SA

Chatto & Windus is part of the Penguin Random House group of companies whose
addresses can be found at global.penguinrandomhouse.com.

First published by Chatto & Windus in 2018

penguin.co.uk/vintage

A CIP catalogue record for this book is available from the British Library

ISBN 9780701183196

Typeset in India by Integra Software Services Pvt. Ltd, Pondicherry

Printed and bound by Clays Ltd, St Ives plc

Penguin Random House is committed to a sustainable future for our business,
our readers and our planet. This book is made from Forest Stewardship
Council® certified paper.

All those who sailed the seas.

*Inscription written by the architect Sostratus; carved on the Pharos lighthouse, Alexandria, 280 BCE*

# *Prologue*

*Nieuw Amsterdam, Manatus Eylandt.*
*The 1st day of April, 1664.*

I am afloat in the Oost Rivier, rocking on the waves, when I hear a
song. Silence covers the city and wraps me in darkness. In front of
me it is still night, but behind me, to the east, all the day stands ready
to arrive. In a moment the sun will burst above the horizon on Lange
Eylandt and the city of Nieuw Amsterdam will wake and stir. By
noon we will feel the thin warmth of April; half winter, and half the
promise of spring. I am happy to be alive on the water and to smell
the salt.

On the sandy shore I find the dry carcass of a horseshoe crab,
hollowed out and turned to the sky. A thousand lives will follow
this death. In a month the horseshoe crabs will come back. The
water will be black with them. Each year they surf the waves,
washing back and forth until they can scramble up the beach with
their blue-and-orange claws. They do not pause after this struggle,
but climb to safety, lay their eggs in the sand and crawl back to the
water. Clouds of seabirds wait for this moment, migrants from
the south. They clatter down and gorge themselves on the eggs,
fattening for their journey. All nature is on the move, restless and
lively.

As I pull my canoe up onto the frosted grass of my orchard, the
song comes again, carrying itself over the lap of the water and my
heavy steps. The melody is unknown to me, but somewhere inside
myself I meet the voice that sings it. I feel certain that it comes from
close by. For a moment I forget where I am, in the New World, in
Nieuw Amsterdam. I feel myself lifted into the past, to the Great
Level, where first I heard that voice.

Back in my own house, enclosed in its walls, it seems to me that the song did not come to me today, but arrived from long ago. The same sound comes and goes, most usually in the quiet of my garret or in the sounds of the flames that murmur in the grate. But I felt certain that I heard that voice today, somewhere between the sea and the land. Then it faded, as it does, and I can only conclude that it came to me on the winds of memory.

And yet around nine by the clock, a boy I know knocks at my door. I answer it myself and let in the sunshine.

'Hendrick.'

The boy takes off his battered beaver hat, worn in imitation of a grown man. Stooping under the lintel, as if he is tall, he enters my hall.

'Mijnheer Brunt, good morning. I have a message from the wharfs.'

'What message?'

'A paper, Mijnheer Brunt. Shall I wait and take a reply?'

The paper he hands me has my name written on the outside, nothing else. The strong penstrokes look familiar. When I hold the paper at arm's length to read I see it tremble.

'Who gave it to you?'

'The boy Frederick, sir. He stays about the wharf, takes messages from the ships' captains into the town and back. He gave me the paper.'

'Why did he not bring it here himself, by which he might have told me who put it in his hand?'

'He said he had no time, sir. There are ships just arrived from the north, as well as the usual traffic.'

I read the note again.

'I want you to return to the wharfs. Find Frederick and ask who gave him this letter. Then come back to me.'

Hendrick nods and turns to go. He ducks under the lintel with a grin that acknowledges his game of being full grown. I watch him run off down the path along the Heere Gracht. He knows I will give him a coin when he returns.

I am an engineer and a measured man of the world. I prefer to weigh everything in the balance, to calculate and to plan. Yet my own heart is going faster than I can now count. I am at a loss for what to do, though the words of the note are plain enough.

*Finding myself in New Amsterdam with business to transact, I intend, if time permits in the next weeks, to pay you a visit after many years.*

The paper shakes again as I stare at it. There is no signature, no place of dispatch, yet I run out of my open door as if I might see someone pass who can explain it. The scene outside is the same as it is every day. At the end of my path I see across the canal and to the houses on the other side. Everything lies somnolent in the morning sun. Nothing has changed except inside myself.

I call for coffee and climb up to my garret. Waiting for my house-keeper's heavy tread on the stairs and knock at the door, I look about the room and place myself amongst the familiar things there, which steadies my heart and quietens it. Feeling the note in my hand now all crumpled and twisted by my agitation, I lay it on the table and smooth it out.

# PART ONE

# Chapter 1

*Nieuw Amsterdam, Manatus Eylandt.*
*The colony of Nieuw Nederland in America.*
*The 1st day of April, 1664.*
*A fair day in prospect.*
*The sky clear, the wind, by my weather vane, from the east.*
*High tide by the Stadt Huys at 20 minutes after 1 o'clock.*

I have lived, for almost a dozen years, here in the colony of Nieuw Nederland, that we call the New World, though it is rightly only new to us, being as old as all creation. This, the city of Nieuw Amsterdam, is sited on the Eylandt of Manatus. It is truly not much of a city: to call it such is the pride of the inhabitants, or the way they talk in letters home. It is a town, most on the firm ground, but in part, as is our Dutch way, on land we have drained. I dare say that before long, if the colony grows and survives the difficult times, we will begin to take land from the sea both as protection and out of habit.

When I think as a Dutchman, if such I am still, I know that it is not other nations that we Dutch dream of conquering, or other peoples. Our real enemy and our best companion is something quite different: the force of nature itself. We have been compelled for centuries to attempt the separation of land and water wherever we find them muddled up. This is our struggle; this our way of being. Here in the New World there is surely land enough for all. Mountains and plains, hills and huge valleys, it is supposed, stretch away beyond the western horizon in a vastness never seen before. They bring fear and entrancement for some. Yet we Dutch turn the other way. We seek out the waterlines: shores, rivers, estuaries and marshes.

So it is no surprise that from my garret window I look down on the canal that my men dug from a filthy stream and embanked as my contract demanded. It's a strip of water, the Heere Gracht, jewelled silver in the morning sun. I ran it straight south to the river's edge, clean and simple, as befits an engineer. At the shore, where once the land slid under the water in a disorderly way, the two are now divided by pilings that have given Manatus Eylandt a firm edge all round its tip. Such is the purpose of embanking: to make an edge, a clear boundary and separation.

Beyond the confines of Nieuw Amsterdam, marsh, sand and river still mingle raggedly up the island's eastern side. There, twice a day, the tide pushes up the ribbony creeks and into the marshes. The glistening brown mud waits, and welcomes the water. When the tide goes out the flats are dappled with gulls and egrets sucking up worms and shrimp. Their cries reach me in my attic in the early morning, and through the darkness, with the casement open, comes the quock-quock of night herons searching for crabs. This is still a small place, two thousand souls. The shore and the sea are right there, beyond the wharfs and the wall. They wait, as once the flood waited, for the call to rise and cover the earth. One day the flood will come again. This is the knowledge that a Dutchman always has.

I have been in possession here long enough to call this place my home, though it is inside my house, more than on these streets, that I am myself, which is all that I wish for. Nieuw Amsterdam cannot be like the old city of Amsterdam, though the people still have the voices of their homes, the *ne* and *ja*, *goedemorgen* and *goedenavond* when the sun sinks beyond the far bank of the Noort Rivier. The very first to come here in the ship the *Halve Maen* also brought the flags that flew from the Fort and the Stadt Huys in bands of orange, white and blue.

That was half a century ago, and Nieuw Amsterdam flourishes in many respects, and now begins to grow. The better sort among the houses, such as mine is, in every way resemble those that were left behind, with gabled ends proud onto the street, high stoops and half-doors for the summer. Tall windows flank the front door, with sturdy casements and the clearest glass to be found here. I have tacked a brass plate to the door with my name and profession: *Jan Brunt, Ingenieur*. Along with the hinges of my doors and the clasps on my windows, this plate is polished so bright that the clouds may be observed running across it, or a face reflected if it comes up close.

On the first floor of my house stand three more windows and another in the gable end where the year of building, 1654, is finely writ in curling iron numbers, bolted into the bricks. On the gable top stands my weather vane, by which each morning I see at a glance how the wind blows. Behind my house I grow vegetables and fruit trees, sheltering them with a fine wall and taking advantage of the western sun. Tulips and other tender bulbs do not flourish here, or flower once only. I lift them for the hottest summer months, when they lie cool in my cellar like gentleman's claret, and replant them in the autumn, yet they come back too tall and without strength.

Inside, too, the houses are much the same as you might see in Leiden or in Delft. New World oak makes good dense flooring, and the carpets on the tables are come from the East Indies as do those at home. Our hearths are tiled in blue and milky white. More than anything, more even than the portraits and little landscapes transported in trunks and boxes, these tiles bring Holland here. Sitting by my fire I can lean close to its canals and windmills, its dogs and children, soldiers, scholars and skiffs at sea. Each blue brushstroke is tender and familiar to me, like a touch on the cheek.

Much is taken from old Amsterdam, but not the light, or the wind, or its long low sky. Even as a child I knew my home, its extent and look on the map. 'That is Holland,' I could say to myself. I knew its shape, the round blue scoop of the Zuyder Zee, and the splayed fingers of the River Rhine that stretched into the sea.

So familiar was the picture of Holland in my mind, that I did not pay it any heed. Only when I came here to the New World did I understand the comfort of that shape, its borders drawn in black or red. Here we are, it says; here we are snug and safe, and beyond the lines lies something different. Here one thing ends and another begins. Mark it well and preserve it well.

In the New World we are just beginning to make our edges safe in this very small part, four or five islands with that of Manatus at the centre. Of the rest we can say little and draw less. We know the rivers well enough, and the great lakes in the northern areas. We know there is another side, and I have seen a map of it; but what lies between, the great immensity of it, is unknown. Sometimes men appear in Nieuw Amsterdam with tales of high mountains and huge animals, but they may be liars or tell fantastic stories for the fame of it.

There was a man here, a trader in furs with a large fortune, who determined to get across to the far coast discovered by fanatic Spanish missionaries. He talked of nothing else but the journey and his desire to make out the whole shape of America once and for all and then to establish settlements therein. The wildmen, with their vagueness in matters of distance, were no good to him in his preparations. He showed them a map of the two coasts and the blank between, but they shrugged, not knowing what a map might be; or perhaps, wishing him to leave that land to them, they turned away. So he would have to do it himself, make the journey and the map.

One fine autumn day about five years ago he set off, crossed the Noort Rivier and struck west. I never heard of him again. Somewhere his bones lie in that space, unless he went south to the French territories or somehow made it to safety. We still do not know what this great land looks like, neither with our own eyes, nor in the way that map makers have it appear, stretched out on paper.

So I live with the unknown at my back, yet happily. I have determined, this April morning, with the note next to me on my table, to record what occurred, and let nothing remarkable escape me. The *wilde mannen*, the wildmen who inhabit the lands beyond the city, say that the sun sees all things. I wish, then, to be a bit like the sun; to see all things, to write them down, and also to record the cloudy world in our hearts that so often cannot come to the surface but shakes life from below.

Today the sun shines across my table onto the inkstand, with my pens and the sand that blots the ink. The pen I hold is my companion, balanced and patient. Words spread from its beak across the paper and follow the twisted ribbon of my life as the maiden Ariadne followed the thread, back to where I start. Word by word my scratches make a shape, a history that comes to me in the form I have writ it.

Oh, how small a word is and how much it must carry. I picture one curled in a basket, weighing almost nothing, though a whole heart might lie in it. Little wonder then that I often score my words through impatiently, or exchange one for another. A man may put a whole thing in language and still find it does not fit what he wishes to say.

It is difficult, but I have time. I am not a man of words, though I have made my peace with them. Often I cannot catch the sort of chatter that falls through the air. I am uneasy in gatherings where talk and laughter are loud and swelling. I aim for solidity, and trust to things that can be measured. I like to pace out the world, understand it with the soles of my feet and my compass and rope. If not that, in other ways, with the tips of my fingers.

This morning, the cuff of my gown moves across the desk with a dry murmur. This gown is deep blue, indigo dyed, and lined in silk the colour of ivory. Layers of wool are packed between the silks like pages of a book. I describe it thus precisely because, wearing it every day in winter and on brisk spring mornings when the wind hits us from Lange Eylandt and the ocean beyond, it is become a part of me. Beneath, I'm all black and white; stockings and breeches black, a fine Virginia cotton shirt – white if the girl Griete has done her work – and underneath there is my own nakedness, as nature sees it. There I am a big-built man, and am in height also much taller than most of my countrymen, who are in the main a squat people. My hair is grey and falls to the shoulder in the manner of men here. I have not grown a beard, but shave myself each morning before the glass, a square of muslin round my neck, the razor sharpened daily on its stone. Facing out at me from the glass I see a man counting through his forty-fourth year. I am not yet old, but neither in the prime of life. I am somewhere in between, though I regard it not. My own person interests me little; it is all beyond me that makes up the horizon of my eye.

Here, as in every place, it pleases me to order the day. I rise early, for I sleep ill, and have done for several years, and do not like to lie in bed. If it is fine and already warm I may throw on my gown and take a turn around the garden, where I check the plants and enjoy the quiet half-light before dawn. On other days, and in the winter, I light the stove in my garret and heat the jug of coffee left from yesterday. Then the day will unfold according to my duties and inclinations.

Once she arrives and has the range heated, my housekeeper Lysbet Thyssen brings me hot water with San Domingo ginger. When she first came to work for me, I showed her how I like it. I snap a finger off the tuber or take a slice of it, and peel away the rind, then cut the flesh to small cubes and pour the boiling water onto them. I have noticed that a tuber of ginger, once cut, puts forth immediately tentative filaments into the world. One might think that the amputated part this way seeks what is lost or, like a person young at heart, straight off puts forth a new shoot.

With the ginger I have a slice of dark bread, with butter at its side and a piece of honeycomb like a rich man's ruff, sometimes from my neighbour's hive, most often from the wildmen who bring it in. I have watched the wildmen harvest honey, contriving to smoke out the inhabitants of the hive before lowering it from the trees. At the appointed time, if I am at home, Lysbet comes with coffee, fresh ground in the pestle – and so we go on in an orderly fashion.

With Lysbet Thyssen I have an understanding. Her husband Maryn having died, she came to work for me some years ago. She brings her apron with her each day, rolled and ironed. Lysbet is a well set-up widow of forty-five, a buxom, bustling woman with broad calves and curls tucked under her bonnet. I know well that she would like more from me than wages, but though I have shared my bed with her on some occasions, I do not allow her a way to my heart, and marriage I can never contemplate. This she discerns though we do not speak of the matter. I have my joys and pains and she has hers. It will do no good for them to be mixed together.

On the hearth before the stove I have left a few shells, delicate and waxy, each half of a hinged pair. They might be wings of angels, white as the moon. On a shelf set into the wall encrusted objects lie scattered. Some are pitted old things – buckles, buttons and keys; others are coins, fused together like bunched petals. Copper gleams green through the ancient earth that clings to them, hard as stone; they seem not to have decayed in the ground, though lying, perhaps, for hundreds of years. Next to them stands a pottery vessel, light brown in colour, scored round the neck and open at the top. It once housed human ashes, buried in the ground from where I took it.

Lysbet asked me once why I keep these objects and I replied that they are a warning that all the things of this world will come to dust. Yet it seems to me today as I look that they will not decay, but rather endure for ever.

It is the two figures propped by the stove that always draw my eye; two women who seem from another world. One is carved from some crystalline rock, the other made of fired clay. The clay woman stands on stumps of legs, her arms insignificant. Most of her is massed round her long breasts and hanging belly. The gash of her belly button looks like an opening to the underworld, that of her mouth like a wound.

The other woman is cut from crystal. She is fish-like and liquid in comparison to the rough clay of the first, and cool to the touch, even in summer. Breasts, stomach, hips, buttocks and thighs grow from one another in smooth egg shapes; legs fused like a mermaid's tail, pinhole eyes. She is a sea creature flung up from the deep, ancient and suspicious. While I write at the table, the note before me, she watches and waits, impassive, through the morning.

Hendrick comes back at midday. He is dragging his heels in a jaunty way.

'Well?'

'Nothing. Frederick cannot remember who gave him the paper, only that the having your name on the front made it easy, and so he gave it to me.'

Hendrick looks at me with curiosity. I cast my eyes down to the path, not wishing him to see anything that might pass across my face, then right myself and dig about in the pocket of my gown for a few coins.

'I thank you, Hendrick. If you hear anything, or if Frederick does, come back and tell me.'

'Of course, Mijnheer Brunt.'

Hendrick takes off his old hat and stows the coins in its lining. He is a boy used to fighting, and spends his days roaming the city. He lives off its scraps and sometimes its kindness, though he takes no heed of that. I watch him put the hat back on his head and run off down the path, and think that Nieuw Amsterdam is a good place to hide things. And this holds true for me as well as for him.

Nature, the whole of our earth, is full of an intelligence that I try to discover. Each day I estimate the rise of the water by the Stadt Huys by means of a device I have set in the wharf there, and so record the hours of high and low tide. My friend, Albert Jansen, a man of parts who built the two windmills beyond the Fort, makes the same observations at his jetty on Staaten Eylandt. These, together with the speed of the wind and the lunar calendar, we compare when Albert comes to my door by the Heere Gracht.

I do more. Each day, if not abroad on business, I write the temperature of the air at first light and then again when the sun is at its highest. These observations I have written in the form of a table each year since my arrival. I am the first man ever to make record of the climate of Manatus Eylandt, its excesses and variations. This precedence pleases me as a toy does a child, though I know it is vanity. The wildmen of this place plant their corn and harvest it without knowledge of recorded time or the months of the year. Neither do they talk of distance as we mark it out along the ground. I have seen them observe me take my measurements, but they do not linger long in looking, saying that everything needful is shown to them by nature.

# Chapter 2

*Tholen Eylandt, Zeeland, Nederland.*
*The 6th day of May, 1649.*
*Wind from the North. Overcast.*

To start, not at the beginning, but a long time ago. Here is a portrait, since we Dutch are so fond of them. Jan Brunt, engineer, painted in words by himself, and so depicted with the mixture of kindness and cruelty we afford ourselves. This Brunt faces out of the picture with as steady a gaze as he can pretend to. He is cloaked in brown velvet for the outdoors, his hair loose over his shoulders, eyes (though the painter may have mistaken them) a pebbly mixture of brown and blue. In his right hand he holds his drawings. Some of them are fantastical, over-embellished with scrolls and flowers, or fleets of merchantmen in the distance. That is to say they are the work of a young man who wants to impress. Yet they offer proof that, as far as embanking and drainage are concerned, he has not wasted his time.

You don't see his feet, just the turned, loose tops of his soft leather boots. And he is standing somewhere known only to the painter, on neither land nor water. We must presume an embankment, which suits him. Behind him a bristling river flows, whipped into grey waves by the paintbrush. A pair of small boats, leaned over in the breeze, work along the waterway from left to right. Tiny figures stand in the sterns, two in brick-red jackets, two in black; flicks of colour against the russet sails. Beyond the river the painter has added a thin grey slice of land. That's my island, Tholen, rising (a very little) from the Oosterschelde estuary, one of the flatlands that sit between the channels of the many-fingered river as it slows towards the sea. Tholen is man's work as well as the river's, its mud solidified with pilings and filled in with estuary silt. Who knows any more what nature gave and what the islanders took. They have protected and farmed it well, built villages and windmills.

A grey church spire and a smudge of gabled houses stand black against the sky. But all this is not the real interest of the painting, and neither am I. A palace of clouds rises through the pale blue, pushed along by the wind. The sky and the clouds are what the painter loves best. He is a virtuoso of the heavens. To be sure I stand there in the middle, but only because I paid the painter and the sky cannot.

My village, dabbed out on the horizon, is reached from where I stand first by a ferry and then by bridges. The ferry takes me across the main river and the bridges straddle the dykes. Once across the Oosterschelde it's about twenty minutes' brisk walk from the bank opposite where the painter places me. Amongst that smudge of houses stands the one where I was born and grew up. It is too far away to show clear in the painting, but just by the open front door stand my mother Beatris, and Isaac Brunt, my father. Katrijn, who is only five, hangs onto my mother's skirts. Anna and Margriet stand by my father, hand in hand.

I am leaving and they are here to say goodbye. My sisters are excited by my departure, and I have told them that when I return I will bring them a present each. 'What sort of present?' Anna asks, and I say I don't know yet, I will have to see what she might like. She is seven years old now, but when I return in a year, or two or three, she will be nearly a woman and her wishes will be fitted to her new age. Margriet, who is thirteen, asks for a fan like the one my mother holds, tortoiseshell and red silk, bound together with ribbons.

My mother does not smile or encourage. She stands inside a velvet gown, its folds full of shadows. My father will send me off with few words. He does not demand to hear from me and anyway, he might say, the stretch of sea that will now separate us is the same water that surrounds our own island. It is not as if I am going among strangers. Across the street live Giles and Sarah Vermuyden. My family is connected to Sarah by marriage, and so to Mr Vermuyden, whose kinsman directs the work I am leaving for. It is Sarah who has helped me; a favour to the whole family, my mother has said.

A chill rests in the air around my mother and father. I have never found a way to them through that cold, and now it is time to go. I kiss my sisters, this cheek, that and this again; first Anna and Margriet, then Katrijn, who runs circles round my legs. I catch her as she ducks past, throw her high and kiss her as she comes down. Then, with my father, a nod. Last there is my mother, who has waited. She does not kiss me, but brushes my cheeks with hers, then steps back into the shadow where I lose her.

Four days later I stand before a polished mahogany door open to a panelled room. I am just that morning disembarked at Greenwich, rowed with the incoming tide to Puddle Dock by the Blackfriars and directed on to St Paul's churchyard. I see the great length of the room signalled by three brass chandeliers that hang at equal intervals. Their branches gleam in a pale sun that comes and goes through four long windows. Even in my unease I count and measure: three chandeliers; four windows; twenty paces. At the far end stands a man in black velvet with a long-toothed lace collar. He is severe, as befits those heartsick days in England.

It is time now to advance towards him. My courage falters when I hear the loud knock and echo of my heels on the wooden floor. The room has been stripped of softness and the noise bounces off the panelling. Alert to the habits of estuaries and seas, I smell the salty tidewater from the river as I pass the open windows. Cornelius Vermuyden waits, and looks me up and down. Then, when I come near, he grasps my arm, pulls me towards him and asks after my parents. It seems impossible, as I look at him, that he ever lived on Tholen or knows its mud and sand. He looks rich and well washed, and too quick in his movements for the patient work we are trained in.

'Here you are then, Jan. Are you ready to start?' He does not wait for an answer, but goes on, 'How do you find London? Nothing compared to Amsterdam?'

How do I find this city? Scarcely seen this breezy May morning, though I walked into the cathedral as I made my way here. A great part of the roof is all tumbled down and lying in piles on the floor. Struts from the vaulting stick up into the sky. Pigeons perch on the brick columns that supported the vaults and clatter away in a dirty arc when I come close. Half the floor tiles have been lifted and stolen. Dust and feathers rise from my boots.

The ruination horrifies me. God has deserted this place. Groups of people huddle in the side aisles where the roofs still remain, indistinct under woollen cloaks. Some use a pew or two to mark a space; others hang thin walls of hessian between the tombs. I realise that they live here. They have been displaced in the late wars, perhaps, too poor to find other lodging. At the end of the nave I find an open preaching place without chairs, benches or a lectern. People here must stand and listen, hats in hand. It is not a place for dreams or napping. It is a place for words alone. The remains of the great organ hang twisted off the wall.

The cathedral of St Paul is broken and the churchyard desolate. Stumps of trees stripped for firewood stand barren over the grave-stones. The sky races above the tapered spire. A wind, as quick as fear, is getting up from the west. It is too cold for spring and the people glance upwards with troubled wonder.

So what do I think of London? I think nothing yet, but I feel unease. I shall not venture a reply because I dislike haste, and am concerned above all to make my way here. I think of Amsterdam, alive with glass and water and the talk of citizens. The Dutch have made Amsterdam from the land, shaped clay into bricks that repel the damp. The city smells of prosperity, of cheese and milk and spices. Damasks and pearls shimmer in the light. Laughter and tobacco smoke pour from tavern windows. In London, rotting timber houses lean towards one another across the alleys. The plaster between the beams and struts is stained with soot. People hurry along in worsted and wool; if silk is underneath I cannot see it.

Mr Vermuyden does not seem much interested in an answer to his question; perhaps he has forgotten it already. His plump fingers drift across the surface of a table next to him. After a pause he asks about my work. His voice has lost the furriness of our Dutch; now it is quick and nasal.

'I have not called you here on a whim, Mijnheer Brunt.'

I incline my head.

'Yet I did not wish to commit the details of my proposal to writing.'

I can only nod again as Vermuyden tells me he needs engineers to take on a task that will be arduous and long. He must know, for he has only to ask his kinsman, that though I have advanced well since I am become a master engineer, I have never yet had charge of any part of a large project.

'You wish to know of my education, sir?'

'Not really, Mijnheer Brunt, but tell me anyway for form's sake.'

So I tell him that I learned the principles of mathematics from my earliest years at school and then, finding that I had an affinity with numbers and measurement, progressed to the Duytsche Mathematique in the Engineering School at the University of Leiden. I stand a little taller as I say these words, finding that I am proud of all my learning, the selections from Euclid's *Elements,* the constructions with ruler and compass, the art of trigonometry and the months spent outside on the practice of surveying. I do not mention the art of fortification, which every student at the Mathematique was required also to study. The wars in England being finished I cannot see that it will be of any use here.

My studies made me skilled at surveying and I added my own talent at drawing upon the best linen paper Leiden supplied. That is to say, I made plans beautiful by adding those fanciful elements that I mentioned. The drawing teachers at the university taught me to give clients a picture of what they want. Though the first map of any place shows the present moment, a plan of works shows the future. Such is the distinction between a map and a plan. Drawings on plans are visions of a place as it will be. I like them to show my work perfected. No wonder they serve me better than any speech, a matter in which, my mother often tells me, I am deficient. I add colour to my plans and roll them out with a flourish. Though I do not speak much I always add that I am first a master engineer and only then a map maker.

Apprenticed to my master Claes Van Nes, I was soon given charge of making the plans and maps. How beautiful I showed the future to be; and how tranquil. I never now draw cannons or swords, never the fields I am going to make trampled by war or made hateful by dispute. For a rich client I like to make three drawings; the first the map, the second the plan, the last the plan perfected into a new world. My drawings offer peace and plenty. They show my clients their desires, not what might be if fortune does not favour them.

There is no table here except that next to Vermuyden, so I can only hold out my roll of papers as an offering that puts me at a disadvantage.

Vermuyden takes it, and carries on talking.

'My sister Sarah has no doubt told you of my work here?'

'She admires what you have done, sir, and has herself shown me the map you sent of your reclamations at Oxenholme.'

'Axholme, since you mention it. Axholme, in the county of Lincolnshire, some hundred miles north of where we now sit. But that was not my first work, Giles and Sarah could have told you. I had to start, as you perhaps have done, with riverbanks; with the Thames here.'

He looks towards the window.

'The Thames is a shifty river, faster flowing than the Scheldt, treacherous and liable to flood. My first work was repairing the sea wall at Dagenham, a neat and simple job of piling and embanking. It served as something to show Joas Croppenburg, though he need not have put me through that, as a relative. You have at least heard of him?'

It is a great relief to be able to say that I have. Our family branches part and then come together again. Croppenburg is not just a relative of Vermuyden but of myself as well, another man my mother has held up as an example. 'Look,' she would say to me (my father saying nothing), 'see how Mijnheer Croppenburg set out for London from Amsterdam with a few fine buckles and some introductions in his pocket. He was soon selling pearls and diamonds and all manner of precious trinkets along with his buttons and bows.'

How quick Croppenburg was, my mother said, to put his profit into land. Here she looked at me to make sure I heard what she said, as a mother and a Dutchwoman. There is nothing more precious than land, she said; nothing more ingenious than taking it from the sea. Croppenburg knew this better than the Englishmen he lived among, and summoned his kinsman and ours – Vermuyden.

'You won't find Croppenburg in London now, Jan,' Vermuyden says, suddenly familiar. 'He has gone to ground somewhere, though he will be back if times change.'

'I see, sir,' I say, although I do not.

'Well, back then,' Vermuyden says, 'twenty years ago now, Croppenburg put me to work on Canvey Island, a wretched pancake of mud at the mouth of the Thames that any Dutchman would long ago have made something of. I strengthened it on the river side – the usual stuff: chalk, limestone, clay, timber pilings, ragstone for solidity. Then, once the river was kept out, I turned my attention to the land, to ditching, filling, draining.'

Mr Vermuyden glances out of the window again. Does he see Canvey Island out there, as if it had been towed into the city in proof?

'Between the embanking and the draining I made new land and enriched old. Croppenburg gave me in recompense a portion of the pasture, which yields a good income from tenant farmers. That's a piece of advice for you.'

Vermuyden makes sure I am paying attention.

'Never take specie payment, young man, if you can get the land instead. You will be familiar with the principle, though too young as yet to go without a salary.'

'Indeed, sir. My mother has expressed the same sentiment.'

'Good. It is no more than I expect of a sensible Dutchwoman. Money passes through your fingers like water; land sticks.'

'Yes, sir.'

'Croppenburg lives on his rents now. The war made his business hard and the King's death has finished it off. Few dare to walk abroad with any jewellery these days, as you will see. It's land that will get him through.'

I nod and wait. I do not say that I have no particular interest in buying land or even in my salary. It is the subtle combat, the tussle between land and water, that catches and holds me tight. Mr Vermuyden also says nothing and a silence gathers between us that I do not know how to fill.

Then he adds, almost in a drawl, 'The present scheme is altogether larger than anything I have undertaken. It is brought about by General Cromwell himself in alliance with several Gentlemen Adventurers. You will have acquainted yourself with its whole history during the late war.'

'Only a little; I know a start was made.'

Vermuyden looks up sharply at this. 'Yes, indeed, a start was made; and a stop too. A very bad business. But now we begin again.'

At that Vermuyden walks towards me, full of energy all of a sudden. 'We are ordered to make a scheme for the draining of the Great Level, a large expanse, being in total area some five hundred square miles in the English way of measuring.'

'That is a vast area, sir.'

'Indeed, Jan, it is. We start with nothing, for it is a great wilderness of fen that stretches from the city of Ely to the North Sea, and as wide again from side to side. That is a great chunk of England. A Dutchman would not credit it lying unimproved. Yet so it is, and now affords little benefit to the realm other than fish and fowl, being for the most part great sheets of water called there meres.'

'Is it a lived wilderness, or at present water only?'

'It is inhabited, yes, Jan; but, the island of Ely excepted, inhabited by a lazy and barbarous people who trap eels and other such trash foods.'

'Does not the place belong in some manner to these people, sir?'

'Indeed not, or only by custom, for much rightly belongs, as underwater, to the realm, having formerly been the property of the King.'

Vermuyden takes a turn around the room.

'The people there are few in number, and of concern only to the Adventurers, who now propose to bring the whole place into proper cultivation. We will make order where at present there is none. No person shall lose their life in floods, no islands drown. It will be an immense labour, the like of which this country has never seen.'

He pauses and adds, 'There is a profit in it for both of us, Jan; a profit in land and standing. You cannot ask that any labour in the world should give you more.'

With the fatigue of the day and the confusion of talk that seems so often to say one thing and mean another, my mind becomes vacant. Although I know that I should feel the happiness that comes with the prospect of work for which I am fitted, I struggle to thank Vermuyden, or say anything at all.

Vermuyden brings me back to the room when he taps my roll of maps and drawings on his velvet thigh. I am proud of my drawings and now wish that he would unroll them. I am looking for praise as a son does from a father, but Vermuyden seems uninterested in my past. The present and the need for speed engross him. Our family connection, and not the work I have done, stands surety for me.

'So tell me now, Jan. Do you wish to work for the Gentlemen Adventurers? Don't dally about. I cannot keep company with ditherers.'

'I am willing, sir.'

Vermuyden nods and then kisses me on both cheeks in a distant way, not holding me close to him but leaning towards me as if to dispatch the action as quickly as he can.

'Well done, Jan; well done. Go now. I will have reports of your progress.'

'Are we not to meet again before I go?'

'I find no need for it. Set out at first light tomorrow. The journey will take you two days, the roads being very bad outside London. Jacob Van Hooghten will meet you at Ely.'

'Jacob Van Hooghten?'

'He works for me and you will work for him. He can explain the whole to you and get you started.'

'I should like to meet others of the Gentlemen who I shall answer to.'

Vermuyden puts my maps down on the table next to him with a slap of impatience. He is a heavy man, with leg-of-mutton calves. He has a dozen children, my mother says, and one of them fought with General Cromwell in the late wars.

'They are far above your head, Jan. You are an engineer; a master engineer, to be sure, and trained in the best schools, but nothing more. These men are not engineers; there is little they can say that would be of any use to you. Some of them know the Great Level, others think of it as they might a plantation in the New World; an empty place that will be a new land. They intend to take a profit from it, nothing more nor less. They are merchants or gentlemen. You might pass them in the city here and they would look like other men. Money is what they offer and you have no need to know more than that.'

'Their names?'

'All on the contract that I will have sent down to you. But it matters little. The chief of them is the Earl of Bedford; a man more merchant than lord, who smells a profit from a distance and has few scruples about heading towards it. But you will likely never see him. General Cromwell heads the company of Adventurers and has himself entrusted this scheme to me. We must begin. Summer is on the way and there is now enough dry land to make a tolerable survey.'

I understand that I have the position and that I am dismissed. I look at the roll of papers on the table and summon my courage.

'You wish to check my drawings, Mijnheer Vermuyden?'

Vermuyden picks up my papers and glances at me, then puts them down again.

'No, no. Van Nes has given his word. Besides, we are related.'

I say nothing and do not ask for my papers, anxious that my disappointment stays inside.

'I have arranged a lodging for you by Charing Cross,' Vermuyden says. 'The Rose Tavern; usually so full of our countrymen you can hear them from the street. When you get up to Ely, find Van Hooghten and put yourself on an easy footing with him.'

So there is nothing else to be done but to bow, and turn, and walk away, which I do with a heart full of foreboding. Had I more experience of such work I might feel easier, but it is not even that, perhaps. It is more a sense of being alone in this city, no person or place nearby that I understand. I vow to begin my work as soon as possible, which is what Mr Vermuyden wishes. Measuring and mapping, steady and patient labour, will give me a feeling of ease greater than any contemplation of the final rewards.

# Chapter 3

*London.*
*The 10th day of May, 1649.*
*Wind from the west with rain to come.*

Outside in St Paul's churchyard I wrap myself tight in my worsted cloak, for the company of the cloth and because now the storm is nearly here. I stop a passer-by and ask, as best I can, for Charing Cross. He looks at me with suspicion, and then, as if to be rid of me, points the way down from the cathedral and makes a gesture for straight on. Past the booksellers' shops, at the bottom of the hill, is a narrow stream, choked and foul, with stepping stones that I take carefully. I wish to avoid notice and walk as those around me do, with my head down. My cloak is a dull brown, my hat the usual felt, with a white ribbon at the base of the crown. You would not take me for a Dutchman from the outside.

At the edge of the stream a woman stops me as if to ask a question, then pulls a bag from the folds of her gown and takes from it a small print, face up so that I can see it clearly. She is silent, just gives me a look and holds my eyes with hers for a minute. I understand; commerce speaks a language without words, and so does secrecy.

No one is behind me or anywhere near. I cannot say why, yet the very sense I have of being observed prompts me to put one hand out for the print and with the other find some coins and pass them over. When the woman rolls up the paper, ties it with twine and offers it to me, I feel none of the usual heart-lift that comes with small purchases; a corner sweetmeat or a pipe in an inn. This is a hurried and furtive thing between us; glancing round, I tuck the print into my sleeve and walk on.

The rain begins as I pass an old mansion by the river; not drop by drop, but in a sudden squall that throws down the storm in a sheet.

Trees whip and bow eastwards. Their new leaves shuffle like an angry crowd. At midday it is dark enough to be night, in which another man might find a portent.

I have read that where there is war it is a shame for a gentleman to say he has read of it only, and has not seen it. There is no war in this city, no havoc of battle; but I am seeing war nonetheless. London is sullen. Soldiers stand on the street corners and beneath the over-hangs of the houses. As the rain begins I hear it drumming on their helmets. Citizens walk past, close to the walls. The women cover their heads with their cloaks and none meet my eye. Fear and mistrust hang in the air, so heavy that I might put my hand to them.

At the Rose Tavern, I find a note from Mr Vermuyden with instruc-tions and money for the journey. My man has already set down my boxes and left, no doubt to find ale and Dutch company. As soon as I have closed the door to my room, I pull out the printed paper from my sleeve and roll it open on the bed. There is no doubt about what it shows. A wooden platform is depicted at the centre of the picture, upon which kneels the body of the King, with the animation of life still in it. His head lies cut off upon the executioner's block. The lines are ragged, the whole cut by an inexpert hand. The King's body, his shoes balanced on the platform, his large hat alone in the middle: these things make a shiver run through me. This was a king once, and I feel sure that the heart of the man who carved this picture lay with the King's, for he made a flat, lifeless thing, with only sadness in it. Even on Tholen – for there, too, the thing was felt – people said King Charles died well. In Delft, a man told me, as if he had been there, that at the instant of the blow a single groan went through the whole crowd. Now, as I sit here, it seems that groan still sounds.

I am a man of solitary habit, yet now I long to leave this silent room and find the noise of life. I'd like a woman to lie with, but I want more the company of men. Downstairs are Dutchmen, shut-ting out the rain with talk and laughter. At the thought my mood lightens, and I remember why I am here. Though without the comfort of family or friend, and though Mr Vermuyden has held my papers (I shall request them with my first report), yet am I determined to seize and undertake this adventure. I call for water, wash my face, and make my way to the parlour.

Smoke meets me, and a thick wall of my own language, mortared with wit and good humour. Half a dozen men sit loosely round a table. Talk flies between them, and through it come jabs of their pipe stems, raised glasses, exclamation and laughter. Straight away, to my relief, a comfortable feeling of Amsterdam and Tholen comes round me; of men who throw their legs apart when they laugh and wear their hair long, as I do.

'Jan Brunt, engineer,' I say, and take an empty chair as the chatter stops and I hear the familiar '*Goedenavond, Goedenavond.*' The circle opens to make a space for me and the day's indignity and strangeness fall away. The man of the inn comes in. I order brandy and a pipe for myself.

For a few minutes the company talks on as if I had not joined it, then a florid man stops and turns to me, wine glass in hand. A diamond flashes on his little finger.

'Your business here in London, Mijnheer Brunt?'

I wonder, even in the company of my compatriots, whether I should speak, as if the mood of this city has oozed inside this cheerful inn.

'To help in the undertaking of a great labour.'

The florid man leans towards me, knees apart. He taps a pipe against my chest. I can feel the heat through my cotton shirt.

'And what great labour might that be?'

'I am to assist Mijnheer Vermuyden with the new draining works in the lands beyond Ely. General Cromwell has ordered them restarted after the years of disturbance.'

Another man turns towards me, heavyset and sprawling on his chair. He lifts his glass so that the wine dances golden in the candlelight.

'Beaver-skin hats, young man – they are my line of work, and I've traded up there, at Ely Isle. Ely was once a fine place, though now much decayed and wretched. Yet round it is strange country, forbidding, a wild place as far and beyond what the eye can see.'

'I have heard it said,' another man broke in, 'that barbarous people live there.'

'Barbarous and godless, too, so I was told,' the hatter added, 'though I never had cause to go in there, the people of those parts beyond Ely having no means to deal in luxury.'

'I know little of the people,' I say, 'except that they are few, and there are five hundred square miles to be drained.'

'Well, Godspeed to you, young man. That's work for many years.'

The hatter laughs with an edge of scorn, or so I think afterwards. The talk then passes to the events of the day and the scarcity of commerce. One by one the merchants complain about the ruinous state of London and no one buying, until a quiet man with folded arms speaks up.

'I myself have succeeded, sirs, right here in London.'

'What is your trade?' The hatter waves his glass again.

'My name is Frans Klaassen, gentlemen. Allow me to show you my stock.'

Klaassen is a lean man with a face weathered in the outdoors and little hair on his head. Alone among the company he wears no hat and has neither cloak nor cane with him. From next to his chair he quietly lifts a box bound in brass with a curling clasp. Inside, trays and boxes are neatly stacked, and alongside them lie three scarlet velvet bags with drawstrings which Klaassen places on the table.

A hush settles on the company, as if we wait for a performance. Perhaps Klaassen is a magician. As we watch he takes three small bowls punctured with different-sized holes and a piece of red woollen cloth that he spreads out upon the table and then, perhaps, several of us understand what his goods are: pearls, from Arabia.

Klaassen tips the pearls from one of the velvet bags into the first bowl. They tremble for a moment before he raises the vessel and shakes it. The smallest pearls, tiny as pinpricks, rattle through the holes and settle into a low mound on the red cloth. Picking up the next bowl he tips the remaining pearls into it and shakes it again. A new mound collects on the cloth, made of slightly bigger pearls. Once more Klaassen repeats the operation. Now there are three piles, and only the biggest pearls are left in the last bowl. These he tips onto the cloth to make a fourth group. We peer at their glowing, uneven surfaces.

We Dutch know pearls. Necklaces and wrist bands, buckles and brooches, stomachers and collars; pearls adorn them all. Pearls are the slow accumulation of beauty and the reward of wealth. We do not mine and cut them like diamonds, or refine them like gold. They are nature's gift, taken from water and brought into the light. We prize their completeness and their milky shine.

The hatter glances towards the door.

'Mr Klaassen, you know these pearls are no longer allowed here? All precious stones are forbidden by decree; the Crown Jewels themselves are melted down and sold off?'

Klaassen shrugs and smiles.

'So much the better for my affairs, since every man desires what is hidden and denied him. Think on it, gentlemen. Is not the most prized part of a woman the most hidden and secret? I sell my pearls in Cheapside by appointment, and the largest sell the best.'

'Why so?' I ask, since measurement will always catch my notice.

From his pocket Klaassen pulls a key, unlocks a drawer in the box and draws out another bag, silk this time. From the inside, when he slides it onto the cloth, comes an earring; a single pearl clasped in a silver crown and sphere. The mount for the ear is fashioned into a cross.

'The King of England wore one such as this to the scaffold. I have them made up in Amsterdam. I could not risk the work here; but many wish to have a copy as a keepsake or a token.'

He shrugs, picks up the earring and returns it to its drawer, then shovels up his pearls. In a few seconds the shining shells – for what are they? The emanations of creatures, or precious jewels? – are bagged up. Klaassen packs away the sieves and scales, the weights and the red cloth, locks the box and stows it again by his feet.

Before anyone says a word, Klaassen raises his wine glass and says with a smile, 'To King Charles and the pearl he wore.'

None of us speak, and strange as it is – for in Amsterdam pearls are bought and sold in the bright light every day and, besides, we Netherlanders have no king nor any allegiance to one – solemnity falls in the room. It settles over all of us, even if, as I think for a second, Klaassen's toast is more a thanks for profit than a prayer for the King's soul.

After a pause the talk turns to the events of the day, and how to pass the evening with the theatres now closed.

'Bawdy houses, too, in case you were thinking of spending your nights under a woman,' says a fair man about my own age.

But I have had enough of company, suddenly, and say goodnight, bowing to each of the men in turn. 'Godspeed, Godspeed,' they say in reply. As I leave I see Klaassen picking up the cards from the table.

'Hombre,' he says, and shuffles them. 'I am the dealer.'

# Chapter 4

*The Isle of Ely, on the Great Level.*
*May, 1649.*
*Wind from the west, with high cloud.*

The next day begins in sunshine that comes through the small dusty window. While the servant is carrying my boxes down the stairs, I rub a hole in the dirt and look out on another city; not the one I saw yesterday. The wind lifts the hem of a grey cloak and I see a flash of scarlet underneath. In the breeze a woman stretches up a hand to steady her hood and a bracelet winks in the sun. Two soldiers walk down the street as a little girl in short skirts, grubby and shoeless, skips through yesterday's puddles. Other children, rag-clad and bony, follow her. The city's ghosts have disappeared.

I take the Cambridge coach at Charing Cross as Vermuyden has ordered, squashed between a silent pastor all in black and a woman whose chatter is soon frustrated by my shrugs to show I do not understand the language. I am glad of the quiet, and peer out at the passing gardens and villages. The inns where we stop to change horses are dirty affairs and the lodgings I am offered in the town of Cambridge little better. I care not, and sleep late, heartened by the flatness of the country and the information that Ely is no more than a dozen miles off.

These last miles I can accomplish on horseback, the road being too poor to admit a coach and only fit for carts and horsemen. A few miles from Cambridge the fields on either side of the road fall away. My journey takes me across a flat and marshy plain studded with ponds. I am going into the fenland.

By the afternoon I am riding along a muddy causeway that crosses a broad silver mere. My mood lifts to meet the distant horizon. I have reached a world where water has its empire still. Frogs croak in the shallows; a heron hunches his grey shoulders on a blackened stump. Up ahead, floating in the fading light, a dark bar appears beyond the water. As I come closer I make out a great cathedral, a black silhouette, high and vigilant.

The town of Ely has lost the splendour it promised from a distance. Many buildings lie ruined and open to the sky. Their walls are pitted, glass has gone from the windows and wood rots in the damp air. Pigeons stand in the empty casements, fat against the squares like portraits ready framed. They rattle up and away as I ride past, and I hear them wheel round and settle again behind me. The streets, in the late afternoon, are empty, but I feel sure that I am followed by dozens of eyes, and am relieved to find the way up into the town immediately.

At the inn by the cathedral I take a room on the top floor and cross to the window as soon as my boxes have been set down. Beyond the low bulk of the island, which by my reckoning must extend some three or four miles to the north, I make out the turning skeins of rivers and expanses of silvery water stretching as far as the horizon. My mind's eye journeys towards the sea, as a geographer's must. This is the drowned country I have come to drain, and I try to get some measure of it before nightfall.

I know not how long I remain transfixed, but darkness falls as I stand there, and then all I can see are pale beams from inside the shuttered houses opposite, and the swinging lantern of a passer-by. The wind has dropped, and the watery air is dense around me. Yet I do not fear this damp as many do. No, I have a sense from home, of being alone with myself, with the green world, and with God. Peace settles on me, and I silently give thanks that I will be tested here and surely not found wanting.

In the morning I send a boy to Van Hooghten at the address given by Mr Vermuyden. I am soon up and ready, dressed in my work clothes, a linen suit and oiled boots. The day is blue and still, and I am eager to start. Van Hooghten is waiting for me by the door to the inn. He proves to be a man of middle height and a few years older than myself. His hair is chestnut, falling in thick curls; his blue eyes deep-set. From the way he holds himself, I feel sure that he is well built and strong, though he stands no higher than my shoulder. He greets me quietly, as if we share a secret.

'Engineer Brunt?'

'Jan Brunt, engineer.'

He nods and says, 'Jacob Van Hooghten.'

'Mijnheer Van Hooghten, I bid you *goedemorgen*. I am ready to begin the work.'

'Walk with me to the staithe and I shall explain it to you. It is best we talk in the open air.'

We speak in Dutch, but alarm runs through me.

'We are surely unremarked; besides, these people cannot make out our speech.'

'As to the last,' Van Hooghten says, 'it does not help.'

He laughs, and I see the wrinkles gather round his eyes.

'Hearing Dutch or another language convinces people, merely, that we are attempting to be secretive.'

'It seems that we are.'

'Mijnheer Brunt, our intentions are already hated by many here. Has Mijnheer Vermuyden not told you that in the late wars the people of these parts, at General Cromwell's bidding, I may say, breached the dykes that had been built in preparation for the great works?'

'He told me only that the works were started and then halted; but also that General Cromwell now takes it all in his own hands.'

Van Hooghten looks at me steadily, and I remember Mijnheer Vermuyden's instructions to listen to him.

'I am ready to take your advice, Mijnheer Van Hooghten.'

He smiles again, and says, 'In the first place, find somewhere to live that is out of the way and unobserved. We start work immediately – our first job, as you yourself will know, being to survey the land, find out its gradients, and so make a map of the whole Great Level. In this I shall be taking overall charge and the middle and northern sections, while you map the difficult part to the south.'

'We will work well together, I trust, Mijnheer Van Hooghten,' I reply.

'I am told you are a fine map maker, so I am sure that we shall. The Gentlemen Adventurers demand maps and plans, as you know. Without them they become restive, uncertain. Though you and I might proceed directly from a survey, keeping the findings in our head and working simply to a plan, yet they wish for fine maps, to pass around, to reassure.'

'The sums of money already advanced perhaps demand them.'

'Indeed so, and the more we can furnish, the more likely we are to be paid our instalments. So we start with a map of the Great Level drowned, upon which we can draw our plan for its draining.'

I begin at that moment to like Van Hooghten, and to enjoy his company. He puts out a frankness that I do not find in myself but yet am drawn towards. As we speak, my anxiety falls away and an eagerness for the work takes hold of me.

'Well, Mijnheer Van Hooghten, I am ready at your service.'

'Good, good,' Van Hooghten says. 'One other thing – call me Jacob, do. There's no point in formality in a place like this.' He takes my arm. 'Now, I shall show you just a little today; how the land falls from Ely Isle, and the general turn of the channels hereabouts.'

All this time I have been following Van Hooghten down narrow streets from the cathedral, and now we arrive at the river, where dozens of small boats are tied up to the wharf. Some are skiffs, their sails rolled up across their masts; some rowing boats and others strange round craft, so light they shift back and forth with the currents and the wind.

Van Hooghten jumps into one of the rowing boats and as soon as I am down into it myself – which movement is as unthinking to us Dutch as mounting a horse – he pushes off from the staithe and into the centre of the channel. A sluggish current carries us away, and for the first hour or so we skirt the island. We pass cattle grazing, my eye at a level with their blue-veined udders. Willows line the banks and our boat sails through their reflections. Behind them bloom mounds of hawthorn and a thousand meadow flowers.

The sun is up now and rises through the sky as we head further into the wilderness. We are soon right in the reed beds, deep and deeper until the last sight of open river closes behind us. The water seems still, though I know it must be flowing seawards, down the gradients. Everything is lush and heavy. I see immediately that my sense, this morning, that this place resembled the Holland of my youth was mistaken. Holland is a land taken from the rivers and the sea, built up and made fertile. It is a place of commerce, and though we fear always the coming of a flood, we battle the power of the water day and night, and for the most part a truce holds.

In this strange land, water is still the master. Here are thousands of islands that come and go, swept away or created at the water's whim, while the channels between them shrink and swell from year to year. No estate can make a claim upon the land. It looks a useless place for agriculture and real husbandry, though I see places where the reeds have been cut, for matting or for roofs.

Still the channel narrows. Van Hooghten has to pull in the oars and let the water carry us forward. I begin, as I never have at home, to lose a sense of where we are headed. Though I know from the sun's ascent that our craft travels in a northerly direction, I soon give up the notion of taking measurements, and let my mind go. In a while – who knows how long or how far we have come – the channel splits and narrows again. There is now no space for oars; I can reach out and touch the reed wall on either side.

'Shift up, Jan,' Van Hooghten says. 'You go up to the prow there, while I move down to the back.'

As I slide forward, Van Hooghten picks up a pole from the bottom of the boat, and stands up in the stern.

A family of coots splutters up in front and as the birds hurry over the water's surface, I am roused by the sensation that someone is watching. There is a shuffling in the reeds, a splash, and then no more. Is there a person, someone who observes us? I glance at Van Hooghten, but he seems unconcerned. He has planted his feet square in the stern, and now throws up the pole, and lets it fall through his hands, leaning forward as we slide through the water.

After a time of this that I cannot quantify, I feel the boat taken by the current and pushed out between the walls of reed, discharged onto an expanse of water, wide and still. It is a great mere, and unexpected, for where are we? The mere fills the view to the horizon, bordered all round by reed and stands of willow. The water glitters, lit by the sun and burnished by the wind. Gold reeds push up into the blue immensity of the sky. Everything is ablaze. Tiny waves slap against the side of the boat; birds sing. The day is cloudless, the world washed clean.

We are alone on the mere, and rock gently with the wind. When I look down into the water I see myself, rippling and indistinct. Below the boat fronds of weeds sway in the current, dense and green, as if I gazed at a forest with the eye of an eagle. So we drift on, quietly. Where does the water end and the sky begin? I cannot say. The whole world floats, and I with it, nearly to the point of sleep, or as if I was transported into man's first kingdom of Elysium. In silence, so that

Van Hooghten does not hear, I thank God for the trust bestowed upon me. Van Hooghten is quite still; perhaps he, too, is almost asleep.

Then over the water comes a sound that breaks the veil; the voice of a woman, singing. It is a strong voice, deep and layered. I do not know the song, nor can I hear if it has any words, but in that instant I am startled back to the day.

'Do you hear that, Jacob?'

'Do I hear what, Jan?'

'A woman singing, surely.'

He pauses and turns to look behind him. The mere is empty. Everything is still.

'Nothing.'

'Yet there was.'

'Perhaps; though it is easy here to be deceived by sounds that have travelled far across the water.'

I wish to believe Van Hooghten, and it is true, in a place such as this a light breeze may carry a song for miles, so that it reaches us as if uttered by our side. But I do not believe him. I sense the singer near and feel, indeed, an apprehension.

'Ah, Jan, I have a sensation that we are watched.'

'I have known many a man, out on the mere, feel there are eyes upon him, though he is regarded by nobody.'

Van Hooghten shunts his pole along the length of the boat, and sits down, letting us rock. Reaching under the seat he pulls out a leather bottle, and drinks.

As he hands it to me he adds, 'It will be best, Jan, if you keep your measuring instruments out of sight when you are upon the water. The fensmen who inhabit this place are an envious people; barbarous, it is said. They live in their own way, calling all others uplanders.'

I smile at that, of course; for we Dutch are lowlanders, which fact, once known to the fensmen, will surely allow us to commune with them upon better terms than in wartime when riot and destruction broke out.

I swallow my beer and let Van Hooghten's remark pass, the day being too young, and our acquaintance also.

Van Hooghten goes on, however.

'At your lodgings, though your business may become known, circumspection is also the best course.'

To this I am able to reply with truth.

'I am not a talkative man, and, further, do not speak the language with ease.'

Van Hooghten now pulls up the oars again and settles them in the rowlocks. He rows quickly to the far side of the mere where the reeds have thinned and an old willow fallen. Easing the boat up against the trunk, he secures it with a quick knot of the rope and hops out on a stretch of bank.

When I scramble up and look about I can see that we have not reached the far side of the mere, but landed on an island composed of silt, built up over the years, reed-circled and self-sown with spongy mounds of grass. I take a few steps forward and straight away begin to sink; or the land begins to rise. Water settles round my boots. Van Hooghten, still standing on the solidity of the bank, calls me back to myself.

'Jan, have a care! Are you a fool? A man can disappear here in an instant.'

'I lost myself.'

'Lost yourself? Sir, you are a geographer.'

Thus, with this sally, does Van Hooghten remind me of the work ahead and my place in it. He is back in the boat by the time I have reached the safety of the bank, and ready to cast off.

'Can you hazard the way back, Mijnheer Brunt?' he says with a smile, when I step in the boat. 'Here, take the oars.'

I row southwards away from the island and across the wide mere, then into the narrow channel and out again into the broader water. Ahead lies Ely Island, where distant lantern lights appear and twinkle. A cowman calls to his cows as he prods them towards milking. A few minutes later the boat bumps against the black wooden piles and we come to rest at the staithe. Van Hooghten jumps out and ties us up with two throws of the rope. As he holds out his hand to steady me I feel myself shrink back a little, wishing not to come to land just now. The feel of enchantment falls away with his touch, yet the remembrance of the day colours my mind as a dream does after we wake.

# PART TWO

# Chapter 1

*Nieuw Amsterdam.*
*The 24th day of April, 1664.*
*The sky overcast, wind from the east.*
*Squalls and showers.*
*High tide by the Stadt Huys at 8 o'clock in the morning.*

Three weeks have passed since Hendrick came to my door with the note. For the first few days I stayed in my house or close by. Hope and apprehension, entwined together, stopped me leaving the Heere Gracht. But no one knocked, and little by little I have resumed my usual pursuits: my trips on the water and walks up beyond the wall; my measurements of the tides and wind, my observations and writings.

My heart, that jumped and shook, has quietened, though Nieuw Amsterdam has sharpened a little in outline, as if I saw it with new eyes or I was showing it to a visitor. One day, on the edge of the Oost Rivier, where unkempt ground meets the water and trees still rise from the marsh, I felt that I was not alone. The sun, low in the west, dazzled my eyes. I persuaded myself then that no one was there, or if someone, then one of the wildmen, who can wait and watch without cracking a twig or stirring the water. I walked on and forced myself into tranquillity. There is nothing I can do but wait, and go on as I have always done.

And so at the edge of the known world I write this my account, and add to it both some events of the day and a description of the place that I have come to. I fancy that painters of portraits, and the writers of poems, no less than men such as myself who measure and record the rivers or the tides, have the same desire. We all wish to bring order to the passing world, to stop the pulse of nature for a second and hold it up for all to see. Here, the portrait painter might say, is your beloved, or a great man, not as you will ever see them with your eye, but as if time was stopped and their features fixed. Thus I, too, record the height of the waters, though the waters do not, at the point of high tide, cease their movement, but turn at the very moment of their height, marvellously, in a way that we can never see. Why else record or paint, when all around us nature streams ceaselessly on?

I live on a crooked finger of ground that slides between two rivers and the sea. Some years ago I might have said that Our Lord, the first geographer, measured and laid it out with all its folds, its vantage points; making all the rivers and inland seas, the marshes and mountain ranges; the whole vastness of America. I would have said that he made this land in many layers, one atop another like the pages of a book to be worn and shaped by nature as he intended. These days I simply record what I see.

It is a hard land that we sit upon here. The sea with the wind in it is a rough beast. Already, since I arrived, it has overwhelmed us twice. This morning the prospect of snow hangs in the air, notwithstanding the lateness of the year. I have known it snow here the first day of May, and in the month of October too. And this despite the observable fact that this city lies near forty-one degrees north of the Equinoctial line and shares its place on that latitude with the island of Sardinia in the Mediterranean Sea. It is a puzzle why one place should have weeks ago announced spring while here the winter teases us still. Some say it comes from the fact of the earth being not quite round, others from the continuity of this little island with the frozen northern wastes. This I cannot say, only assert that when I have asked the wildmen where the cold comes from or the heat, they laugh and give no opinion, but seldom mind the temperature of the air, frequently walking out half-naked in the snow.

This is the worst of Nieuw Amsterdam; this and the close hot summers when mosquitoes swarm up from the flatlands, and hang in grey clouds over any shady place. There is no remedy against them in the evening though the natives smear their naked bodies with bear grease, and I myself have done the same when far from the eyes of my countrymen.

Such are the irritations of this island. Yet it has great wonders too. When the wind drops on a cloudless night, the stars draw close, shining newborn. That's a sight to make me fall on my knees from the beauty of it.

When I first arrived here, in the year 1652, I called at the Stadt Huys, not so much to offer my services, as to register my presence. I wished still to be known by the name of engineer; if not to practise then for some pride in myself. I had money for several years of solitude and careful living, which was what I planned when I set out from the old world. I wanted nothing, and no one, or no one I knew living. I had no acquaintance or friend, and many seemed to fear me. I was the ghost of myself, and the inhabitants of Nieuw Amsterdam sensed it. Men, women, children – everyone – moved away if I came near them, so that I always stood alone in any room I entered, and lost the habit of even saying *goedemorgen* or nodding if I passed a person in the street.

From those first days I did what I knew how to do, more from habit than from a desire of gain. I began to measure and to map the marshy ground around the city, and this work, with my instruments and papers that I held in my hand, passed the time and gave me a familiarity with myself. After some weeks I left the city and began to venture beyond the wall, to discover and record the composition of the whole island. Then one or two curious men began to talk to me. The surgeon, Varreranger, a man with an understanding of instruments in his own trade, made my acquaintance. Others began to stop and ask what I was doing. Soon, I suppose, a story about me went around.

The Director-General, Pieter Stuyvesant, called me to his house, where I found him leaning on the gate, resting his wooden stump. It being the first time I had seen him, I did not know he had only one good leg. Stuyvesant took me into his parlour and told me that his men had seen me about and I was known to be an engineer. Did I have any experience in the map trade?

'Mijnheer Stuyvesant, the two go hand in hand.'

'Very well. I need a map. In fact, I need a map that will show people the virtues of this place.'

'Does a map ever show anything else, sir?'

The Director-General looked at me with a belligerent eye, then leaned back in his chair with a grin. We understood one another. What map of a colony pictures its hardships?

'The fact is,' Stuyvesant went on, 'Hendrick Kip is selling parcels of land up in the north-west of the island. The man sees only a quick profit. A village is forming, and I'd like a proper plan for it.'

Stuyvesant, who puts himself forward as a practical man, is in truth a dreamer who dreams in maps and pictures. He wanted the new settlement put on the footing of a Dutch village, to be called Nieuw Haarlem, with plots of equal size going back from the streets. This picture of Nieuw Haarlem came from the old world or perhaps the world of the landscape painters whose pictures make our flat land hilly and our skies and acres vast. Did he see his home village, wherever it was, where pears ripened to gold against brick walls and the women always had their pails and brushes at the ready?

'We need more people, Mijnheer Brunt. I wish you to make a map to entice them here. Have you done such a thing before?'

'Not exactly, sir, but I know what it is that you require, and am trained in the art.'

Stuyvesant talked on, and lit up in me the desire to excel that I thought extinguished. I took the job, my first considerable commission here, the contract signed at the Stadt Huys by Stuyvesant and myself. The next day I went straight to work with my notebook and measuring rods. I surveyed the ground up in the north-west of Manatus Eylandt and drew a map that would have pleased my younger self. It showed the village laid out in blocks and streets that might grow out into the countryside. All round the edge, as I had done long ago, I drew Pieter Stuyvesant's dreams and visions.

At the top of the map I drew two whales, blowing out the sea, and in the distance three frigates of the West India Company leaning into the wind. Then, for fancy's sake, came a pair of curled-tailed sea creatures. Down the left side ran the fruit of the land, down the right the harvest of the water. None of the capacity I had as a young man deserted me. Vines with entwining tendrils danced across the paper and the boughs of plums hung heavy with ripe fruit. Heads of corn stood proud as torches. A roe deer lifted her head trustingly, as if she intended to lie down straight in the hunter's path.

I drew no wildmen, but rather a curled salmon as it leapt from the river, a lobster and a codfish. Along the bottom walked Nieuw Haarlem's people: Dutchmen, their wives and children. At the last I drew myself sitting on the top of a canal bank. My hat, in three ink strokes, was outlined against the sky.

This, my description of the world that might come to be, framed by all the beauties of nature, was much admired, and passed from hand to hand in the office of the Director-General. I made a copy, and sent it to the West India Company in Amsterdam. I heard that it was engraved and sold to people dreaming of another life, both those who might make the crossing, and those whose walls already hung with other worlds.

Stuyvesant praised my map, and the drawings also. Several men from this city bought parcels of land around the village, and built houses for their sons and daughters, it being cheaper to set them up at a distance than build a house or buy a farm closer to the wall. So Nieuw Haarlem grew, though it is not quite the paradise that the Director-General dreamed of, menaced as it is still by the wildmen and its roads often impassable in the winter.

Other work came after, piece by piece, and I have never been without a map to make, a new arrival to advise or a piece of draining and embanking to undertake. It is my fortune that the lands and rivers of the English colonies to the north are marshy and muddy and with my help the colonists may put them to productive use. I am often sought out, but take no more work than I need, preferring to have sufficient time for my own thoughts and studies. It is one thing to survive in Nieuw Amsterdam, another to live; and though life may take different shapes for different men, the life I cherish needs less wealth than time, and thus I arrange it so.

If the day is fine, or the season further advanced, and I have no work to attend to, I may put on my beaver hat and take the paddle that stands against the wall by my front door. On such a day I step out onto the path to find the whole Heere Gracht sunning itself, supine in the early morning. The canal seems motionless; the tide on the turn. It is my custom when I leave the house to lean over and examine the water, as a mother checks her sleeping child for rashes or signs of a sickness.

Most times I turn north with a skip in my step, for I am to this day pleased with the work I made with the canal, and know the citizens of this place have cause, in better health and firmer ground, to thank me for it. I cross the bridges over the Begijn Gracht and the Heere Gracht itself, and make my way down the lane past the Red Lion tavern to Smee Straet. This street, though it lies within the protection

43

of the wall, is nonetheless insalubrious, distant as it is from the safety of the Fort and flooded if storms come with the spring tides. Stink covers it in summer.

Free slaves and other people without steady employment live here, crowded three or four to a room. In recent years some natives who have been drawn into Nieuw Amsterdam by trade or by their own curiosity have set up alongside them. Once introduced to the city life, they seldom return to those they lived amongst. This habit of wandering, it seems, was implanted in Adam and Eve, our first mother and father, who left their home to live among creatures unknown to them, and never returned. Such a habit I have never observed in the animal kingdom, for the birds and even whales that cross skies and oceans each year, leave and return. Men and women, having sailed the seas, as I have done, or struck out for a new place, seldom make the journey back.

Here on Smee Straet, Gertie Stoffels keeps her house. On warm mornings she sits outside, knees apart under a thick skirt and apron. She wears a dirty cap and keeps a pipe in hand. Gertie is free with words, and knows me for a man who is never loose in conversation.

'Hey, hey, Jan Brunt,' she says when I come round the corner. 'Still no woman after all these years? And you a man in the prime of life?'

You see, we have an understanding.

'I look after myself, Gertie.'

How Gertie came here I do not know, but she has a brisk business that keeps her handsomely. She owns this house on Smee Straet and a homestead beyond the wall, and has plenty of credit with the merchants at the wharfs. Her respectable business is to find maids for prosperous residents, girls new off the plantations, come here with freedom and nothing else. Some disdain to serve again and prefer to stay with Gertie, or so she says. Any man who wants a woman comes here, and since men outnumber women in this town, she turns a fair profit. Any time I pass Gertie's, I am likely to see a sailor coming out and a townsman going in.

Well, there is someone here for men of every taste. Turn the corner to Tuyn Straet and then left into Prince Straet and you find another house with the door ajar. On the stoop sits a young woman with mother-of-pearl breasts, her skirt up around her thighs. Fresh young boys line the parlour fire, their collars loose; but they are not clients. In the bed in the wall lies a man, locked in because a town commissioner might come by. The girls joke that they have the easiest job in Nieuw Amsterdam. They are the decoys; in this house it's the boys who work.

Either way, as Gertie says, the money comes in. Her girls, she declares, are the best in town. Besides those off the plantations, there are girls who are natives to this place and others from Holland or the English colonies. The native ones are taller than the Dutch, and often better made, their limbs being straight and smooth and their skin unmarked by the pox. Their colour may be attributed to the sun, which they revere, and let shine on them, generation after generation. I have no doubt either that, were they to be instructed as our women are, they would be quite as accomplished, being curious and quick to learn and knowing their own histories without writing, but as a kind of chant that has many different stories in it.

I bow to Gertie as I pass. She takes her pipe from her mouth and waves it towards me as if she wants to tie me in its smoke. We get along, with little need to speak. At the end of Smee Straet I walk along by the shore until I come to the wall. This wall marks the boundary of our city, a division between Nieuw Amsterdam and whatever lies beyond. It was built to keep the wildmen from coming here, they being thought to menace the small colony from their greater numbers and savage ways. These days, the wildmen seeming fewer from their land being taken or sold for farms, the wall is more often spoken of as a barrier against the English, who press down from the north. Beyond the wall sits my orchard, or what I call my orchard, though it is more a meadow that I leave to nature.

I keep the meadow almost in its wild state, having there only a couple of large apple trees and a sturdy wooden seat that I have constructed. This I sit upon in the shade on warm afternoons and in the winter too, when snowfall has silenced all of nature but the sea. Several men have tried to buy my orchard from me, the land having acquired in recent years a greater value, but I like it as it is, with tall grass in the summer and bees that come and go amongst the flowers. Here I keep my canoe, turned over under a tree.

It was with the wildmen that I acquired the skill of making a canoe and preserving it watertight. A Dutchman, or any person familiar with the water, might easily do the same. The wildmen have great skill on all manner of water and say that there is nowhere they cannot reach in their canoes, for they are so light that they may be hoisted shoulderwards and carried overland from one river to the next.

Though my own canoe is long enough for two men, I propel it with ease and with a single paddle, first one side and then the other. The wildmen like to face forwards in their canoes and see clearly what they are approaching. I do the same yet still prefer the pull of the oars, and to look, as we do in memory, back to where I started. I fancy that therein lies a difference between an old world and a new.

Once launched on the Oost Rivier, I may let the tide take me down the marshy coast of Lange Eylandt, which is a larger island than any I know from Holland, or any I saw on my travels. On the shore lie piles of stranded bladderwrack that in the summer heave with clouds of flies. There are plentiful small rivers running into the marshes, with otters in them, new-crowned kings of the water with the beavers mostly trapped and gone.

In the summer I may paddle on for days. I catch fish and travel as the wildmen do until I reach the far end of the island where it breaks into numerous inlets and beaches. Then I walk down to the open ocean and feel myself to be not a man but a part of nature, as is a star, or a dolphin that leaps for joy out in the bay. Far away round our earth lies the old world, while here I stand on the new. Waves rush up to my feet and then pull back, marbled with sand and foam.

# Chapter 2

*The Isle of Ely, upon the Great Level.*
*The 20th day of July, 1649.*
*Wind from the west, the sky overcast.*

It is a month before the dog days when the high summer comes to an end and Sirius shines bright in the sky. I have been on the Great Level for two months now and I am beginning to get the measure of the place. Its contours are no longer strange to my eyes. The town of Ely falls away into green fields after five minutes' walk. Herds of cattle now surround the town, brought across the causeway to the island to fatten on the summer grass. Before the autumn rains set in they will be on the move again, driven down to London and the slaughterhouses of the market there.

The woman I lodge with is no more than civil. Mrs Suckling is her name. She takes my money with ill grace and never speaks of the war, though a rough print of General Cromwell hangs inside the door. I stay with her some evenings and begin in a halting way to speak English. She sits in a high-backed chair and smooths down her linen pinafore with short hard sweeps, as if it stood for me, and I were a small boy, poor at grammar, in need of correction. Other times I stay in my room with my books and my figures from the day's work, or meet Van Hooghten in his lodgings to talk and smoke a pipe.

I do not go to cathedral services in Ely, though I am told that every person should attend. I dislike the curiosity of the people, and soon find that my separation from the world around me is not uncongenial, being in keeping with my understanding of myself. For the most part I am met with silence or a nod and a stare, but at night

I walk quickly, and fear to be attacked. In the daytime children follow me along the streets, darting in and out of passages and doorways and trying insults.

'Boer.'

'Hey, Mr Herring.'

Bold as crows, boys in gowns run out from the school building by the cathedral, and pull at my sleeve.

'Made of cheese?'

'Go away, stranger.'

'Yes, back to where you came from.'

I smile to show I wish them no harm, and walk on like a deaf man. If I commanded the language better I might tell them that the place I come from is not so unlike this one, flat and circumscribed by water. But I do not try to speak to them. I smile over their heads and continue on my way. Later I hear their words again, and surprise myself with the thought that, despite such taunts, I am happy to have left my home in search of adventure and fortune.

Soon I notice that I am not alone in my cowl of silence. There are others as quiet as I am; men and women who hide their faces and go hunched about their business. These are they who sided with the King and now they are the debris of war, abandoned by its retreat. Here are young men discharged from the King's army with half a limb; traders who supplied the losers; widows and children without support beyond a reluctant parish. They are not wanted and are now called traitors. Most people here were Cromwell's from the start.

Yet though victorious, Ely is not a place of ease or laughter. The wars have left the town in want. Taverns are closed, at least to the street, and there never was much other entertainment, I fancy. Perhaps a fair will come in, but now all I see are the pedlars, clad in cast-offs. Some sell ribbons and pins, scissors and needles. Others tout vials of medicine, cordials, scorpions from the east, potions of all sorts. Above the bed where I sleep, a dry bunch of herbs hangs suspended. Does it ward off spirits or stop my aches as it gathers dust?

This is the time of the ague, too. From the standing water of the meres bad air rises up and brings the shivering sickness into town. Some say the ague sits in the air, others that it is heated by the sun, others still that it is brought by spirits who come at night. When the fever rises, people dose themselves with an infusion made from poppy seeds. Whether this has any effect I cannot say, only that Mrs Suckling lives in great fear of the ague, and with good reason, for I have seen it carry off children in a few days from the first sweats. It is a haunting disease; once it enters, there is no getting rid of it. It comes back with no warning, making prisoners of its victims.

To a man who knows Amsterdam and Leiden, this is a miserable poor place, with scarce a book to be seen in the few good houses that I have been in. Yet, to my surprise, the meres and bogs supply a multitude of foodstuffs and other goods. Stacks of peat stand in the yards by the jetties, taken from the islands that emerge from the water in the summer, friable and easy to cut. Alongside them lie bundles of reeds, the best for baskets and matting, the rest for thatch. The fensmen are now landing many thousands of eels, that are carted in wooden barrels to London for sale, alive in water and tangled together like the hair of the Medusa. These eels are mysterious creatures, with wide lips and roving eyes. It is said they come from across the ocean and return there in the winter.

Then, a few days ago, great flocks of geese were driven in from the islands to be plucked by the townswomen whose employment this is. I watched a woman at her task, the goose trapped neck first between her chapped calves. In a few minutes she pulled out its feathers, working both sides of the bird from breast to tail, and then released it, pink and naked, leaving by her feet a pile of feather and down. The bloody tail feathers are cleaned, cut and sold for quills. The lightest down plumps up pillows and mattresses. All day the air is filled with feather fragments that float through the narrow streets and settle on my clothes. Five times a year, I am told, the geese are brought to be plucked, five times returned to their island homes.

The people of Ely Isle like to stay upon their upland. They mistrust outsiders, not just foreigners such as I am, but all those from other places, especially their neighbours, the fensmen, who live out on the meres, and come to Ely only to trade. Though they are close as to miles, the fensmen are spoken of with lowered voices. I have seen townspeople cross themselves in the manner of the old religion when the fensmen pass. Witches are said to be common amongst them, and many, I heard an old man say, still practise the pagan religion that long ago held sway across these islands. Upon my enquiring what this might be, he said that the fensmen make offerings to pagan gods, and declared that no traveller who wishes to return ventures into that treacherous place. Wraiths and spirits live out on the meres also, he added. At night their fires burn and the fensmen pass through them without harm.

The world beyond the Great Level arrives slowly, carried by chapmen who hawk their goods in the streets and bring sheets of printed paper with the news. London news is also told abroad by the carters who go back and forth with eels, goose down and quills. London, I am told by one of them, is a place of felons and dissolute persons. War is again in the air, the struggle between the royal cause and those who want no king. Ireland declares for kings, and the old religion, and rebels against the republic. One day, as I walk up Fore Hill towards the cathedral, I chance on a detachment of soldiers fifty strong on horseback.

The sound of hooves on the flagstones rings loud off the sides of the buildings. A thickset man rides at the head of the group. His long leather coat is spotted with grease and a heavy helmet jogs his knee. I stand in the entrance to a mean shop and measure him with my eyes. He is of middle height and age. With little presence on a horse, he slouches in the saddle and holds his head poorly. He has no air of either modesty or grandeur. Sparse grey hair falls about his shoulders, through which his scalp is pink and visible. Even from a distance I see that he has a growth between his chin and lip that draws the eye to it as to a sore, and others over his lips and brows.

I turn to a native of the place who stands by me.

'Sir, do you know this man?'

'What is it to you?' he asks and considers me keenly, as if I might be the agent of a foreign power. Though I know myself to be a stranger here, it is unpleasant to be brought up close to the disdain of one man for another, where war begins, and might begin at any time.

A young man turns to me as if to suggest without words an acceptance of my presence in this place, and says with kindness in his voice, 'It is General Cromwell, come to raise troops for new wars abroad. He once lived here, in St Mary's Street, so I know the look of him, though not every man does, or wishes to.'

So this is General Cromwell, who commands the army and was principal among those who killed the King. Many here were his supporters; but war has dulled their admiration and their joy at victory. Few run forward to thank him, or kiss his hand. No one cheers or presses close to his horse. General Cromwell does not have a face to love, or even a face to be afraid of.

The horsemen halt at the cathedral door and several foot soldiers come up. A table is called for and set on trestles. Cromwell does not dismount, but carries on towards his old house. Like the man of property he is, he has come to make sure it is in order before he leaves these shores.

Though at first reluctant, a few young men now begin to press up to the table. The harsh weather of the last winter has taken its toll. Food is scarce and most of those who push forward look ragged and poor. I watch one of them, urged on by his companions. As he approaches the table he stands up a little straighter, throws back his shoulders and tips up his chin. Looking at him, I see myself, two months before, advancing in that London room towards Mr Vermuyden, my maps and drawings in one hand.

The boy signs, and is gestured to one side. Others come up. One man jumps down from a passing cart and approaches, as if possessed of a sudden whim to leave his life and take another without a thought. The helmets of the soldiers glint behind the trestle; the horses sweat in the summer heat and stamp on the cobbles. They dip their heads and flick their tails to drive away the gathering flies. Swords poke out from the soldiers' long leather coats. The sight excites those who are watching.

Someone shouts for General Cromwell, and more men press forward. Even I, a Dutchman with no notion of the past histories of these islands, feel that what has brought them here, besides hunger, is more than the hatreds that fester from the last wars and now burst out again. In this ruined place people long for something to happen. Men are restless creatures, and tired of standing at street corners, hungry and casting about for work. They chafe at inactivity. The horses, the arrival of General Cromwell, a sense of the danger that is to come: all this stirs the crowd like a sudden squall over a field of corn.

A young man, little more than a child, breaks out of a group, approaches the table and leans over it. A soldier holds out an old quill, but the boy seems to turn away. Then, right there, one of the soldiers comes up, pulls his hands behind his back, pushes his head down and marches him off. Though the boy screams and calls out no one runs forward to help, and I stand there, immobile like the rest.

I look round, but General Cromwell has not returned. The men next to me have already gone. Quickly, the whole crowd breaks up and disperses. I walk away not wanting to encounter a soldier. This is how an army is built, how young men go unsuspecting to war; and the people of this town, after years of fighting, do nothing to stop it.

Later, Van Hooghten, who has been here long enough to know, tells me that many are turning against Parliament. People are sullen. They do not speak out, but look to their own safety. Under the cloak of darkness rich men flee, he says, some to the colonies of Virginia and Maryland, where the planters wish to proclaim Prince Charles their king.

The Prince has got clean away to The Hague, and waits for destiny to pick him out. His court grows daily. In ones and twos men of ambition loyal to the late King arrive there, and bring money, which they lend to the Prince in the hope of future reward. It is said this court is a racketing place, built upon all possible licentiousness. The more such tales are told here, the more the Dutch are reviled by sober men. Van Hooghten's demand for vigilance now begins to gather sense. We are doubly spied-on and disliked, as improvers and as Dutchmen. I am the most careful of men, yet our purpose is now well known. Worse than this, I believe that my travelling box, which contains my instruments and contracts, is opened when I am out. The woman Suckling denies it, the girl who works for her being, she affirms, a drudge who would never give herself the trouble of disturbing a gentleman's effects. I do not believe her, say nothing and plan to move my lodging as soon as I can find another. We continue our conversations in the evening and I begin to feel the words of the language separate from the general noise and sound one after another plain and clear.

As word of our work gets out, some dozen of the Ely Islanders come forward to offer us their services. Some say they know the meres, others that they worked on the embankments that were destroyed and so can be useful to us. Van Hooghten refuses every offer. None of the people native to this place are to be trusted, he says, as their conduct in the late war plainly shows. Discretion demands that we find our workmen from outside.

When at last we have the men we need, come from Holland and skilled in the arts of triangulation and drawing, it is past midsummer.

The days henceforward are shorter and the tides higher. We must quickly map the islands and the watercourses before the rains come and the summer landscape sinks underwater.

I take great pleasure in making maps and charts and know that the creator himself is my guide. When he created the earth, it was without form and covered all over with water, just as this land is in winter. On the second day of the world, he made the firmament that is heaven, and divided the waters with it, so that half the water lay under the firmament and half whirled beyond. It is beautiful to know that, drawn on a map, nature takes the shape and outline that only heaven sees. When he makes a map, a geographer lifts the surface of the earth, as an anatomist might lift the skin off a skull, and pegs it out flat. It gives me joy to think that I will do it.

# Chapter 3

*The Isle of Ely.*
*The Great Level.*
*July and August, 1649.*
*Fine summer weather.*

And so our work begins. Van Hooghten, with some of the two dozen men come from Holland, geographers and navigators in equal numbers, has the charge of surveying the whole of the Great Level. He and his men will determine its outer limits, which task means covering it with their triangulations, all five hundred square miles that Mijnheer Vermuyden spoke of. His geographers will begin also to survey the middle and northern sections, while I and my men take the southern part.

To redeem the drowned land it is necessary for us to understand it; that is to say, to measure it. I will measure the breadth of every channel and all the islands as we find them. We will calculate also the lengths of the channels and the gradient or fall of the water to the sea.

For us earthly geographers, the job is compounded part of science and part of imagination, for in this place the line between land and water is not as clear as the map must make it. It is a line that wanders and shifts with the seasons and the years. One summer an island comes up clear from a channel, only to shrink away when the rains arrive. Another year a river decides on a new turn, gambols about and abandons its old course.

This is the nature of the Great Level, and it has never before been fixed on paper. The reason is simple. None of the natives of these parts has need of a map, neither the people of the islands such as Ely, who fear to venture into the fen, nor the fensmen, who know all the watercourses as they twist and change and all the islands as they rise and fall. This land, since the creation, has slept sound under its watery covers each winter and thrown them off in the heat of summer.

Now everything will begin to change. The land will wake and emerge, as improvement demands. With the maps of the middle and northern sections, and Van Hooghten's survey of the extent and perimeter, we will make one whole map of the Great Level drowned, and so proceed to a plan of its draining.

In the heat of the summer I begin my task. We start each new day where we left off the day before. At precise intervals of distance we tie up the boat to measure the depths of the waters as we map them. This, in a river, is a simple matter, easily accomplished, the depth varying only with the time of year and the fall of rain. But north beyond Ely Isle is a place of meeting that alters the case. Twice a day at high tide there is a mingling of salt and fresh waters, the heavier seawater sliding below, the lighter river water turning lazily above it, trying to go on its way, yet pushed back towards its source.

In the summer, when the fresh water is low and idling, this conjunction is a benign one, two old friends tipping their hats and nodding as they pass. But in the autumn and spring, at the highest tides, Van Hooghten tells me, they may come up fast against one another, and neither has the space to yield. The water then overflows the banks of the channels and rises through the reed beds and above the tree roots. Sometimes all in a rush, or sometimes with a slow and steady elevation, the waters grow until the meres are enlarged and joined and sheets of water like the great flood of old spread out under the sky all the way to the grey horizon.

These great winter meres I have not yet seen, only the meres that are permanently established. Yet even a small mere seems large to the eye close up. The water takes in the azure of the sky and gives up its shining light so that at the horizon solid and liquid cannot be prised apart.

I lean over the stern of the boat as it sways by a reed bed, and drop a plumb line. When the lead touches the bottom, I can read the depth from the marks on the line and record the place in my book. In this way we will chart the course and fall of each channel. Once all are plumbed and mapped, Van Hooghten and I will decide where best to make a cut, a new watercourse to gather and drain the water from the land and carry it to the sea.

This is not the simple matter of a map only. The land here is not all of one substance. At points the clay comes to the surface and there are islands of more solid ground upon which grow a multitude of bushes and small trees. There are other islands, too, such as that to which Van Hooghten took me on my first day. These float upon the water, platforms of spongy vegetation. Still a third form of land, upon which grass grows plentifully, appears only when the spring waters have subsided. This summer land, peat-black and flat as the mere-bottom, will be most fit for farming.

A serenity comes upon me as we begin the work. I am sure in my knowledge and my skill, and the exercise of it calms me and takes away the feeling of being naked and observed that I have in Ely. Each day we push out a little further from the town, and work our way towards the sea. We part company and work alone on the smallest of the channels, with walls of reed about us. I take pride in the task, and recount it to Van Hooghten when we meet in the evening.

It is three weeks after we begin measuring that the first thing happens. I have left my men and taken a coracle such as fensmen use up a winding channel away from the main current of the River Ouse. This coracle, of the sort that I first saw by the wharfs in Ely, is a curious round craft, made of skin stretched over a frame of willow, and tarred black inside and out. It is small and shallow-bottomed; so light that I can hoist it onto my shoulders if land appears where I do not expect it. Paddling first one side and then another with its single oar I can nose my way up the narrowest of channels. In the height of summer when the water is low, the coracle floats easily over the shallows. When I work alone I use it almost every day.

Now we are in the dog days. Summer heat holds sway over the whole of the Great Level. Land and water, warm with sunshine, lie lazy and still. Reeds sway as I edge between their russet walls. High above, a lark sings its warning to the blue. Plumb line, measuring rods and ropes are stowed in the bottom of the coracle, my papers and chronometer in the large pocket I have sewn into my jacket for the purpose.

I am ready to lower and lift my line; to measure, check and write. Instead I let the coracle go, and drift with it, half asleep. The narrow channel empties out suddenly into a pool. In a splash of sunlight on the far side I see two or three women on the bank, indistinct in the dazzle, drying themselves after bathing, perhaps.

Nearer to me in the shade of a willow is another woman. I see her in the water, the hem of her shift loosely gathered in both hands. She does not notice me or hear anything, for at that very moment, before there is time to move or say a word, she bends forwards and pulls the garment over her head. So I see her as I have never seen a woman, her whole nakedness, half in my plain sight, half reflected in the water.

And the same instant, or so it feels, she lifts her head and sees me there. Her furious eyes strip me of everything and make me as naked as herself. The coracle floats closer to her. What can I do in that moment? Nothing. I cover my face with my hands. I cover my eyes, my nose and mouth. I want to block the operation of every sense. But it is too late; her look hits me like a spear. I cannot, even afterwards, give that look a name. It has a presence, and sinks inside me as surely as my own plumb line sinks into water. There is no pulling it up again. It is down in my stomach, ripping through my organs, settling into my flesh.

When I wake up, or take my hands from my eyes, the world has tipped sideways, and there is a confusion of shouting, and I too try to speak, to defend myself from her sight. What can I say, in that whirl of legs and arms, as her companions reach to pull her up, water slapping the coracle as she scrambles on to the bank? Nothing. I cannot speak or steady the boat, only see through a mist as the women snatch up her clothing and cover her. Besides, she is already gone, or going, through a tangle of low bushes into a parting in the reed wall.

Silence falls on the afternoon. Coots sound their sirens round the meres. Feet first, a flight of ducks skids in. Water droplets catch the sunshine. The reeds shiver and sigh. For some minutes I sit there and then with an effort lean over and check my instruments and ropes. They are still there in the bottom of the coracle, and the sight brings me back to myself and slows the beating of my heart. When I look up I see the mere, the water and the sky, all unchanged. But I know that everything is altered and translated. I spin the coracle, work abandoned, and paddle back to Ely, heavy with whatever is inside me.

From that day on I live a different life. Something has happened to me, though it feels neither a curse nor a blessing, but simply a change. Straight away I accept it and ingest it. The woman I saw, who saw me, has taken up residence inside me. I begin to wait, though I scarcely know who I wait for. I cannot say with any certainty that I would know her again if I saw her in the street in Ely. I caught so little of her features, transfixed as I was by her piercing look.

I am the same Jan Brunt, engineer; a tall black-haired man, given to silence and sitting alone in speculation. It is only to myself that I am different. The men I work with say nothing. At my lodgings, Mrs Suckling regards me with the usual suspicion. In the evening we continue our conversation and now work through lists of plants, then the names of animals. Gradually I begin to make out sentences in English and find myself understood. It is in part a matter of pronunciation. Lay our two languages side by side and the resemblance is clear; they must at one time have known one another. It is only the speaking that makes them such strangers.

I say nothing to Mrs Suckling about my box, which I find one evening with the lid up, but return with a new one that has a strong lock. In this I store my papers and take the key with me when I leave, hung on a string around my neck. Still I have the feeling of being watched and followed, though I never see a man behind me, and, our purpose becoming known, I can see no benefit in it. In Ely some of the people talk openly about the works. Opinion divides, as do the water and the land upon our maps. Some see good profits in draining the Great Level and the increases in all kinds of business that will follow. Others, who stand neither to gain nor lose, are indifferent.

I know not if it was people from Ely, or fensmen, who destroyed the earthworks and turned the last scheme into ruin, but Van Hooghten tells me it was a combination against the King whose business it was. Now that the war in England is finished the temper of the people here must be different. This being the case, I tell myself that my sense of being watched and my papers disturbed is imagination only, and comes about from feeling myself a stranger in this place.

★

Steadily the work advances. I start each day at the staithe as the sky lightens. Autumn comes towards us; the days shrink and the sky darkens early on the horizon. We are now bringing every creek and mere, every turn of water and curve of land, into being on our maps; giving the Great Level an outline and a form. Sometimes I work with other men, but I am often by myself. I tell Van Hooghten that I am watched, but he shrugs me off, and assures me that it is the place itself, the great wide feel of it, that oppresses me.

'There is no one here concealed,' he says with a smile. 'It is your own loneliness that conjures watchers, as wanderers see phantoms out of fear and hope.'

He is mistaken, or has forgotten where we come from. I am a Dutchman and an islander. Water and sky are safe to me as my mother's skirts. I know an empty silence and a full silence. Stand still in a full silence and it's loud with noises. A heron takes flight; he creaks like a ship in sail. Ducks scuffle in the reeds. I hear the beat of wings, the movement of creatures in the grass, water rippling, and the wind that accompanies me everywhere, sighing and roaring. Nature, that seems so quiet, pours out its songs. Even in the darkness there is a velvet purr of sound, of moles underground and field mice above.

An empty silence is quite different. If I hear a silence as quiet as the earth must have been before all things living were placed upon it, I know that something is amiss. Something has stopped up sound. Then ill-ease comes over me; a drawing-in of breath.

This is what I hear one hot afternoon towards September. I have the boat tied up, and have laid upon the bank a plumb line, a measuring rod and chain, triangulation poles and the chronometer that will confirm the calculations I make concerning the speed of the water. Next to them sit a compass and my papers with the figures written in. Clouds move slowly across the bleached-out sky, everything lit from my left hand towards my right. In the distance, seawards, I see a group of men, hear their words as they float over the marsh as I have seen angels' words writ in ribbons in the churches of the old religion. They are fensmen, come to lift wicker traps and empty the tangled eels into nets that they pull behind their boats. I hear the splashes as they throw the traps back into the mere. If they have seen me they show no sign of it, take no notice of what I do, and soon drift out of my sight.

Alone with my instruments, and engaged in my work, I forget myself. Even as we map this wilderness of mere and reed, we talk and plan how to drain the whole. Van Hooghten and I are in agreement. The whole of the Great Level must be scored across from south-west to north-east. Two new cuts will take the water from the present marsh and mere, stop the overflows of the rivers that now flood whenever there is a heavy fall of rain, and discharge the excess water into the sea. The first cut, though yet marked even upon the map, we call New River.

To plot a course for this new cut, I must first measure every shift in the gradient, and map every curl and tributary of the Ouse that already runs here. Today I am some miles north from Ely at a place where the last works were destroyed. I can see the remains now, a long line of hillocks and depressions. Nature is quick to take back what she might consider stolen from her and already they are covered over with bright summer grass and encroached upon by water. If you had no notion of history you might think them natural formations, or that the mounds concealed ancient ruins such as have been left by antiquity.

This afternoon I am calculating how high the embankments of the New River will have to be. Almost lost to the world, sitting on the grass, I pick up my papers and begin to write. At this moment I hear the silence empty behind my back. Apprehension presses on my senses and the feeling of being watched steals over me with a shiver and a lurch in my stomach as if I have dropped from a great height. When I look up, there she is, though how she has arrived at this place I cannot make out.

She stands at a distance, alone and without her companions. Though I wish straight away to speak so that she must reply, I cannot. No words come to me, either Dutch or English. I jump up and then see that my instruments lie scattered on the ground. I bend forward as if to gather them and go. In that instant she picks up the chronometer and turns to me, at the same time taking a step away.

'This – what do you use it for?'

Instead of asking how she came here or what she wants from me, I answer her, as if such a meeting as this might happen any day.

'It records the passing of time.'

Indeed, though I cannot think it then, while I turn my eyes to her, a chronometer does more. It snips up time, as much as if I were to take a pair of scissors to the air itself. And then it drives us on, towards tomorrow and the very moment of our extinction. I should look at my chronometer with distaste; it is keeping time with my dissolution. Yet I do not fear or dislike it. On the contrary, it is a source of joy to me; the newest to be found, Leiden-made. Its case is silver, egg-shaped and burnished to a soft brightness. As soon as I saw it in the palm of the watchmaker I determined to have it, and saved to buy it. The movement, under the oval face, turns with the earth itself, obedient to the same force.

It is not in my hands now, but in hers, and with a sudden gesture she hides it behind her back. I wonder if a woman such as she seems to be, from the unimproved part of this land, has seen a chronometer before. Does she know its beauty and its value? I am filled with a fear that she will throw it in the water and so I put out my hands towards her.

'I beg you, give it back.'

At this, she smiles, though her eyes remain steady upon me.

'You believe, sir, that no man or woman has a timepiece here?'

Lost for the English words, I stay silent.

In that moment I begin to see her clearly, and that she is not a girl, but a grown woman, tall and solid on her feet. Her face is brown from the sun as if she scorns to wear a bonnet, her hair cut short and stiff above her neck. Everything about her is golden and brown. She is without a scratch or a mark. She is dressed in a bodice and skirt that meet at her waist in a manner rough but serviceable. Except for her shoes, which resemble a man's boots, and the lack of stockings on her legs, she might step unremarked into my mother's kitchen.

Now, as if my chronometer is not enough, she picks up my measuring rod and holds it out to me.

'And this – how do you use this in your profession?'

I am considering how I might answer with the English words I know, and in a way that will not reveal my purpose, when she walks towards me across the spongy grass. For a second I fear that she will throw both rod and timepiece into the water, but she does not; she goes on holding them as if they are now her possessions. We are close by one another, and look into one another, eye to eye. I am the taller, but not by so much that I can see over her head, as is usual in my case with women.

A shadow seems to pass over me at that moment, not of darkness but of some material that I cannot see. After an instant of time that my chronometer might not register, I come into myself again and wish to speak. Or rather, it is a stranger within who bids me to talk; as if another man entirely has been resting inside me, waiting. This stranger is not a man such as I have known myself to be. He is a man without calculation, with a forwardness that I have never had; and yet he is a part of myself.

When I speak it is with his voice, not mine own that I know to be so halting and behindhand.

'I have seen you already.'

'And I you.'

'I have wished to see you again.'

There is no reply, but the stranger within me is bold.

'What is your name?'

'Eliza.'

I am a prudent man, embarked upon this task to advance in my profession; sure in purpose and firm in outline. Yet at this moment I feel none of that. I wonder if the heat has invaded me, caught me off-guard. I know that I am disordered. Believing myself alone and unobserved, I have rolled up my sleeves and tied them above my elbows. My stockings and my shoes lie in the boat.

In the drowsy heat, and in the glare of her presence, my bare feet begin to sink into the fen. The space seems endless, though if I stood in the boat and turned to the south-east I might just make out the grey bulk of the cathedral at Ely even from this great distance. But now my eyes follow the low contours of the numberless floating islands, and trace the winding river courses by their borders of dense alders. Everywhere towards the northern horizon lie the meres, one after another, flattened to silver discs in the sun. Only to the west is my eye stopped, for here the reed bed is so high that I can see nothing beyond it, just the sky above and the sun blazing in it like an emperor.

You are Eliza; not a girl, but a woman. Not out there beyond me, but here, at my side. I feel you present, already, from your gaze, inside me, alongside the stranger who spoke.

I stand back for a second, and see you again, as if for the first time. You look straight into my eyes, and I know again that things have changed, and that a part of my life will be addressed to you.

You have come here from somewhere in this expanse, and somewhere must lie the island on which you live, for you are a native of the fens, of that I am at once quite sure. It does not seem strange that you have appeared or that straight away I begin to tell you how I use the measuring rod and the chain that lies coiled on the grass of the riverbank. As well as I can, I explain the principles that my countrymen Snell and Van Royden laid down when they invented the system of triangulation that we now use to map every feature of a landscape with perfect exactitude. I even show you how it is done and explain the way I measure and calculate, and how, knowing distance, I can with the chronometer find the speed of the water at any time.

I tell you all this, full of my own knowledge and pride in my work. You listen with stillness, though my speech is rushed and my English imperfect. In truth my answers are just talk, language that bubbles up through my confusion. Though the stranger within me is bold, the man that I am finds that this is all he can say. A greater thing hangs between us that has nothing to do with the words I use.

Then, as suddenly as you have come, you lay down the measuring rod and put my chronometer back in my hand. For a second your palm closes over mine. The touch of your skin is warm and rough. In the moment that I bend to stow the instruments in my bag, you turn and walk away. The opening you make in the reed wall sways and closes; you are gone through into another world.

# Chapter 4

*Ely Town.*
*The Great Level.*
*August and September 1649.*

When I meet Jacob Van Hooghten in the evening, I hope that the darkness of the inn will make it easier for me to tell him what has happened. I want to open my heart to him, to show him that it beats faster and more strongly. In this strange place Van Hooghten has become my friend, the first that I have found, and I have placed my confidence in him more than I have dared with any other person, either man or woman. But I stumble before I can find the words, and at that moment feel my courage drain away. I say nothing, and the evening goes on in the way of countless others. We drink the weak beer of the country and smoke a couple of pipes of rough tobacco. Through the fug we talk of progress and how, if our surveys proceed with speed, a map will be ready by the winter.

So I do not speak out, but hide you straight away from the world. From a small boy I have been easy with secrets, neither my mother nor my father having looked to talk about themselves or hear what was in my heart. So I have become apt to hold both joy and insult fast inside and grow them as grit grows pearls.

I do not then think to myself I will continue to hide you, or whether you will yourself come out of the shadows. Though in all things a methodical man who plans step by step, putting one foot before another, I do not look ahead, but simply fail to speak out. If Van Hooghten notices my halting speech, he says nothing; besides, he is not a man to force a confidence from another.

*

By this time, Van Hooghten is the picture of a healthy man, with skin as brown as his chestnut boots. Whenever we meet he clasps me close and smiles. His teeth are very white now in his round face, his eyes deep blue, and his mood is high. We both sleep soundly, a circumstance he attributes to the nature of the work, which is arduous and steady. We measure and draw, calculate and note, he with his band of Dutchmen on the drier ground from where they can triangulate with ease, I with mine on the water. We are the first engineers to map this whole wilderness, and take pride in that fact, as if we were explorers out on the ocean.

I send my men to the south, and spend days out on the meres alone. I sleep under my upturned coracle, concealed in the darkness of its shell. You tell me later that spirits live on the meres, but that my coracle protects me. Its skin, taken from a living being, serves as a shield. This I do not believe, and yet the rough feel of the wicker frame brings a kind of comfort, though there is no animal abroad large enough to menace me. My instruments and food I keep with me, and I myself, should it rain, am preserved from damp and ague. In my schooldays I have read of the sage Diogenes, who lived thus in a barrel, and understand, as I lie alone, that his folly was less than I thought it as a child.

With this comes a picture of the school on Tholen, my parents' house by the canal and my little sisters Katrijn and Anna, head to toe asleep in the large bedstead in the parlour wall. The bedstead doors open a crack for air, but like me my sisters lie in their wooden box, warm and safe. A quilt covers them, sewn and embroidered by my mother. Sometimes they up-end and lie side by side. In the gloom they whisper and tell stories. Seated at the parlour table my mother pretends not to hear. She leans her sewing into the candlelight. Her brow is golden in the brown room. Katrijn and Anna have a life snug and far from wars.

A letter in the hands of the postmaster at Ely goes aboard ship at King's Lynn and arrives on Tholen in a few weeks. To my mother and father I send greetings and to Margriet I write that I have discovered a tiny iris here, its petals cream and blue with yellow splashed down inside. It grows on the damp banks, scarce higher than my finger. I tell her I have sent it to a learned gentleman of my acquaintance in The Hague and that if it is indeed undiscovered I shall name it for her. Beyond this, I find that I have little to say.

I think of my mother pushing me, her only son, forwards from the shadows, too sparing with her love and praise, and understand that I am looking for another life.

Jacob Van Hooghten also writes home. With his customary regularity he sends news to his widowed mother and three brothers all making their way in the world, one a sea captain with the West India Company, another a lawyer in The Hague, the last a schoolmaster in his village in the north, as their father was before him. He writes also to his betrothed, Maria. He tells me about her in his eager way, smiling as if he sees her in his mind. Van Hooghten never doubts her love and says simply that they will be happy when life allows their union. He has no fear about the future.

'This is Maria,' he says, and snaps open a leather case. Inside, an oval portrait nests on its velvet bed.

'Once the work is done here,' he says, 'I will have saved enough to set up on my own.'

Life spools out ahead of Van Hooghten, a straight sunlit path. Time, also, in his imagination, is a steady progression, facing forward. Beyond Maria he sees children, then a good house with a piece of fertile land under a wide sky, credit at the bank, and his projects, one after another into the distance. Neither sickness nor death disturb the outline of this vision.

'Look at her, my Maria,' he says, holding out the portrait. 'I'm a lucky man, Jan.'

I agree, and draw the small painting close to me so that I can see her, though in truth I feel no presence there. Eyes – blue; hair under the lip of her bonnet – fair. A young woman stares out steadily, though whether it is the painter who looks at her that way, or whether it is her own habit of looking at the world I cannot tell. I hand the little portrait back to Jacob, and nod my approbation, for that is what he wishes.

Although I have said nothing to Jacob, you are now always there in my mind. Whenever I am out on the water and closed in by walls of reed, my whole self and body is tensed and waiting. I can feel from the silence when I am observed. The white butterflies fly up and away and all around me the murmur and chirrup of the fens is lowered, leaving only the sounds made by the wind in the leaves and the gentle lapping of the water as it runs against the banks.

Sometimes the feeling fades away, but at other times, there you are, quiet and sudden. I am certain that you have watched for a time and then parted the reed stems to appear beside me. If I ask whether you have a coracle nearby or have come across the islands on paths unknown to me, you shrug and say nothing. The very way you stand, straight and solid on your feet, your head up on your neck, eyes nearly level to mine and shimmering in your face, has a challenge in it.

You watch me work, and little by little we fall into snatches of talk. You show me summer flowers and tell me the names of those that are particular to your people.

One hazy morning I am bold enough to ask, 'Where do you come from?'

'Around.'

'But where is your home?'

At that you laugh.

'Here. Where then is yours?'

I turn and point to the north-east where Holland lies.

'It is beyond the sea.'

'A place beyond the water?'

You turn in that direction as if Holland might be visible.

'Tell me about it.'

So that day I sit on the grass and neglect my work, making a picture for you of Amsterdam and then of Tholen. You stay very still as I talk and say nothing. To speak of myself in this way is new to me, and the words come even more haltingly than usual. Each word in this unfamiliar language is an offering that I wish you to take.

Another day as you stand behind me I feel your hand on my back, distinct and strong against my spine. I am ready to turn and pull you towards me, but hesitate. I fear to anger you, as I did that first afternoon. So I tell myself it is my own desire that I feel, not anything that comes from you or runs between us.

This desire has grown with your curiosity and your presence and I have let it. I do not wish to contain it; but I fear that if you feel it in me you may disappear and never return. I do not know where you come from, and you have turned away my questions.

Then, in the last of summer while the days are still warm, there you are again, standing tall far away along the bank of the river. Once again I am in a manner struck dumb, and can only think to carry on my work and wait for you to come up to me, which you do along the narrow path that runs by the riverbank. You squeeze over and through the willow branches, solid and sure-footed.

'Good day, Eliza,' I say then, when you are right by me.

You say nothing, but I know suddenly what is to happen. I cannot remember how or how much time goes past before we move, but only that we are onto each other, and fallen to the grass, and I have one hand on your back pulling you towards me, the other already under your petticoat, and you, Eliza, though I do not say your name then – you, the same, your hand in my breeches so I gasp; and then we are together, and though everything about me is disordered, everything is at the same time clear, and it is not as if I am dreaming but rather as if the whole world is bursting into life, and all of nature standing still.

Then I am lying on the grass, breeches gone, everything gone. We are down to the bones, to a nakedness that seems to have stripped away flesh. There is nothing between us. You are lit up by the sun, lying on the grass with the light pouring down onto your back. My arms run right round you, and after everything you rise from my chest, and finally I look up and see in your golden eyes first a tenderness, then an absence, as if you were one moment with me and then in another you have already left. Quite in silence you put on your shift and shirt and walk away along a path that leads through the reeds, never turning back. Such paths are not safe for me to use, but I do not in any case attempt to follow you or see where you are going. I just lie there and perhaps I sleep, because by the time I come to myself the sun is dropping into the water. The mere is glazed with beauty, the reed heads dark against the red to the west, and lit up in feathery flames to the east. The notion comes to me that God is here, and walks near me; but I sit up and find myself alone and naked still.

I gather up my things that are scattered about. The moon is rising to guide me back to Ely Isle. I row over the darkening water until I arrive at the jetty and tie the boat to its slimy stump. Then I see the river flowing north and the great dome of night coming up. I stand and watch as the light goes and the stars become a hundred, then a thousand, then too many to count, and throw their light all over the black sky.

From that day the sun shines on everything in the world. It feels to me as if I have a new knowledge, and that the change that came over me when you first fixed me with your glance was the beginning of it. This knowledge is not from a person or a book. It is a knowledge of what is, neither sacred nor profane, but just the world itself.

Later, the day comes back to me, sometimes in fragments, sometimes to my moving sight. Though I see you and hear the sound of the whole Great Level as it lay stretched out in the summer sun, my mind is not the only vessel that holds the past. In my flesh and bones memory stirs and wakes. You have not gone from me but wait beyond the round curve of the earth, a part of it, and alive to my touch. With the beat of my heart life quickens and time falls away to the other place where we live as real as waking day. Then I can see into your eyes, not from afar as memory sometimes sees, but there, lying beneath you. Your shadow falls onto me from above. My fingertips run up your back and move bone by bone up to your shoulders and down over your breast to where your heart beats. The sunshine runs through your hair like living gold.

# Chapter 5

*The Great Level.*
*Autumn 1649.*
*Fine warm weather.*

That autumn, while it is still warm, we find each other often. You sometimes come over the fen on foot, sometimes in your coracle across the water. I might be at the start of my day's work, or you might arrive halfway through as I sit across a stump with my feet over the water, the willow leaves trailing in the current and my mind with them, when suddenly there you are. So we begin a sort of court-ship, in which words and flesh take equal parts.

On the fen and under the sky we are alone. We might be the first two people in the world, except that Adam knew Eve, who was fash-ioned from himself, whereas you are everything that is strange to me. I do not guess when you will find me, or how you do so, or what you will say when we meet. At first I ask you little, fearing that you will take flight at any question, though everything about you excites my curiosity and interest. You seem to have come complete across the fen, and though I wonder, I know that you are a part of this world, and do not belong in mine. It is I who have come here to the Great Level and I approach you with a reserve and diffidence that are familiar to me, careful to remain at a distance. At the same time I am recording and noting, as my habit is, and determine to understand you as a geographer does the shifting land, with patience and by study.

I say your name when we first meet and then over and over as we lie together – Eliza, Eliza, Eliza. I trace your outlines until the surface of you in a manner gets under my own and I am not sure, lying on the grass, where we begin and end or that there is any division between ourselves, the water and the pale sky. On the inside of your broad wrist I can see and feel the veins that run beneath your skin. It comes to me that your body and my own, with their caves and hills, declivities and safe places, are part of the earth. This feeling fills me with a tenderness so that I want to hold you close and feel the soft hair on your arms stand at my passing touch. Our being together comes to be nothing strange, and concerns no other living being.

Lying with you my most secret self opens out and I begin to talk of notions that I have long kept close for fear of ridicule. Strange as it is, it seems that you, a woman from this rude place, can better understand what lies in my heart than any man of genius I have met. One day I say that I am sure we are present to God and approved by him in our nakedness. You do not scorn me or call me blasphemous, or tell me I am mistaken, but simply laugh, rich and strong, as if the subject is absurd, so that I soon come to think that having made this beauty, the creator loves it still.

Another time I explain my fancy that this east part of the nation of England was surely once joined to Holland. Great forests covered everything, scored through by rivers that flowed to the north perhaps, or to the south, but did not end, as all these rivers now do, in tangled meanderings and mud. Men walked freely over what is now the sea and mingled with one another in the time when there were no nations. So it was that these people used the same language. How long ago it was I cannot guess, but I am sure these two lands were only parted when cut in two by some huge storm or sea-surge that brought this island into existence and made the coasts of Holland too.

As the weeks pass you tell me something of your people and how you live together on islands in the meres; how if two people quarrel they will part company, one staying, the other travelling to a different part of the fen to join others there. This, you say easily, is quite a frequent occurrence, and ask if the same happens amongst those I live with. I deny this, but later see that it is indeed so, and only the way we describe such an event is different. We prefer to call a separation in a family something else, an opportunity for advancement, or a need to trade; but its effects are the same.

One evening you point out to me dots of light in the gloom. They get brighter as darkness gathers, and then they vanish. It is my uncle, you say, with some other men. They are catching eels that make their way down the rivers and out to sea, lifting the eel traps and sliding the eels into buckets of water. One man holds up the lantern, the other raises the traps and empties them. When the lights disappear it is because they have put them down in the bottom of their coracles while they return the traps to the water.

As the weeks pass I stop wondering about your appearance in my life or why I keep it a secret. It is simply that a light has begun to shine where there was none before. Everything about you fills me with happiness. I leave Mrs Suckling in Ely and take lodgings in a damp farmhouse that sits above the old river in the south of the island. The two rooms have a charm to me, though they are nothing more than a bedroom and a parlour, furnished scantily with a wooden bed and chairs, a table and hooks on the walls for my clothes. The farmer seems more interested in the money I give him than in my person. Secure on the island, where his two dozen cattle graze the rich grass and feed well on hay through the winter, he knows my business but keeps that knowledge to himself.

The whole landscape, that soon will begin to change, now comes to seem magical. When I wake in the morning and fold the shutters open, the dark horizon and the sky meet in an opal glow where the sun will come up. I rise very early, eager to get out, tense with desire. My movements have quickened, charged with vitality even as I am measuring and writing, full of the task.

In the first weeks of autumn I begin to assemble the map. Van Hooghten joins his own drawings to it and together we sketch upon it the course of the two cuts that will carry the water to the sea. They will be magnificent structures, such as have scarce been attempted in Holland even, and never before seen in these lands. Each will be a hundred feet wide and be boundaried with fine broad banks to serve as both bulwarks and bridle paths.

The first cut will be made to the east of the River Ouse, with a high embankment on its eastern side, matched by the western bank of the old river which will rise to meet it. It is simple when I draw it upon fine linen paper. The new river slices straight through meadows, meres and marshes. The old river winds close by, as a slow old man walks mazily by a nimble youth.

As the weeks go on and the autumn advances Van Hooghten and I both shift our place of operations to the town of King's Lynn that lies on the furthest edge of the Great Level, closest to the open sea.

Towards the sea the whole landscape becomes indistinct. It cannot with any certainty be mapped and is scarcely traversed. There are no permanent islands here, no certain channels. Everything shifts and changes with the seasons, the years and the tides. Salt and sweet water run up against one another, rivers turn to estuary, islands to salt marsh, peat to mud.

In the marshes, where there might be a boundary, but is none, the two elements are fused. The land is water-soaked and the water carries its heavy load of silt. Yet we know that it is the water, not the land, that we must tame. Water is subtle; it must be drawn out from the land, never forced, but offered new channels and insinuated into a clean division of liquid and solid. As I make a map which turns the infinity of meres and streams, rills and islands into two elements only, rivers and dry land, that is my task.

In Holland we have for hundreds of years coaxed land from the sea, or joined new land to that we have already reclaimed, but this place is far stranger. Here the fens people make islands, not to add to dry land, but to float upon the water. There are hundreds of these islands now in the meres, or it may be thousands in such an extensive landscape. They are hidden by ramparts of reeds that grow too high for any man, even standing in a boat, to see over them. Now I begin to see many of these islands in the course of my mapping, and examine their foundations. This task I undertake with a degree of fear, knowing that behind the reeds the fensmen place their houses and draw up their coracles out of sight.

One afternoon when you find me at this work, I ask you about the islands.

'It is plain, Eliza, that your people make these islands. How is it done?'

'Over years, for we do not command the water,' you say. 'We do not cut the land. We make an island not by draining, but by an opposite sort of work.'

'Tell me.'

'The first thing is, to call upon the water.'

You tell me how you entice the passing water to give up its cargo of sediment and leaves. The first year there is a ragged accumulation of sticks and vegetation against the willow stakes. In the second year it thickens up. In the third, mud begins to stick and by the fourth the sediments start to harden. Then, once a kind of rampart has made itself, the fensmen capture silt and vegetable matter to build the interior. At any time they may have one or two near grown, several in their infancy of sticks and mud, and several halfway fixed. Sometimes an island is overwhelmed in floods and swept away, but, tended by the fensmen at its birth, it grows to permanence with reed beds and willows of its own. One plant offers a home to another; birds, insects and the smaller creatures likewise.

My own labour continues until the rains come, and the rivers and banks that I have been mapping disappear. The waters rise, and begin to bury the summer islands. I can see the grass waving underwater if I peer over the side of my coracle as I paddle along. In these last weeks before winter I am full of the wonder and delight of you. In my imagination I see the great lust and joy of God as he made the world out of himself. When everything was dark God's spirit moved about over the face of the waters, hovering to and fro, deciding. There was then, in those first moments, nothing that God could not do, or make, and the first thing God did was to shout yes. 'Yes,' he shouted. 'Let there be light.' And his shout was so powerful and lusty that light appeared, and darkness with it, and then he pushed the light to one side, the dark to the other and called one the day, the other night.

I now give my attention to the beginning of the world. Out on the fen, with nothing but the mere about me, I imagine God's joy, the way the spirit of creation rushed up through him when he had made the light and the darkness. Of course he went on; he could not resist, especially when he had made that most beautiful thing, the sun. With a huge roar he separated the waters too, half above the firmament and half below, the waters above whirling beyond the planets in a great spiral of snow and ice that we see as the blackness there.

That was the work of the first day, the evening and the morning. But he didn't stop; life possessed him and gave him the whole strength of the universe. With a great lunge he gathered up the shining waters and made the dry land appear, rising up in mountain ranges and islands, deserts and volcanoes; and he dipped his bucket into the oceans he had made and flung the water across the earth. Lakes collected themselves, emptying out into rivers, and he plunged his hands again into the warm earth that he had created, the loam full of insects, the roots of plants streaming out from the tips of his fingers, pushing down and up until great forests grew, the branches opening out one from the other, everything multiplying together and ceaselessly.

But now he was aflame with the power of creation and it poured from him, so he pulled out clay from the land to make all the living creatures. They grew from his hands and ran scuttering and pattering and galloping over the new meadows and up the trunks even as the bark formed and the fruit ripened. Seeing his creation God didn't stop; no, he shouted his joy so that the heavens rang with it, and the stars shook, and it bounced off the lid of the firmament and ran off into the void beyond. In this way all the sounds of heaven and earth came into being.

And in the third and fourth days this lust grew stronger and the forms God created were more extravagant: sea monsters; and lions with shaking manes, golden like the reed beds here; and great whales with grilles for mouths; and tiny fish to feed into them. He worked on and on, the colours of his creations getting more beautiful and unlikely. In one burst he made the peacock and its shimmering tail that brushed the ground as it walked its uppity step, and rose high and trembling with desire; in another great waterfalls issued from his hands and he threw them down precipices and into lakes so that spray filled the air and danced in the sun with every colour he had ever wrought.

But neither the tiniest shrew nor the leathery rhinoceros was enough; nothing could appease the urge to make more. He wanted noise and heat, the crack of lightning and the roar of forest fires. He started the earth spinning and the winds following on, and he piled great clouds up and up with flinging arabesques of his hands and he stooped down to make tiny spores and seed heads, mushrooms that came up whole in the dark, and perhaps he might have stopped there, but he did not. On the sixth day he made a man, and gave him a name, the first name ever given, for God himself did not have a name, or anything attached to him, since he was the creator.

East of Eden God conjured a garden for Adam to walk in and planted it with all the most beautiful and fertile trees and plants he had created, and, as a last burst of creation, God added Eve. And this, I think as I go about my measuring and plumbing for depth, was the creation of the world.

God's lust for invention waned after that. He was tired, and sat back and watched everything that he had made. He threw Adam and Eve out of the garden and set them to wander across Eden and into the world and have children, but still man disappointed him. Then God went back to the beginning, to water. Water was God's great love, the first thing, the dry land only a second thought. So when he decided to rid the world of the evil of man it was water God turned to. In his rage he opened the floodgates of heaven and let the fountains of the deep pour over the earth. He made it rain unceasingly until all the earth was covered in water, men and children and women whirled away in the flood until only a few were left. Just in time he repented and ordered a ship made, men and animals saved, a voyage and a settling on Mount Ararat.

But that was much later. I feel now as God did on the evening of the first day when he put down his strength and saw the sun he had just made set for the first time. The spark of his creation has got into me and I feel the meres spill over with the same joy that God felt. The whole universe streams towards me. I have the sensation when I see you that I am looking as an astronomer does when the stars in all their majesty are suddenly brighter and seem to come down and touch him and draw him up.

This is your gift to me, and God's to the world. This I see as I have never seen before, that we were not made to be the lords of creation, but a part of it, together with the stars that come close to us as we lie together. The life of all the things under the firmament surges through us then; we are filled up and replenished and time itself is stopped.

# PART THREE

# Chapter 1

*Nieuw Amsterdam.*
*The 10th day of July, 1664.*
*The sky clear, wind from the east.*
*Oppressive hot.*
*Low tide by the Stadt Huys at 10 o'clock in the morning.*

There is much I find in Nieuw Amsterdam that I wish to record along with my story. Though I might say little aloud, inside I speak. As I walk by the Heere Gracht, or beyond the wall where the English farmers have bought out the Dutch settlers and now clear the land for crops and pasture, I take note of what I see. When I sit in my garret with my gown tight against the cold, and the wood whispers in the grate, I talk to you; and you reply. I can hear your voice, low and always to me strange as all the English voices must be to a Dutchman, and yet in its upswing and the laughter caught in it, not so.

From here, this bright morning in Nieuw Amsterdam fifteen years after that first day, I can see that life does not proceed as we were taught at school, that from the first day of the creation of the world, one day follows another; the past and our history piles up as if we have laid one sheet of paper upon another until the last page. That is what I believed: that time nibbles away at the future, and in that moment puts the present behind its back. The past retreats as each present moment joins it, on and on.

Yet that is far too simple. Inside us, time sways backwards and forwards from now to then, here to there, and nothing of it is lost or goes away, but it all hangs everywhere, translucent in the air. Some men turn away, and walk on, saying that the past contains only their former selves and ghosts of people and deeds. Others, like myself, live every day with it. One minute I am in Nieuw Amsterdam, the next pulled on a string into the other time that comes with me, so that here on the Heere Gracht, or as I walk across the marketplace, you and I talk. I may pause to greet an acquaintance, and then we go on with our talk, so that I see this place but also that other, and you are both here and there.

For twelve years I have kept you alive beside me. I have heard your voice, touched your skin. Then came the song and the note that lies on the table in my garret; two such ordinary events that have often, surely, slipped past with the day and gone unnoticed. This time sound and hope jostled in me for weeks. I thought I caught sight of you once, in the crowd on Het Marckvelt, tall and bare-headed as you always were. Now hope has subsided, and left me by myself.

It is not the first time. Over the years I have sometimes found myself alone, without your voice. Then it seems that loss tunnels holes inside me. I feel loss exactly; it is displacement, not death. To strangers I appear solid and upright, the tall engineer they have come to know in this place. 'It's Jan Brunt,' they say one to another. 'A useful man, honest with his prices, careful to execute commissions well.' And to be sure, I am to them no other, though they shun me in the tavern if they want only light conversation. Jan Brunt, engineer, residing for a dozen years now by the Heere Gracht at number 12. They can pull my doorbell any time and as like as not find me at home, upstairs in my garret, or by the fire in the parlour in winter. Yet when I cannot reach you, I know myself to be a man unmade from within. Then, after some days, or in an instant, you return. The world opens again, and in my garden a ladybird shines scarlet in the sun, placing its crooked legs with care across a leaf.

This morning I have paddled my canoe to the tip of Manatus Eylandt. I am sheltering in the lee of the wharf that faces onto the Stadt Huys, the paddle across my knees. The brisk wind carries a tang of Atlantic salt and seaweed. Around me several ships ride at anchor. From the stern of a West India Company merchantman glass windows glitter and wink, and the Company's great silk flag ripples above them, striped in blue, white and red. Beside it are anchored three ships from the English colonies. One has hoisted the Red Ensign, in obedience to the English King, but the other two fly that flag without the cross of St George, in open rebellion to the restored monarch.

When I come here, I like to let my canoe drift up to one of these great ships as they shift on their anchor chains. It is a dangerous pastime, and draws shouts from the men aboard, who take me for a wildman or lunatic. As I bump against the oak belly of a merchantman, I hear the whole boat groan, and though I have no wish to take another voyage further than my profession demands, my heart lightens with possibility at the sound. If I took passage for Boston and then headed north towards the ice, or went south and continued on past Recife towards the end of the American continent, I might find wonders.

I glide round the ships and into the shelter of the harbour wall. Here the world is loud with noise. On Stadt Huys Laan a baby pulls at his mother's breast. He snorts softly as he drinks and his throat clicks as it opens and closes. His mother settles herself and rocks him to sleep, and her chair creaks on the oak floorboards. Over on Het Marckvelt the steady tap of a cane suddenly stops. That's Tonis Jansens, a full-blown man given to the gout and a limp. Like as not he has run into his friend Peter Wand and now leans on his stick to pass the time of day. Peter Wand sucks his teeth in sympathy when Tonis Jansens complains of the high price of beaver pelts this year. By way of saying goodbye, Jansens raises his hand to show a fist full of carnations he has just bought for his wife Johanna. The flowers are warm with sunlight and rustle like paper as he lifts them.

Through the hum of voices and the clink of change in the market-place comes the thud of a hammer. North along Heere Straet, new houses rise, with fine crow gables and birch-wood cladding. This is the very edge of the town. On an empty lot, summer flowers have planted themselves in the cleared ground. A purple vetch straggles over the sandy soil. How tenacious it is, undeterred by lumps and stones in its way. Bees advance towards its flowers and the plant leans towards the bees when it catches their hum, so the pollen can make the leap from the flower throat right into the open collecting pouches.

In the morning stillness these sounds drift over the water and curl round the rigging of the *Prinz Willem*, the slender hull of the *Leopard*, just in from Antwerp, and the *Salamander* and the *Patience*, run down from Boston. The ships from the north, like these two, are ever more numerous and bring trade and English goods to this place. A Dutch ship like the *Prinz Willem* is a rarer sight. Many say that Nieuw Nederland has been left to fend for itself in these last years, and that our English neighbours increase in numbers far faster than do the colonists here.

Yesterday I shared an evening pipe with William Sharp, an English trader who comes and goes from Massachusetts Bay. Sharp is a short, wiry man of discernment and well worth an hour's conversation. He drinks my coffee sitting by the unlit stove in my garret, where I have opened both windows to tempt a breeze. He asks me why it is that our Company governors care so little for the colony. I answer that I cannot say, not being privy to the thinking in Amsterdam. Perhaps, I add, the Spice Islands in the east that ooze easy profits now engross speculators instead, whereas this hard spot, this little worm of an island, is scarce worth the trouble.

'Indeed. It is barely defended,' he says, and raises his eyebrows.

'The Company maintains the Fort and battery.'

'Your fort, Mr Brunt, will deter no one. Where is your militia?'

He laughs and adds that the doors of the Fort were wide open when he passed it earlier in the day. Boys ran in and out, and not a soldier in sight.

'Nothing seems in order here.'

'Herr Stuyvesant, our Director-General, is most at his ease when he quarrels, and quarrel he does, with the Company as much as with us in the city. So things come to a halt.'

'Meanwhile, you are in grave danger of being overrun, Mr Brunt,' Mr Sharp says, 'and not because Director-General Stuyvesant is a difficult and hot-tempered man. You must reckon with greater things.'

'What greater things can there be, Mr Sharp, than the pastimes of boys, and where better place to play than a fort that lies wide open?'

He taps my knee with the tip of his pipe, his hand curled round the bowl.

'Governor Winthrop some weeks ago declared that the King now grants him rule not only of the new Connecticut colony, but all the land between that place and Virginia.'

'Indeed so, sir.'

Scorn crosses Mr Sharp's face, as if I have shown too little interest in his news.

'Do you know anything of the customs of the English?'

'Not so much, Mr Sharp.'

'Neither us up in New England, nor those wretches who still hanker after the old world in the south?'

'I care nothing for the quarrels that you English have brought to the New World.'

'You have never been in England?'

'Never.'

I do not like to find myself in deceit, and hope to stop the conversation there. I do not wish that any man or woman should know my history, or pass it round like a dish of meat upon a plate.

'Yet you speak the language with ease.'

'I have learned your language doing business for Englishmen.'

'Drainage business?'

'Indeed, sir. There is profit in buying marsh or mudflat and conjuring a farm from it. That is what I have been able to do for your countrymen as well as my own.'

'Very good, sir; there's no end to my countrymen in these days.'

'Indeed, Mr Sharp, and I collect new forms of language from them. I am a curious man.'

'That is indeed true, Mr Brunt. I notice you have the habits of an antiquary.'

With this he gets up and begins to cast his eyes round the bare walls of my garret.

'No portraits or landscapes,' Mr Sharp remarks, with his back turned from me. 'None of the pictures so common in the houses here. No pretty women or cheerful taverns.'

It is indeed the custom amongst the Dutch to crowd their walls with pictures of people; husband and wife in their separate frames, family groups with children sitting round their parents and dogs weaving in and out. No end of people, and landscapes too, that make crowded Holland much bigger than it is.

Though we are a practical people we are also gripped by the imaginary scenes our painters make for us. Fantastic pools and waterfalls, that flat Holland can never boast, cool us in the heat of summer. We love maps, because in them the ocean is everywhere fixed to our walls and ships speed us to strange new shores where waves scour great rocks and palms stand over silver sands. No wonder many of us have thirty, forty pictures to a room.

Why do I have no pictures? people ask. It hurts them to see my walls so bare and speechless. I shrug and smile. Perhaps I am not a Dutchman any more, I say. But the truth is that my mind teems with pictures. Without even shutting my eyes, I see landscapes. People, sounds and scenes flash past. I can walk into any one of them and find myself in another world, twenty years ago, yesterday, or today, its colours vivid, its sounds alive.

Pictures do not help me remember. Those few I had I left behind willingly in Amsterdam. A painting fixes a person or a place, freezes them in a moment. Life is trapped. Even you; beyond a few small drawings that run down the margins of sheets of paper filled with calculations, I have no portrait of you. I do not wish for you captured and framed. I want you alive.

This is what I am thinking as Mr Sharp starts on my collections, going from one thing to another and returning at last to the hearth by the stove where the two goddesses stand. Now I become uneasy. I am accustomed to Lysbet and her duster, but otherwise wish my goddesses undisturbed.

Mr Sharp has lost interest, sits down and returns to his theme.

'Mr Brunt, you need to look amongst your own acquaintance to take the temper of the times. Look to Mr Miller, who buys house after house here, or Mr Peabody who now owns half the ships that go between Nieuw Amsterdam and the New England ports.'

This indeed I heard, I say, but it is not a matter for me but for the English.

'Wake up, Mr Brunt. Events move at a great pace. Governor Winthrop is already overtaken. In Boston the news is that King Charles has thought better of his last gift, and has revoked it in favour of his own brother, the Duke of York. He now decrees that all the land from Maine to Delaware is granted to his brother, and names especially the Noort Rivier, that they call the Hudson.'

Mr Sharp eyes me again, and says as he gets up to leave, 'To include this city, Mr Brunt.'

Rumours run along streets and round corners; then trickle away. After a few days Nieuw Amsterdam settles back into itself. Now heat lies on Manatus Eylandt, thick and insect-filled. Men loll in the shade. Work and chatter slows. The sun sucks up steadiness and endeavour. We battle summer.

Then Lysbet tells me there is digging and piling at the top of the street here. A makeshift embankment is rising. I walk up by the canal and find plump Martin Robben, who prefers a spoon to a shovel, throwing sandy earth up the slope. Ezra, a freed slave, labours next to him; and with them a ragged bunch of men from the wharfs.

'We need to add another ring of defence,' Robben says. 'Colonel Schuyler's orders.'

The city is stirring, woken from torpor by the English King's decree. Muskets will glitter at the top of the new embankment, pointing north. If the first wall fails, the fight will come to my door. Walking home, I pass the quiet houses along the Heere Gracht, shuttered against the sun.

Minutes later, a knock at my door. Philip Schuyler, once colonel of the garrison, stands there. His grey beard glistens with sweat.

'Mijnheer Brunt, *goedemorgen*.'

I bow. Schuyler is a hotheaded man I only pass the time of day with.

'You have heard that the English King now declares Nieuw Nederland to belong to his brother?'

'Yes, indeed, sir, some days ago, from the furrier Sharp.'

'Director-General Stuyvesant being away, I have ordered our defences strengthened. On behalf of the Company and citizens I ask you to check the embankment.'

'I have just been there, Colonel. It looks in order. You can carry on.'

I close the door to him and take slow steps to the garret. The goddesses stare through their slitted eyes. Apprehension comes over me, the grey feel of London long ago and the city full of ghosts. I ask myself how much it matters which power, on the far side of the world, takes it upon itself to be our master. Looking from my window along the Heere Gracht I see through it to a picture of St Paul's cathedral, wrecked and gaping, and fear that war being brought to this place.

With the new embankment up, fear of the English is set aside. Now rage at the West India Company sweeps through the city. Where is Director-General Stuyvesant when he is needed? Not here: he's gone to Fort Orange, a week's sail upriver, and taken most of the garrison with him. The winds of talk shift and veer. More news arrives from Boston. A squadron of warships has put in there with orders that the colonies of Massachusetts Bay and Connecticut now place themselves under the sovereignty of the King. Just as Mr Sharp said, King Charles declares his intention to subdue all of Nieuw Nederland, join it to the English colonies and to bring the whole of the settled area of this place under the English Crown. What belonged to the West India Company will now belong to him.

It seems to me impossible: to own a mountain or claim a river with a flourish of the royal hand. The ambitious spirit of the English has indeed begun to run fast round the world. More than this small city, the English settlers have always wanted the land. Mountains, marshes, acres, estates, plantations, woods and forests, the rivers that run through. They want the land, and with it the beavers, the bees, the healing plants, and the careful shy deer. They want to own every living thing in this new place and still it might not be enough.

This thirst for possession is furtive amongst the colonists in the north, who pretend to a pure feeling for God and declare they make a paradise in his name. It breaks out more easily in Maryland and Virginia. The first men from these southern colonies I met in the way of business were taut and bitter with loss. The burning ashes of defeat came with them to the New World. The fire glowed under their new lives. Nothing, not even wealth, could put it out.

I remember one such smouldering man who came to see me some years ago: Captain Maybrick, a landowner in England and formerly of His Majesty King Charles's army, as he told me; now a planter on the Chesapeake. Maybrick had enquired in the city for an engineer and been directed to me. The destruction of his English estate during the late wars still pained him, he said, and with the King dead he was unable to return. General Cromwell was sending over plenty of troublesome Irish; he had fresh labour and was resolved to use it.

'I plan to clean out the swamp and put the land to use. Improve it, Mr Brunt. Your line of work, I'm told. The whole swamp is useless now, and floods in the high tide.'

'You know the rise and fall of the tides at your estate?'

'Yes, yes; all of that is calculated.'

Maybrick seeming vague about the size of the task, I suggested that I come down to Bellevue, as he named his estate, and accompany his engineer in making a proper survey of the land and waters. The idea did not please him.

'I have drawings made already,' he said, 'and a plan for the works. I only wish to know if they are sound and the improvements give me a return for my money.'

We sat in the Ship Tavern, an inn much favoured by the English, being run by one of their number. Maybrick unrolled his drawings and spread them out across a table. The map of his estate was sketchy, and the ground inadequately surveyed, but the plans for drainage were neat and careful.

'They have evidently been drawn up by a man who knows something of drainage and irrigation.'

'Of course, Mr Brunt,' he said, though the look on his face belied his certainty. Perhaps he had paid a man unqualified and now sought to remedy his parsimony. Such a method of proceeding is common everywhere. I have little respect for a man who is not prepared to pay for lasting work from the outset; nonetheless I am prepared, for a fee, to put right what has been hastily done.

'I cannot say if this scheme will work. I will need to go over the ground, make a fuller map and a detailed survey also of the river and its rise and fall.'

'You want to pay a visit to Bellevue?'

'Indeed, sir. To be certain of success, I should have to come several times. Nature may resist what we propose.'

Maybrick looked astonished.

'Nature resist? Why then, Mr Brunt, it is your job to vanquish nature, as I do on my land.'

I nodded, as I have learned to do with choleric men.

'To be sure; yet water is a subtle partner.'

'Partner? Why cannot you simply tell me whether these drawings can be implemented?'

'To be sure, I should need to have an idea about all the powers nature might summon before I can make any recommendation.'

Maybrick looked uncertain, and then shook his head.

'No, no; I cannot have it.'

'Very well. As you wish, Captain.'

The look upon his face was now one of hesitation.

'But you think that this might work?'

'It might, with the right man to oversee the works and due care taken in their construction.'

'Thank you; that is all I require.'

Maybrick fumbled in his deep velvet pocket and drew out his purse. From it he pulled a handful of coins of high value, which he put on the table between us. Then he rolled up the drawings, nodded a curt goodbye and left the inn. I never saw him again.

Looking now from my window over the canal, down the slope to the Oost Rivier, I see where Lange Eylandt begins, stretching away towards the old world, while behind me stands an infinity of land, all shining in the summer heat. It will never be enough for those who want it. Now I see that it never was, neither here, nor in the Great Level, when it lay that winter under its liquid covers, quiet in hibernation.

# Chapter 2

*King's Lynn.*
*The Great Level.*
*Spring, 1650.*

With the end of winter, the flood begins its retreat. I watch the meres shrink to pools and the rivers take their narrow courses once more. Land emerges slick and waterlogged. Meadows form in the spring light, bright with flowers and noisy with geese. Dragonflies flash and career across the water. Nightingales and warblers sing the day down.

In the long wait over the winter many of Van Hooghten's small band of Dutch navigators took their wages and went home. Their job is done, their maps and plans drawn and settled. Two new rivers will be dug, and, in the north, other cuts will carry away the flood waters of the Rivers Nene and Welland from the meres all about them. Straight seaward lines will replace the meres and islands, that now to my eye look like silver discs scattered across the landscape.

We put the word out for engineers, men who will turn our flat drawings into the new land. Van Hooghten writes to his acquaintance in Amsterdam and round about that we are looking for men familiar with the building of run-off channels and sluices, windmills and locks, as well as the digging of watercourses. Engineers are men accustomed to travel in order to find business. Moreover, their work runs from one project to another and is paid at a rate higher than work that is fixed and certain. For these reasons, and the Great Level being close to Holland, Van Hooghten is confident of finding his men. But word of the strangeness of this place and the failure of the last works seems to have got about. A few men trickle in, but along with eager youngsters who travel for the first time, Van Hooghten has to take on some whose greater experience comes at a price.

One is Adriaan Renswyck, a tall man with sunken cheeks and rheumy blue eyes. Renswyck has years of service in the West India Company behind him and the flux has worn him thin and bad-tempered. His clothes are greasy and black, his beard likewise, a circumstance notable amongst us Dutch, who are a people much given to cleanliness. An earthenware bottle hangs in the pocket of his frock coat and pulls it down on one side. He has no family with him besides a bony orange-coloured cur that follows everywhere at his heels. He is only come, he says, because the wages are good and the work familiar.

By the end of April three dozen Dutchmen are here, in different lodgings all over the Great Level. I place those who will work in the south in the biggest towns, and to each give a copy of my plan. Between them they divide up the work. Four men in Ely take charge of the start of the new river, four in Downham Market have the middle section and the sluice at Denver, four in King's Lynn the stretch from Denver to the sea. Van Hooghten puts Renswyck at the head of the King's Lynn section, knowing him to be a man who has experience of command.

Hundreds of labourers must clear the land, lay out the cuts, dig and lift the soil and build the great embankments. Van Hooghten considers the extent of the works and says that hundreds may not be enough. Thousands in the end may be required. Where shall we find them? The mood in the towns is sullen, though we pick up a few dozen men in each, and contrive to begin with them.

When word of our scarcity reaches the Gentlemen Adventurers, General Cromwell offers a solution that solves two problems with it, his own and ours. He will send us prisoners from his wars in Ireland who have been taken in great numbers. They are costly and threaten to escape. He will deliver them to us, Cromwell says, and furthermore will add soldiers from his own army to guard them. He keeps his promise smartly. The first men arrive a few weeks later at King's Lynn, packed into the holds and on the decks of such merchant ships as Ireland could provide. Many have died on the way. The survivors are ragged. They are insolent men, proud in their hatred of General Cromwell, Van Hooghten tells me. To my mind they are no more than slaves.

We keep the men in barns and storehouses near the towns. General Cromwell sends more soldier guards, tense men who keep one hand on their swords as they walk. Contempt for the Irish sits in them and shows itself in blows and insults that I do not understand. It is the disdain the soldier feels for one of his kind who has been captured, the swagger of the victor, and mixed in with it a resentment of their present task. The prisoners are set to work straight away to build camps for themselves. They put up wooden huts thatched with reeds to sleep in, food stores and depositaries. Adjoining each they build huts for the soldiers. Nine camps in all are built over the whole Great Level.

As the weeks pass, the two camps by King's Lynn begin to look like a settlement, with paths between the huts and noxious privies dug here and there. The prisoners' camp, bordering the river, is stockaded round its edge in a rough semicircle. It houses three hundred men in thirty huts. In a few weeks a market establishes itself by the soldiers' camp, food laid out for sale on thick reed mats. Milk and summer greenstuffs from the fields of the islands; even meat is to be found. Fenswomen walk through the market wrapped in their cloaks. They sell wildfowl, eels and all manner of fish. The market soon turns into a kind of town. Makeshift taverns and bordellos spring up. Soldiers off duty saunter down the two dirty lanes; anyone who has money or wages is inclined to spend it after hours. At night the river flows through sheets of smoke that glow like orange muslin in the firelight.

The mere is still alive with songs and noises, but I hear them less often now. The world of men is pushing in. A web of other sounds stretches out across the Level; the push and return of toothed saws; shouts, hammers, voices of complaint, wood-groan from the wagon wheels, the dart and snap of the whip. Boots bang on the wooden pathways and Renswyck's cur barks at the rats that have come off the ships.

Out on the water are the groups of fensmen, watching. I see men pause as they put out their eel traps, unbend and turn towards the camps. They stand in their boats, collected against the horizon like bottles on a shelf. When we begin the works I feel a change in the air. It has the quality of a threat. This feeling I try to ignore and rather look forward to the moment when my plans will bear fruit in the pastures and wheat fields of the whole redeemed land.

Once the works start I no longer feel safe to meet you out on the fen, so I leave my lodging and move to a dark lane on the edge of King's Lynn where I have two rooms with my own door. It is at first an odd circumstance that we are closed into a room with a roof over our heads; but here we can pass the evening together. Here I wait for a soft knock, or to hear the latch lift from its iron bed. When you come to me our nights begin to take on a settled feel. I always have food ready, the coverlets smoothed, and the floors brushed clean. These homely habits delight me, though I know that you will leave before sunrise. In the morning all that is left of us are two plates and knives, and two glasses that stand side by side next to the wooden washtub. Often I leave them when I close the door, so that I can return to a sign that we were here together.

In the small parlour you walk from wall to wall. You pick up one thing after another and ask questions. How is this used, how that? You open the covers of the books that I keep on a shelf and study pages while I say nothing but wonder to myself how a mind might be that has no letters in it. You know about reading; how, you do not say. It is only that you lack the skill. I see that you observe my face when I read. Your eyes follow mine.

One evening I hand you the only English book I have, *Mathematical Magick* by one John Wilkins, and watch as you run your finger across the biggest letters of the title page, up, down, up and down the bars of the M, withdrawn into concentration. You feel your way round the black letter where the type has pressed and the ink puddled in its shape. Then you hand the book back to me.

'I wish to learn now.'

It is not a statement, but a demand. We sit side by side at the small table. I write the letters of the alphabet in order on a bare sheet of paper, spaced far enough apart that you can trace them with your finger, and sound them out as I write. Though my Dutch makes me a poor guide to the sounds they make, you learn most of them in those first evening hours. The next day and the next we go on, until you have them easily.

I feel myself a woeful teacher, having no memory of how I myself learned my letters or turned them into words. My English is weighed down with the earthy thickness of Dutch. You seem not to notice, but set about the task with care, not moving from the first group of letters I have written until you are sure of all their sounds.

On the fourth day I make the letters into words and try to explain how they group together in sound. You laugh when you make the first word entire: moon. I put another next to it: fen. You laugh again, with triumph and with joy.

Another day we make a list. You say a few words, and I write them in my own imperfect English: Jan, Eliza, mallard, bread. I want to write all the words that crowd my mind and hear you sound them out – desire, beauty, tomorrow, together – but this I forebear to do, only adding others from the place we are in: mere, sea, eel, heron. You wish to know the useful words of my work and I write some of them for you: cut, embank, washes, tides, sluice, drain. Others, too, that I no longer remember.

My teaching is muddled and inexpert, the sounding of the words and the writing of the letters mixed together. The foolish book of mechanics is all I have to teach you with, but it does not matter. I write out the alphabet and hand you pen, ink and paper; you return with the paper forested with letters with their curls and hooks ready to join to others in the manner I then show you, so that you write in the way of the Dutch, for the English hand I have never mastered.

Though you learn and I teach, I do not simply put words down your throat as a mother feeds a child. Something else happens. We learn together. I see a wonder in you that reminds me of a school-house game, writing in lemon juice, and bringing the paper up to the candle. Near the heat each word came to life and revealed itself. So it is with you, as if the words are already present and now come to the surface. Your delight we share, and both of us are changed; you by the knowledge, I by the joy of the knowledge in you.

When I see that joy cross your face and flash through your eyes I feel a tenderness to weep, though I do not, but rather gather you to me and hold you tight to myself. If afterwards we explore one another by the candlelight, it seems just as if one way of learning takes over from another and enlarges it.

# Chapter 3

*King's Lynn.*
*The Great Level.*
*Summer, 1650.*
*Fine hot weather with wind from the west.*

As soon as they are confined in the camp the prisoners try to escape. Groups work to tunnel under the stockade or push it down. Soldiers walk the camp perimeters from riverbank round to riverbank. I see them stop at intervals and dig their pike heads into the ground to test for disturbance in the soil that might show a tunnel beneath. In the middle of the stockade a wooden tower rises and a stair winds round it to the top. This is the idea of Adriaan Renswyck; he has built such a thing often in our colonies, he tells me, and is quick to point out its uses. A secure camp, he says, is the first condition for the success of the whole enterprise.

'Put a pair of soldiers up there day and night, in four watches of six hours. Should any man escape by day he can be fired upon. At night a man cannot go without a lantern; the meres will swallow him. Follow the light when a prisoner breaks out at night and you can get him back.'

Renswyck carries the point with Van Hooghten, and then orders the addition of two more watchtowers, one at each end of the stockade where it meets the river. Lanterns are set to burn at their tops all night. They swing in the breeze and throw shadows over the whole camp. Still not satisfied, Renswyck orders an embankment built beyond the path that runs around the stockade. Any man who slips out must now clamber up its earthen sides and slither down the back, where water collects in a ditch. That accomplished, a prisoner finds himself either straight into the treacherous meres and creeks, or in the makeshift town that has collected round the soldiers' camp.

From the moment he builds his first watchtower, Renswyck takes on a kind of alertness. The camp begins to absorb him. Although he has little of this country's language I see him often in the company of two soldiers, Captain Townley and Major Wade. If these two chafe to be off to the wars in Ireland they do not show it. At the camp they have their own world to command. In the morning they round up the work parties and hand out the spade and wooden bucket that each man carries with him to his place of labour. I pass Townley and Wade sometimes when I am in the camp and bow briefly in acknowledgement. They nod back but do not stop to talk. I am a man who holds nothing for them; it is Renswyck who captures whatever attention they have.

The camp is now well guarded, both on the land side and along the river, though the prisoners rarely hazard an escape on water. Few can swim. That skill is rare, and these men are mostly from the damp middle of the island of Ireland. Still, they are prepared to hazard a water escape. After a group untie one of the boats and slip across the river in it, Renswyck insists that all the boats be brought into the lee of the watchtowers and tied up there, so that they fan out like a pack of beagles on leashes, and bang against each other through the night.

A few prisoners do get away each week and make it to Lynn to creep aboard a boat leaving; but most are picked up from sheds and barns. No Englishman, it seems, loves an Irishman. They are returned to the camp with little ceremony. Some men disappear, swallowed by the meres. One step into the reeds, one slip in moonless darkness, and they are gone. Water closes over them.

The atmosphere in the camps is sullen. The prisoners work and the Company of Gentlemen Adventurers feeds them. Everyone expects that at the end of the hostilities the prisoners will go back to their country or be shipped to the colonies of the New World as indentured labour, a state little different from that they live in now. General Cromwell cares not where they go as long as they can never again fight against him.

A couple of months after the prisoners' arrival Renswyck takes delivery of a cartload of boots and leather jerkins, part of a convoy that also brings embanking tools. One day in August we begin in earnest. We are arrived at the moment when the lines come off from the map I have drawn and stretch towards their destination across the ground. This is the time when an engineer, who has perforce been surveyor and map maker, too, becomes himself. This is when the new landscape that I have seen in my mind will begin to come into being.

On the first day of laying out the course I arrive early at its northern end and sit on my horse facing the sea. From the path by the Ouse I look down into the river and watch the force of the tide as it pushes up to meet the water that comes down. The two foes meet, and push up against one another, with no yield from either until one slides over, the other under, and they mingle together in eddies and waves. We will build the sluice at Denver to manage this daily combat and calm the flood.

Van Hooghten rides up, and stops by a circle of carts piled with axes, ropes, saws, spades and bundles of wooden pegs I have had made in the camps in the last weeks. I take a deep breath of the mud-heavy air.

'Good morrow, Jacob. Now we start.'

'At last, yes.'

Behind him I can see Major Wade. He leads a line of prisoners, with Captain Townley at the rear.

'I am ready,' I say.

'I'm glad of it. You will see me often, though I must visit in turn all the works that are in train, here and to the west.' Van Hooghten leans over and puts a hand on my shoulder, then turns his horse away; and so we set to work, I to my part, he to his.

The path of the new river will be laid out with rope and pegs, following my plan through reeds and marsh, across the meres and streams. Everything along its route will be cut down. When the new cut is deeper than the existing river bed, water will collect in it and the meres start to drain. Thus we proceed layer by layer, the deepest cut left to the last, and build the high embankments for the new rivers and the old at the same time. Later we will cut divers smaller drainage channels to lead the water to its new outfalls. Lastly we will build the great sluice and its run-off channels. Windmills, as necessary at intervals, will lift standing water from the fields and carry it into the new rivers at times of heavy rain.

The prisoners cut stands of alder and beds of reed and lay the branches across the marshy places. Foot by foot they peg down the rope until the whole river course is stretched out across the land. Soon the washes between the rivers are a morass of mud, pitted, scarred and hardened in the summer heat. New grass struggles to push through; here and there a daisy flowers. In my mind's eye I see a picture of the new landscape, its fields bordered by ditches, stretching away to the horizon. Cattle graze the pastures, and fields of shining grain ripple in the breeze. But this beauty I imagine is a long way off. Instead the landscape turns grey, thick with dust that rises from the churned-up land. The sun shines weakly through it.

Shouts and curses hang over the Level. The men from the towns around dislike working with the prisoners and many collect their wages and leave. The soldiers beat the prisoners with wooden sticks if they throw down their spades. After some weeks it is found expedient to tie one to another those prisoners who try to escape, both as an example to others and as the only way to be sure of them. Such men have then to work as one, lifting their spades and bringing them down together; otherwise the rope between them slackens by one man, tightens by another, and impedes them all.

Worse than the cries of the men and the commands of the soldiers are the times of silence, when the prisoners neither shout nor sing, but push their spades into the ground, lift the soil and throw it without a sound to where the embankment is building. Their acquiescence is tinged with a sullen acceptance of fate that I shrink from despite myself. The weakest prisoners fall ill with the ague that rises from the meres. Many become too sick to work and lie damp and feverish in their huts. Some die, and are buried by their fellows in accordance with their rites, though no priests are allowed them.

But this is not all that is askew. You are now also a part of myself and of the work here. For the first time in my life I have found my drawing, calculating, planning, and the beautiful execution of all, to be insufficient. I wish, also, to be close by you, to eat my dinner and spend my nights with you, to bring to you the best examples of my labour – a piece of land tilled and made productive, a straight and well-lined canal, its water making a picture with the sky above. When once it was enough to know that I worked in accordance with the will of God and to the satisfaction of my master and my family, I desire now to offer you all that I do. This I cannot, for the fact of having agreed a measure of secrecy with Van Hooghten. Though the generality of our work here is known and the courses of the new rivers now plain, the exact sites of the sluices and outfalls are kept hidden. Van Hooghten reminds me of what happened in the late wars.

'We have no need to go into details with anyone, Jan. Mijnheer Vermuyden has that task, and we only the work of carrying out what is agreed.'

It occurs to me that Van Hooghten's injunction need not apply to the generalities of the works or to the map we have made of the Great Level drowned, and this I show to you one evening, rolling out the paper on the floor of the little parlour in my lodging. Pride fills me when I look down on the map, where the slow curling rivers are shown with a line for each bank, while thinner lines enclose the large islands. The winter meres, which turn to pasture in the spring, are shown as marsh is on all our Dutch maps, with close-marked dashes. The thousand islands in the meres such as your people make are shown as dots and circles; the towns outlined and coloured grey.

The words written upon the map you can now make out easily without the letters falling over one another, and it is the words and not the map itself that capture your attention. You go from one to another, from the towns to the rivers and the biggest islands which have their names written upon them.

Now that you read so well I encourage you to write yourself, and not just for the practice of it. I wish myself to read what you write and so learn, perhaps, something of what you do not say aloud.

'There is nothing for me to write, Jan,' you say when I make this suggestion one evening. Your eyes are full of their challenge.

'You might write a letter.'

'A letter such as you receive from the messengers?'

'Yes. Or from any other person who writes to me.'

'You suggest I write to a person?'

'Yes. Not a letter to send out, but as an exercise in writing.'

'Yet there is no need to write, Jan, since you are here beside me.'

'Write to another.'

'There is no person I can write to. I have no need of writing.'

'Then you may write for yourself.'

'What should I write for myself?'

'Many people have written the story of their life, or related some of their days, and you might do the same.'

This notion hangs in the air. You do not pluck it out, or talk of it again, though you go on with copying and making lists of words, which you add to one by one down the length of the paper I have given you. Strangely enough, it is I who seem to take up the suggestion of relating a story. While I stir the vegetables in the pot, and you sit at the table, I begin at last to unfold my closed self; to talk of the life I lived on Tholen and in Leiden, and soon, in a way vague enough to satisfy Van Hooghten, about the progress of the works.

One evening I describe the cut of the new river that runs straight and proud across the land, and the embankments along both the new and the old rivers.

'How does the embankment hold in the water?'

'By its strength. We build so high and wide, and so solid, that the water is constrained to flow between embankments when it rises.'

'Yet I know that water is stronger than anything.'

'Not if we build properly.'

'Does it ever happen that the embankment fails?'

I pause then, and remember my childhood. I know the force of water; I have seen it.

'Only if we build badly, and leave a weakness for the water to gnaw at. Then an embankment can fail.'

'Water works its own holes.'

'Only if we give it a start. A weakness that water pushes at. That is why my calculations must be correct.'

But my pleasure, though it grows when I talk of my work, has a darkening edge. It has come to me that for one world to be made, another must die. Now, as my vision begins to come into being, I am filled with sadness as well as joy. I have seen that this unimproved world has its own way of being which will be lost. It has, even, its own splendour. I determine to tell you this, but you have turned away and then it is too late, for joy has awoken in us and is roaring round now, and you come to me, very close so that I can feel it in you, and I lower my head and kiss you, and feel the thought as I do so that with you everything opens out as we gather one another in and then all thought is washed away.

# Chapter 4

*Near King's Lynn.*
*The Great Level.*
*Autumn, 1650.*

The works go on while columns of insects sing above us. Fevers run through the prisoners' bodies, and into the soldiers and numbers of the engineers. Any place other than the Great Level now seems far away to me, as unreachable as a mirage across the desert. It is many months since I wrote to my parents and my sisters. My father's hand on my shoulder, my mother's anxious admonitions, the laughter of Anna and Katrijn: they seldom break into my mind. The Great Level, though I know it to be a small part of the earth, might stand for the whole of it.

In October the camp is swelled with hundreds of prisoners from another war, waged by General Cromwell in Scotland. Covenanters, I am told they are called, taken at a battle by the town of Dunbar. These men are short and tangle-haired. They dress in all manner of ragged clothing and many speak a language that some of the Irish can understand in part, but none of the English soldiers. I try to make out one word from another, but, having no success, allow their talk to surround me as if it were a kind of music.

So this land gathers strangeness as well as change. With the new prisoners the works progress fast, but they bring difficulties with them. The two bodies of men, the Scots and the Irish, must be housed in separate quarters, for they are of differing persuasions, the Irish of the old Roman religion, most of the others its sworn enemy. Notwithstanding the remoteness of our situation, where a pastor is rarely seen, the prisoners talk of little else than their faith and the battles they fought to preserve it. I am told that when the Scots and the Irish mingle they come easily to blows over the nature of the sacrament or the power of priests. New huts are therefore hastily thrown up for the Scots. It is getting crowded inside the stockade, a circumstance that worries the apothecary who comes regularly to the camp. He brings bags of herbs and medicines that he sells to the soldiers and to us Dutch who know from long experience that the ague can be held off by such infusions as we can make from his wares.

Adriaan Renswyck finds a new way of bringing order to this place of strife. Each morning before the work parties are assembled, he orders the men to stand in a line outside their huts. Then he walks by each line and counts the men in it. He is seldom alone now, and comes accompanied not only by Wade and Townley but also by a sort of secretary he has picked out from amongst the Dutch. This man carries a large pocketbook, leather bound. At certain points in his inspection, the same each day, Renswyck stops and gestures for his book, into which he deftly writes his tallies, hoarding prisoners as if they are gold.

One morning I pass a number of the Irish prisoners who stand in the half-darkness, and see a grizzled old man cup his hand over his young neighbour's upturned palm. Something glints before fingers close over it. Curiosity pricks me, and an undertow of fear. Perhaps this sleepy boy has a knife, or some other rough weapon.

'What do you have there?'

Tiredness makes me suspicious. Here are men whose hatreds slow my work and place at hazard my reputation.

'Nothing,' he says, and puts his hand behind his back.

On an impulse I call a soldier. He is on guard, but has turned away to stare towards the stockade, waiting perhaps, as I have so often waited, for the sun to glide up above the fen and bring the comfort of daylight to the camp. He comes with reluctance to my summons and waits by me as I talk to the boy.

'Give it to me.'

Slowly the boy holds out his hand and opens his fingers. Red rises in his cheeks, and, at the same time, in mine. From his flat palm I pick a thin, cheap medallion; tin, and imprinted with the face of the Madonna, picked out with the sharp tip of a nail.

'Take it, take it.'

I close the boy's hand over the metal scrap, and wave the soldier away. Shame fills me that I felt fear of so little. My apprehension has overcome me. The day has started with feeling running too high, and ill will follows it. If a Scot should come across a man with such a charm in his hand he may try to pull it away, such is the Covenanters' hatred of the old religion. The Latin prayers of the Irish also draw the anger of the Scots. When I hear a Scottish and an Irish prisoner in dispute, and the shouts and growls of those who quickly gather around and add their angry faces to the crowd, I turn my back and walk off.

The men's resistance is complete. The guards hurry them to work each morning. They tie those most likely to flee and patrol the length of the works all day. The ground itself seems to take the prisoners' part. Near the middle section of the new river, where I expected an easy cut through peat, we encounter gravel, which slows us down. Then storms drive over the whole Level, one after another. Soil in the washes runs off into the cut just made, clogs the bed of the new river and destroys its gradient. Again the atmosphere darkens and I have the feeling of the watchers getting closer in the misty nights. Some days I take to sleeping under my coracle near the works. Van Hooghten teases me, saying I am become a fensman, or a savage, or a Scot, wrapped in my blanket under the sky. The solitariness of the night will do me no good, he adds, and the bad air after the rains will bring the ague.

Then, as the days shorten towards winter, an insurrection breaks out at the works north of the new sluice. One sunny afternoon I arrive to see a long line of prisoners sitting on the ground, their tools lying beside them and a soldier standing by. Adriaan Renswyck walks up and down, and as I approach slaps one of the men with his glove. The man flinches as the leather whips against his cheek, but he does not move. Renswyck turns to the soldier in rage.

'Make them get up.'

'There are too many, sir,' one of the soldiers says. 'They cannot flee, to be sure, but they refuse to stand.'

'Why have they done this? Tell me; you were here.'

Renswyck throws up an arm so that his cloak flares out behind.

'Do something. Take a man out of the line and beat him in sight of the others.'

The atmosphere is thickening and needs patience to thin it out. Renswyck is already beyond sense. The soldier silently refuses to obey him. These men have no love for the Dutch. Most long either for real soldiering in the vortex of war, or for their homes. This half-life of keeping order is neither. It is, one told me, a humiliation, and unhealthy at that.

'Upon what grounds do they stop work?' I ask. I make my voice quiet and level.

The soldier turns to me and I add, 'What is your name?'

'Ralph Cooper, sir.'

'I am Jan Brunt, the engineer here. Tell me what the prisoners say, Mr Cooper.'

'That things are coming up from the ground, Mr Brunt, strange and wondrous things.'

'Where?'

'Just along the embankment, sir.'

'Very well, Mr Cooper, let us go and see for ourselves, and speak to the men there.'

Renswyck turns to me and says in Dutch, 'Speak to them? You need to restore order. Make an example of one man and the others will pick up their spades soon enough.'

I feel sudden rage. What is Renswyck doing outside the camps, which are under his authority?

'Mijnheer Renswyck, might I ask why you have come here? This stretch of the works is looked after by Aelbert Mortens, who answers to me.'

Aelbert Mortens is a taciturn man apt to spend the evening with a bottle of brandy in one hand and a bible in the other. He says little and keeps his opinions close, though I should like to hear them, for he has worked in Suriname in the New World, and in many other possessions of the Dutch West India Company. Van Hooghten thinks him steady, despite his moroseness; another man who has seen better times and now seeks to recover his position.

'Mortens –' Renswyck jerks his head away again. 'He's over there, shaking. I happened upon him and have assumed command.'

I walk across to Aelbert Mortens, who sits on the bank of the new cut. He is about forty years old, bull-headed and solid. A ragged velvet coat hangs from his shoulders. His face has fallen into deep lines. I tap him on the shoulder.

'Aelbert; it is I, Jan Brunt. What is passing here?'

Mortens turns to me. Terror streams from his eyes.

'We have disturbed the dead. Their spirits walk abroad as a judgement upon us.'

'Do you see them, Aelbert, these spirits?'

Then I understand what Renswyck sees; that Mortens is deaf to human speech and speaks not to me but to himself.

'Aelbert, do you hear me?'

He says nothing, only continues to look wildly about him. It is not within my power to bring him out. I turn away, and leave him to sit on the bank alone. I must talk to the prisoners and coax them back to the digging; force them if needs be. The work must go on, advance by the calendar we have laid down.

As I walk away from Mortens, my eye catches the raw edge of the new cut. Twenty feet below the surface the peat and silt stop and another formation begins. I know immediately what I see. I cannot be mistaken; it is as if a drawing I have long studied has come into being. I am looking at the layers of a road sliced through by the new cut as clean as a cake. It is of ancient construction, but as fresh as if just laid down. I stand and stare, forgetting all about the prisoners and their fears, then jump down to examine it close up. The flint at the top is familiar to this place, and used by the fensmen in their knives and axes. But I marvel at it, for though an extreme hard stone it is yet compacted with the finest gravel in the way set forth in every book I know upon the science of engineering. This top surface lies on sand and gravel mixed together to the depth of a foot, and the whole rests on a bed of branches and twigs, tangled to a dense blackness. It is a firm road, yet built beautifully to float upon the marsh.

I remember from my books of study that this is a road such as the Romans built. Scrambling up out of the cut I look around me and see the prisoners, who sit on the ground, tied one to another with rope. Beyond them, and beyond the excavations of the works, the meres stretch out on all sides, like silver coins thrown into the mist. This land looks as if it has always been like this, uncharted and unchanged. Yet here is a road, and surely, down this road Roman legions marched. In this desolate place, where had they come from; where did they go?

And before any soldiers walked here, engineers came, men such as myself, strangers to the place. They must have measured this ground, as I have done, observed its times of flood and shrink, and calculated where to float their road across. Perhaps they lodged hereabouts, or at a fort hastily constructed, for the people of this place could have had no good intentions towards their conquerors. At this thought I feel something of the spirit of these my ancestors enter into me. By my shoulder I sense a man such as I might have been, though more likely born in Spain or some other southern place. I see him rise up out of the fen and come towards me across the expanse, an arm raised as if in greeting, one engineer to another. He is young and dark-complexioned; full of his knowledge as I am full of mine. His gestures to me are at once eager and supplicating, as if he wishes me to tell his story, to rescue him from that place where the dead of his religion journey in the end.

The road is well done, and would be still serviceable were it lying now upon the surface of the land as it was when built. I feel a joy to see its beauty now brought by chance into the light. Yet had we not cut through it, it would have lain undisturbed in its sleep of centuries, down below the vegetable world, no conjecture to be made of it. My fancy brings forth ghosts; yet they are everywhere, if only we could see them. Perhaps this is the very thickness in the air of this place, filled with the souls of those who lived here, or passed this way.

This jumble of thoughts rushes through me in an instant. I had thought the meres untouched, but this cannot be so. Nature has swallowed what man made, dragged it beneath the water and the mud. So our eyes deceive us. We think we see all, or can discover it, and yet we see so little. Time has covered over what men made here before, and all the habits of their life.

As if in a dream, I see inwardly the whole skin of the earth peeled away. It is a picture only, yet for a second everything is discovered and placed before me, both the works of man and the hidden works of nature that only seldom burst forth as volcanoes and hot springs. For if a Roman road may hide here unsuspected, my own work might at some future time drown also, and lie forgotten.

I walk back past the slumped figure of Aelbert Mortens, to where Adriaan Renswyck still stands with his sardonic look. Only a minute or two has passed, but my ill humour has turned to wonder.

'Have you seen the road we cut through, Adriaan?' I ask.

'You have been dreaming, Mijnheer Brunt,' Renswyck says. 'What road? You are seeing things.'

'Indeed I am, Adriaan; great things.'

There is no profit in talk with Renswyck, so I turn to Ralph Cooper.

'Come, Mr Cooper,' I say. 'Pick up your pike; let's go.'

Ralph Cooper leads me along the roughly thrown-up embankment of the new cut. Below on the mere, the reed heads are brown and the hawthorns heavy with scarlet berries. After a few minutes the ground is firm beneath my boots again and I am come back into the world of our day. In half an hour we reach the northernmost extent of the works. An angry murmur of voices rises up from beyond the new embankment; spades, entrenching tools and hessian sacks lie across the ground, piles of muddy soil stand at intervals. Another ragged group of prisoners sits on the grass. Two soldiers stand guard.

'What passes here?' I ask.

The prisoners reply all at once.

'The work of the devil.'

'These are witches buried here.'

'Or this is the work of witches.'

'Or sinners with no Christian burial.'

One man makes the sign of the cross on his breast, rocking forward as he does so. Another says the same words over and over. The rest just sit, and raise their eyes to me in accusation.

A tall soldier, who himself appears discomposed, points to a patch of turned-up ground a little way off. Walking over I see new-broken shards of pottery. Dusty ashes veil the grass. Beside them a rough-hewn pot as high as my knee lies quite out of the ground. It is full of grey fragments that make a kind of gravel. All around, the tops of many more jars have been uncovered. Rightly they must be called urns, for there is no doubt that this is a place of burial.

'Go back to Mr Renswyck,' I say to Ralph Cooper, 'and tell him that work is finished here for the day.'

Then I tell the captain in charge, 'Escort the prisoners back to the camp, but leave me half a dozen of your men. I wish them to excavate these things and remove them from sight. We will work tomorrow in the usual way.'

When the prisoners have been marched off beyond the embankment I kneel down to look at the excavated urn. My heart is full within my chest, for I see easily that within the ashes that have spilled out onto the mud are human bones. Man, woman or child; perhaps a whole family is mingled here, the ashes of one person poured on top of another.

I cannot resist plunging in my hands and drawing out a handful of grit and other stuff. When I open my fingers the heaviest particles fall to the ground, coating it in patches. The lightest rise into the air, a million motes in the shafts of autumn sunlight. The dust moves and turns gracefully. I watch it fall, then come up again, pushed by the resisting ground. Minutes pass as it comes up slowly and then sinks again until finally there is just a slight haze left. The sun shines through it, filling the air. The sight is as beautiful as God's grace, or the light that will open to the heavens when all souls rise at the Last Judgment.

I part my fingers and see that a few lumps cling to my skin. One of these I pick out and rub on my breeches as I might do to a pebble from a beach. The dust comes off and I see that it is a tooth, ivory white, perfectly formed, brown in the hole where the root once grew. Wonder turns to horror and I dash the other teeth off my hands. When they fall onto the grass the story of the sowing of the teeth comes into my mind, so that I fancy for a moment that a legion of Romans, fully armed, might spring up to fight. My ears fill with sea-sounds and I forget where I am.

When I come to myself I order the soldiers to dig out all the urns. They do not move; they have seen my horror. It comes across me that we are in a sacred place and that the spirits of the dead, now disturbed, may remain here with malevolent intent. This I know to be a superstition, and tell myself so, yet fear fills me.

I grab one soldier's pike from him and lower it towards the others, advancing on the group without a thought in my head.

'Take up the urns. Carry them beyond the new embankment and bury them again. Cover them well. They are pagan remains, merely. No Christians lie here. Put them from your minds. Now get to work.'

Slowly the soldiers bend to pick up the spades abandoned by the prisoners.

'Do this and you may return to the camp afterwards. I give that as an order.'

I leave and walk slowly down the new embankment in search of Van Hooghten, who is riding this way from Ely. I will tell him how the Roman road has come to light and show it to him before it is washed away, as it will be. The discovery of the urns I will keep to myself; I do not want Van Hooghten to share my fear, or see it.

# Chapter 5

*Near King's Lynn.*
*The Great Level.*
*Winter and spring, 1650–1651.*
*Days and nights both cold.*

Colour drains from the islands and the meres. The last red berries are eaten by birds or wither and turn to black. After the winter solstice the golden heads of the reeds fray and thin, until the reeds stand grey and seedless, bent westwards by the bitter wind.

I now insist that the more docile prisoners are unroped when they arrive at the day's place of work. They do not thank me and still labour in anger. Round their hands they tie rough strips of hessian taken from the sacks which they fill and tip out to build the highest parts of the embankments. By midday blood seeps through the hessian and drips into the mud. I demand leather gloves, and order them handed out with the spades and returned at the end of the day. This measure helps the men's hands, but not their feet, which, from standing in the mud, turn black and rot.

For want of doctors and space to nurse them these sick men are sent away, I know not where. When I look at the prisoners, so miserable and far from their homes, I remember the captivity of the Israelites in Egypt, that I read of in my childhood. As these men are, so were the Israelites in captivity, forced to build great works and labour without reward.

I think of the buried road. Was it also built by men such as these, taken in battle and enslaved? What a great desire men have to take the liberty of others with scarce a thought. And more, what pride man has in the conquest of all living things, the smallest creatures as well as the mountains, valleys and seas, which are alive in their own fashion. This idea will not leave me. It fills me with unease. Like the Romans long ago, the Adventurers now subject this place to their will, as if the whole world is part of an empire like that of Rome.

The urns, and the ashes within them, squat in my mind, a mystery and a threat. The remains in them are not of Romans, who built tombs for their dead. Who were these, then? Another people from this place? The silence of the urns unsettles me. I have breathed the dead, taken them in. I want to exhale them, but find that I talk to them instead.

'Who are you?' I ask. 'What customs do you have, what beliefs?'

One night I return in the darkness to the place where the soldiers buried the urns, and dig about until I find a small one that sits as high as my hand. This I empty and carry to my lodging, where I put it out of sight in my box.

When I was a child the world appeared a safe place, made by God and explained by him. But now uncertainty has entered my heart with the dust of the dead. Nothing is as it seems; much is covered up, much washed away. Yet when I turn to God I cannot see him. I tell this to Van Hooghten, feeling safe to confide in him, far away from home as we are and with no priests or churches near, only our bibles to read and to guide us. I am losing sight of God, I say to him, and this dimming of the light appears progressive, as blindness can be. There is no single cause; it must be borne. Perhaps it started with the discovery of the urns. Perhaps it has been going on longer, but it was only then that I noticed it, like the faint tremor before an earthquake that has long been building its force under the earth.

Van Hooghten is alarmed at my confidence. His kindly face is covered over with fear. He says nothing and I guess he hopes that I will say nothing also. That is our habit of life. Though there must be many Dutchmen who have lost God, no one amongst us speaks out when he walks away.

In my childhood I knew God. I knew him as I do my mother and my father and all those whose acquaintance I make and who leave an outline on my soul. God comes through my skin, down my throat and into my heart with each breath.

When I learn to read, I hang on to my mother's red woollen skirt, feeling its rough weave and the softness of the white muslin apron tied over it. I am a thin, dark boy, tall already for my age. I stand and cross one shin over the other so that I can lean into her as much as I dare and breathe her cool, musty scent that soon gets mixed in with the very idea of God. My head rests on her and I feel her chest rise and fall. My heart beats in time with hers, steady and strong. My mother sounds out each word of the prayer book, and points to it as she reads. Soon it is as if she and God are speaking at the same time and in the same voice. I can hear his voice inside hers, and his presence shimmers with the words. I love him and, though I do not have the thought, I know that he loves me.

Later, when my sister Margriet is old enough, we two sit at the table in the parlour with my father, he in an oak-armed chair, Margriet and I on four-legged stools drawn up close so that the wooden edge of the table presses against us. From then on there is no leaning in to my mother and feeling the warmth of God. When my father reads the prayer book God's voice becomes stern and distant, as if he speaks from far away. Now God is in the firmament of heaven, high above us, and looking down. Then I often make mistakes with my reading, fearing my father and God together, for this God will chastise me if I fall into error or fail in any tasks at home or at the school.

Each Sunday we go to the church in the village and the pastor preaches forgiveness, or repentance, or obedience. The nave of the church is high and columned, filled with the light of God that comes off the water in the canal outside. There are no paintings on the walls; it is cold and white and golden. The pastor speaks of the great flood and tells us it is needful to be as Noah was, righteous and obedient and the only man to survive. Every Dutchman lives in fear of the flood and must be as pure as he. If I am a sinner I will not be saved as Noah was, but drowned and lost.

Though this God makes me fearful, I bargain with him, promise that I will learn my tables if he makes sure that my father treats me kindly, and if he will save me when the time comes. Sometimes he agrees, but at other times, though I fulfil my side of the promise, he fails in his, and then I am angry, and fear him and know that I have fallen from the path.

All through my childhood, though, the kindlier God comes back when I am alone with myself. He and I talk together – or, to be more exact, I talk to him – and he sometimes speaks to me in reply. I tell him what I am doing, as if he might not be able to see; describe to him my daily walk along the canal to school. If I notice a carp rise to the surface, or see that a calf has been born in the water meadow and is lying damp and surprised on the grass, I make sure to bring these things to God's attention.

'Look at that,' I say, as if directing his gaze.

'Yes, I see it, Jan,' he replies.

'See the way that calf's legs are tucked under him, so he can push up and walk.'

'Ah, yes, Jan, it is wonderful how ready he is for life.'

'My sister Margriet did not walk like that. She was useless for so long, lying on our mother.'

'Why might that have been, Jan?'

'I cannot say,' I tell God in answer to such questions, for these things I puzzle over as I lie in my bed at night with the curtains tight shut across the opening to the room.

It does not come to me then that God, having made the world, must know it and see it all. No, I am sure that, just as I see a new wondrous sight, so must he, or so must he if I point it out. I wish him to cast his eyes on this small corner of the earth; the island of Tholen itself, my village of Sint-Maartensdijk, and the things I see. If a new crop is sown, or slice of land reclaimed, I bring it to God's attention, not just for the joy of it, but so that he can change the great map of the world that he must have created from the beginning.

We understand one another well enough in those early years. Sometimes I know God walks beside me. At other times I talk to him while he stays in heaven. From my schoolboy years I begin to show him my scholarly efforts, and to strive to be worthy of him. The first works of drainage that I accomplish I share with him; they are my gift to him and his to me.

And this goes on until now, and his gradual disappearance. Now I turn to him sometimes, and find nothing, or it seems that the voice in which I was used to speak to him is no longer serviceable. God is leaving my life. I notice that I do not attempt to make him stay. Some people, when God stops speaking to them, or does not answer an appeal, will call out, Stop! They will entreat, pray harder, beg God to chastise them, to break open their hearts, batter down their defences and walk back in.

I do nothing. I let God disappear slowly. He thins out and dissipates – as if, towards the end of a church service, the organist plays more and more quietly and then simply ceases altogether. There is not so much a departure as a lack of presence.

And so he is gone, and I find myself changed. When I used to speak to God I was always stretching up, enlarging myself so that he might see me; raising my voice and justifying myself to him. Now that I have stopped, the world remains, just itself. A curtain has been lifted, and the gauze that stood between myself and nature melted away. I feel a part of all that is. If now I see a creator, it is nature itself, in every particle in all the earth and skies. I see it in my flesh, and in you.

In December ice creeps along the streams and across the meres. Snow settles on the frozen water and when the ground turns too hard for digging the men are confined to the camps, restless and quarrelsome. Nonetheless, at the turn of the year, I am able to travel to London and report to the Gentlemen Adventurers that the works are remarkably progressed. An eagle, high on the eastern winds, might see the new landscape coming out of the old, an orderly world being born from the wilderness. The new rivers are now laid out and partly dug. The run-off channels for the sluice at Denver are also near complete. Two more years will see the whole endeavour finished and the Great Level drained and ready to be farmed without the smallest difficulty, for all land that comes up from underwater is level or only very gently inclines, and is composed of the finest silt and peat with gravel here and there.

You and I never talk of the time when the works will be finished and I will have to leave this place. I know clearly why I am reticent upon the subject. I am anxious that if I speak out you will leave as you first appeared, without any warning, and that I shall not see you again. I fear that you will refuse what I have in mind for the future. Or perhaps it is that I do not have the language to speak of it, our relation being so much of the present tense.

So it is that when we are next together, from habit now entwined together like branches so that I hear your voice soft upon my neck, I do not say what I had intended. My hope hangs there just out of reach. For this is what I wish to say, then and since, that it is a year and more since I came upon you, I in my coracle, you near naked in the pool. Since that time the feeling within me has only deepened. I have been with women before, Dutchwomen who wished for the life my mother has, but with none did desire grow and join us together or spread out into stillness and peace. I want to say this, and that I have come to understand that I do not want the life my parents live.

I think of us together as Adam and Eve were, in Elysium, alone. I want more, though. I long also to be as Adam and Eve became: adventurers who had to discover and make the world for themselves.

One day I find the courage to ask you, 'Eliza, why do you come to me? Why do you stay?'

At first you say nothing, but turn and look away, and I think you will get up and leave; but you do not. Instead you say, 'Because your life is different from all I know.' With a leap of my heart I hope that your curiosity is for me also. From there is only another step to ask you if you will come away with me to another, even more different life when the work here is finished.

I do not ask you that, but I say, with teasing in my voice, 'And do you like what you find?'

'I cannot say; I never knew another life, Jan. The way the uplanders live is closed to me.'

'And now?'

'And now with each step I take I move away from something that I can never leave behind.'

'That is a riddle.'

'No, Jan, it is just as it is.'

You say no more, and turn away, but not before I see sadness sweep through your eyes. This conversation brings me hope and unease in equal measure; hope that we are making something new in our fashion, unease that you see no other life than this one here today.

I have taken a new lodging on the marshes at the edge of Lynn. It is a fisherman's cottage with a chimney running up the middle, the kitchen on one side of it, that is also a small parlour, and on the other the bedroom. Besides my horses in the stable I have a cat that chases mice across the floor and brings them to me, half alive, when I return in the evening. I like to light the fire to warm your arrival. For the kindling I have hung bunches of reeds from the ceiling so that the heads are dry and friable. I layer them on the hearth and sprinkle sulphurous powder on them before bringing my flint and steel close enough to send a shower of sparks to ignite the fire. The roar of the flames up the chimney fills me with a childish joy, though I know not why, except that fire is man's alone, and with it began his conquest of all nature.

To the reeds I add the willow logs I have cut, and soon have a good fire going. I fill the lanterns and hang them from the beams. You often find me bending in, careful not to bang my head on the rough mantel, to turn a chicken or stir a pot of cabbage and barley. On the table I have laid out bread and cheese, two knives, two spoons, two rough pewter plates and a jug of beer. When you come close you brush aside my hair and kiss my neck beneath it so that I turn and circle you with my arms, and feel you steady on the ground. This little room, low enough that I must duck as I go through the doors, grows bigger with you in it. It stretches to everything.

Some evenings I sit one side of the fire, you another. We feed it with squares of peat cut from the fen. They glow long into the night and fill the cottage with their comfortable vegetable smell. Though at a distance from you, my fingertips run over your skin from afar, over your skirts, under and up, and you might then raise your eyes to mine, and from them streams a deep light that calls me to your side. Then I sit beside you on the floor, my cheek against the linen of your petticoat. I draw light circles on your sun-browned skin. Everything is warm and secret, and what comes next is not oblivion, but, as the ancients thought, a way for man to share the gods' divinity.

At other times you sit at the small table with your writing. You practise with seriousness, as if you have no time to lose. When I mention this you say that you are eager for this skill that you see comes so easily to me, and you wish to acquire it so well that you never forget it. At first you sound the words you wish to write, one by one, and turn each letter into its mark upon the page.

You still copy from my books and my pages of figures, but when I say that one day this new knowledge will be useful to you, you deny it. 'I do not think so, Jan; nor that of reading neither; but I wish to know it.'

One dark winter evening I see a light burning in the cottage as I come near to it. You have lit the fire and sit at the small table in the yellow pool of lamplight. I put down my instruments, take off my cloak and put my arms around you.

'You are writing, Eliza?'

'Yes, Jan. Just words; practising the writing of words.'

I glance at a loose sheet of paper on the table. You have written on it, over and over, *mother, father; father, mother.*

'You want to write to your mother and father?'

'Just the words.'

I draw up a chair and sit down.

'Will you write their names?'

'No. I cannot.'

'Why not, Eliza? Why not? You may tell me; I shall not take anything you say amiss.'

You draw back and pause, then say simply, 'I cannot. They are dead. Both dead.'

Your voice is flat and final; it has a warning in it to come no closer. I can only take your hand and hold it until, after a few minutes, you sigh and lean yourself against me. Feeling the fast beat of your heart against my chest, I determine then not to ask any more. I will wait. The time may come when you decide to tell me about your parents and the world you live in. If you do not wish to talk, I shall not demand to know, neither now nor in the future. I do not seek to force you to anything, but to love you as you are and as you wish to be.

No one knows of the time we spend together in my cottage through the long winter. Van Hooghten wonders aloud that I have abandoned my town lodgings for such a dismal place. He has cut his chestnut hair right to his scalp, as if he does not want the bother of it any more. The wrinkles round his eyes have deepened in the cold.

'Are you such a hermit, Jan, in truth?'

'You think me rather a sultan, with a harem here, and a great stable of the finest horses in the world?'

He laughs, and I feel a sudden fondness for him. Van Hooghten takes the world easily. His ambition is to stand well, to rise higher, and to marry when he is able. He looks on me, who entered our profession with no fixed plan of advancement, with puzzlement, yet for the most part asks few questions, and leaves me to myself. In this matter, though, he is not turned away so easily.

'You did not return to Holland this winter, as I took the chance to do.'

'I went down to London, Jacob, and gave our report to Mijnheer Vermuyden.'

'To be sure you did, Jan, and I have not forgotten it; but I am guessing that was not your motive for staying on here.'

'I did not feel the pull of home; it seems lost to me and over the horizon.'

'And your sisters that you have spoken of?'

Margriet, Anna and Katrijn come into my mind like a painting, flat against a white sky. They stand on a sliver of grass and seem to float above the ground, far away. I cannot see their features, or if they smile at me. Margriet is in the middle, Katrijn and Anna to either side. It is now many weeks since I wrote to them or to my parents.

I look at Van Hooghten and wait for him to add what his voice holds back.

After a while he says, 'It is rumoured that you have a woman here.'

I do not deny this, but do not wish to speak of you.

'It is common enough in this desolate place.'

Van Hooghten comes forward and puts his hand upon my sleeve.

'What do you know of her, Jan?'

What do I know? I know as an engineer does, who understands the body as a place of channels, of liquid contained within veins. I know as a geographer does, who studies and describes the surface of the earth, its valleys and mountains. But I know also as a man who longs for your company and for the force that fills you, which is the same force that drives all of nature.

Every night, when I am returning, I imagine that you might already be at my cottage; I look forward to the moment when I will open the door and find you there and that very act fills me with a future that opens out to the horizon in my mind. If the kitchen is empty when I lift the latch and step in, I go about my evening tasks still with a sense of you close by, and if I hear you open the door I turn to hold you not as a delicate thing, but tight, feeling your solidness. You are a woman with the strength of a man, and this too I love.

All this I might say to Van Hooghten, until I remember that he would take me for a madman or a fool, the people of the fens being spoken of as savages. Van Hooghten seems to consider me with a mixture of sharpness and sympathy. 'These are not the times for holding yourself close, Jan. You need to look about you. The fensmen do not wish us well. Have you not seen groups of them watching, and lights at night? Have you not heard sudden sounds behind you, then turned to find no one?'

'Those are the sounds of the mere, Jacob. You told me so yourself.'

I think again to take him into my confidence, to tell him that I have come to find the Great Level a place of wonder, and so I go on. 'Besides, Jacob, there is much to be admired here. Have you not ever felt the beauty of the place, the expanses of water, the stands of reed and the sky that mirrors it all?'

Van Hooghten leans forward.

'We are here to work, Jan, not to look as painters do and imagine things. Besides, you are not talking sense. The meres breed the ague. The people are barbarous and hostile; the land scarce productive of anything more than a few eels and grazing in the summer. You see that?'

'Indeed, I know it. Yet though it is unimproved, this place sometimes seems to me finer than the greatest work of any engineer I can think of.'

'False sentiment, my dear Brunt. You have forgot your profession.'

'Then we'll say no more of it.'

The conversation ends, but I feel uneasy at my own reserve. Van Hooghten is the only friend I have in this place, and I should like to explain to him the beauty I now find here. My feeling for this strange place has grown with my love and now its beauty and your own are intertwined. As for the rumour that I have a woman, I do not know how it might have got about, and suppose that it is a supposition merely, because of my own reticence. I am sure that no one has seen you in my company. Yet Van Hooghten has noticed some change in me.

The boats at King's Lynn bring us more ragged men furious at their fate. Van Hooghten says it is at General Cromwell's command; others that the Earl of Bedford, who will profit by the draining, insists the most. The Gentlemen Adventurers pay for the transport of the prisoners, it is said, and for the keeping of them here.

Adriaan Renswyck demands some of the prisoners to build quarters for the new arrivals. I hand over the men with reluctance. He puts them to work no matter what the weather, and takes no notice of sickness amongst them. In a few weeks the camp by King's Lynn is twice the size it was last year. The first stockade Renswyck built has been breached; a fenced corridor now runs from it to a new camp that bulges out beyond the market streets, once again stockaded and towered.

One early spring morning I follow Van Hooghten's muddy overcoat as it swings up and round the stairs of the furthermost watchtower. We come out into chilly dawn at the top, where the sentries stamp the wooden platform to keep the cold from their feet.

'Good morrow, gentlemen,' Van Hooghten says in his slubby Dutch English.

'Good morning, sirs.'

The soldiers nod at us but their eyes go past our hats and out over the camps. Though Van Hooghten and I can command them in the matter of the drainage works, they hold us in low esteem.

Van Hooghten and I look down at the snaking wooden walls that define the camps.

'Look at that.' Van Hooghten points at the new stockade of the second camp.

'Listing from the vertical, and only a few weeks built.'

It is obvious; a section of the new stockade is leaning inwards like a drunkard. The second camp, built out on the marsh, has already begun to sink. After rain, peaty black water seeps into the huts. The prisoners fill hessian sacks with sand and pile them by the doors, but the water takes no notice, flowing through the holes, easy and unheeding.

Next the prisoners raise their rickety bunks above the floor, where they sleep two together, head to toe. Fever and sickness weaken them. A doctor arrives from Ely and moves into a small house hastily constructed for him by the Adventurers Company beyond the stockade. He checks the men each day for rashes and signs of wasting fever, and orders the sickest moved to a hut that is set aside as a hospital, where other prisoners tend them. He demands volunteers for this job, but none come forward. I choose a dozen men who lack the strength to continue labouring outside, thinking that I am easing the burden of life for them.

A day later, two of them have squeezed through loose planks in the stockade and run onto the fen. From the watchtower a soldier sees one of them splash through the icy water of a small mere nearby, and try to conceal himself in the reed beds.

'Tell me, why have you fled?' I ask when he is brought back and stands before me.

He refuses to speak, and I turn him over to Major Wade, who has the authority to order a beating and will use it. There is a belief, Van Hooghten tells me, that strangers come into the camp in the dark, and go from hut to hut, speaking of destruction and the fires on the meres. These fires are marsh lights, the strangers say, will-o'-the-wisps conjured by spirits. Such talk inflames the prisoners; and since we continually turn up strange axe heads and other metal objects of no known use, the fear of spirits grows as the works progress.

Warmer weather brings no change. The prisoners are apathetic and live in mud and lice. Every morning after they have collected their tools, they file past the cookhouses. Pease pudding, boiled up, cut in slabs and slapped between slices of barley-bread, is their food for the day. I eat the same while I am at the works or ride from place to place. Beer is served to the soldiers and engineers, and everyone drinks the water from the mere, or from the streams and rivers. It appears wholesome enough except around the camps.

We Dutchmen supplement the local bread and eels with our own supplies, brought from Holland. A barrel of salted herring stands in the corner of my larder, and from a shelf hangs a yellow Gouda cheese in a muslin bag. In the evenings I cut slices from it and nibble them with pleasure, feeling myself to be a student in Leiden again.

In the camps, prisoners and soldiers, Scots, Irish and English, all begin to look alike. Peat sticks to their clothes and works its way into the weft. Beards make old men of everyone, and fear of sickness walks beside them. Now only the Dutchmen take care to display their cleanliness, as if they were in their own country with the neighbours looking on. Van Hooghten orders his housekeeper to brush the mud from his clothes each evening. I hang my own cloak before the fire where it dangles almost to the floor. I brush it myself. I do more, as if I were a man of fashion; upon advice I send to the city of Norwich for new boots finely made there, knee-high and supple. I buy two pairs and wear them by turns. Each night I scrape the mud off one pair, stuff them with dry rags and grease them with oil. Fearful that the rats will gnaw them, I air them in a wooden box with holes, while wearing the second pair, fine and dry, upon my feet the next day.

'Quite a courtier,' Van Hooghten says, to tease me, which, though I know it derives from his affection, I take also as a hint to draw me out.

Adriaan Renswyck is one man unaffected by the squalor and discontent. Since the discovery of the urns he has lost all interest in works; the camps engross him. One evening I notice that his slovenly cloak is gone, replaced by one of plum-red worsted, fringed with rabbit fur. He wears a beaver hat, black with glints of moonlight. Seeing my glance he takes it off and holds it out.

'From Nieuw Amsterdam. The best skin to be had.'

In this empty desolate country, in the mud and sleet, Renswyck begins to look like a townsman. He buys a malacca cane with brown-stained knuckles, and plants it on the ground at arm's length like a rich man in Dam Square. I come across him one morning running his palm back and forth over its silver top with a dreaming look. Even his low cur is fattening up, and though it skulks behind him still, its hair is brushed and clean.

From the top of the camp watchtowers one evening I look south along the length of the cut, and then turn round to the north, where the works stretch to the site of the new sluice. The air is heavy, the meres grey and darker grey where the wind is passing clear over them. A layer of orange lies under the cloud bank on the horizon. If I turn westwards the scene is as it always was, the silver meres streaked with the sunset, and the dark coming down. The scene is peaceful, but this evening I am filled with unease. A dozen fires burn in a ring around the camps. These days the fensmen are always out there, on islets that only they can reach. Are they watching? Can they see me up here? I wonder.

I imagine that they might advance with stealth on my cottage and look through the windows. At night I take care to draw the battered shutters up and bolt the door.

'The watchers who set the fires,' I ask you one evening. 'Do you know them?'

'They are my people, Jan. Uplanders have many names for us, we ourselves none.'

'What are they doing?'

'They are working, waiting for fish to rise. They are always out on the mere when the moon shines.'

Now there is impatience with me in your voice. I cannot stop myself from speaking again.

'They ring the camps, as if to set a watch upon them.'

'That is a trick of the eye, merely. They go about their labour in the night when some of the best fish are to be caught, and the fowl, too, as they sleep.'

'Yet they never approach or greet us, neither during the day nor at night.'

'You do not concern them.'

So absorbed am I in the strong sense of you, that I do not say what I have thought, that such reticence is curious; that I feel I am watched, day and night, though I never see anyone close by; and that this sense is just the same as that I had when you first appeared to me, silently, more than a year ago.

'The women who come to the market by the camp, do you know them also?'

'Some of them.'

The little parlour is safe and yellow in the candlelight. I am emboldened to go on by your closeness to me.

'Do you talk of the future when the meres are drained? What rights to fish or graze the land do you maintain?'

'The right of custom. We have always been here.'

'You have a lease?'

'A lease?'

'A document.'

There is a silence, and a look of confusion passes across your face before you say, 'I do not know, Jan, and do not wish to talk of it.'

It is as if a door has closed. Fearful that you will get up and leave, I do not pursue the subject but ask instead about the urns.

'Have you ever seen such urns as have been turned up this winter?'

At that you laugh suddenly, as if I have brought an absurdity into the space.

'They contain only dust.'

'Whose, Eliza? Do you know who buried those urns?'

'Not people of today, but those who came before.'

'Do you know who?'

'No, I do not; but it does not matter. They are here, listening; and the spirits also.'

There is no feeling of fear in you. You speak as if it is as obvious as a chair, this rug that we lie upon, or the fire before us.

You say you know about the God of the churches that the uplanders worship. Your people do not find God in a church, but consider that he is everywhere and in everything. This solid fact is simple, not open to a question.

'It just is,' you say.

The whole world, you tell me, is divided into three regions: the sky, the earth upon which we sit, and beneath us the watery underworld. No living person can pass the borders, but the spirits and the souls of the dead go freely from one place to another.

'Do you see them, Eliza?'

'Mingled together sometimes. A star that travels through the sky has a tail like a sheaf of wheat. We see it composed of spirits in flight.'

I wonder then whether you will begin to speak of your parents, but you do not, and I ask you no more. I summon up my patience. I remember to wait. There is time, I say to myself; I have a lifetime.

# PART FOUR

# Chapter 1

*Nieuw Amsterdam.*
*August and September, 1664.*
*Wind from the south, very light.*
*Great heat throughout the days and nights.*
*High tide by the Stadt Huys at 5 o'clock in the afternoon.*

From there on the Great Level, where we are sitting together by the fire, to here in my house on the Heere Gracht, is no distance, just a moment of reordering. The layers of my life lie stacked in my memory. Every day, and in my dreams, they are shuffled. One stratum slides over another, is laid down and brought up again, existing both then and now. Truly we are alive there in my cottage, where your skin is warm to my hand; and truly I am here, walking along Stadt Huys Laan, where a trickle of people soon collects into a crowd.

It is a bright August morning, the 27th of the month. The heat of the day is still at bay, the colours of the city full and brisk. I am wearing a muslin shirt, and no stockings on my legs. Any other clothes would be a folly when the air will soon get close and hot; nakedness would be true propriety. The women have left off their petticoats and stockings. Here is Hendrikje Beck, who lives a few doors down from me, her pale bosom quite uncovered, and here old Cornelia Vort, airing her red calves with a grunt and a smile. She is come with a slave child who wears nothing but loose pantaloons and a shirt with the sleeves cut off. Only the merchant Asser Levy is dressed correctly, as he always is, in black.

Hendrikje talks excitedly, waving a piece of paper.

'Ah, Mijnheer Brunt,' she says when I come up. 'Here is news.'

I incline my head, but Hendrikje needs no permission from me to keep talking.

'News from Lange Eylandt, brought this morning with the milk.'

Hendrikje has a farm on Lange Eylandt, though she lives here in the city, letting her son Dirk make the journey each morning across the Oost Rivier with the milk, butter and hard cheese. These she sells to householders all about, is done by mid-morning, and then gives herself over to gossip and her pipe.

Yesterday at first light four English ships sailed into Gravesend Bay by Breukelen, and rattled out their anchors to swing with the current. They are not merchant ships, but men-of-war, Hendrikje says, and pauses in her dramatic way. Dirk, up early with the cows, watched everything from a field by the shore.

Once they secured the warships, the sailors wasted no time in lowering a tender from each boat and then soldiers into them, helmets and pikes as well. The ships' captains must have known that Gravesend Bay has a good firm jetty. The people of Gravesend came out of their houses, some with their guns, some to marvel as the crowd of soldiers grew with each passage of the tenders until they numbered three hundred.

The English soldiers were far too many to fight but they carried no weapons, just sheets of paper, printed in Dutch. These they handed out in the crowd and to every person standing on their stoop. Dirk took one.

'And here it is,' says Hendrikje, waving it above her head. 'An offer of fair terms for those who make no resistance to the English, who declare the whole colony of Nieuw Nederland now to be theirs.'

As Hendrikje reads a shout goes up from the edge of the crowd.

'Look, look, coming up towards Noten Eylandt.'

People scatter and run down to the wharfs. But I can see them from here, four dots out in the bay, bearing north. If they are warships, all we can do is wait. The city is undefended, the determination of Director-General Stuyvesant uncertain. People spill out from their houses and mill about outside. Noise and confusion fill the streets. Rumours rush from mouth to mouth. It is a hostile force; no, it is an expedition merely; Governor Winthrop of the Connecticut colony is on board the flagship, to what purpose it is unclear, but it cannot be a good one.

Instead of listening to gossip, I go home to my garret where I have a good view of all the waterways. I pick up the ships in the circle of my telescope. They are frigates, built for speed. None of our ships go out to meet them; no warning shots are fired. Little by little their shapes and colours resolve until they are clear and present to my eye. From the main masts, the gold, blue and red Royal Standard wrinkles and stretches against the shimmering sky. At mid-morning I walk down to get a closer look. The scene, as the ships heel over gently in the breeze, is magnificent and, to the children who run around in excitement, joyful. Leaning over the wall by Op't Waeter two boys with a spyglass pick out the names carved on the ships' prows: *Lion, Guinea, Perseverance, Endeavour.*

By the afternoon the little fleet is anchored by Noten Eylandt in plain sight of the Fort, though not so close as to provoke the few soldiers inside. With many others I walk over to the Prince Gracht by Schreijer's Hoek for a good sight of them. Gerrit Philipse, a trader whose doors open onto the marketplace, comes out to join me.

'Mijnheer Brunt; good afternoon,' he says. 'No doubt what the English are up to, I suppose?'

Hans Dreper, from the tavern on the Heere Gracht, strolls by, wiping his hands on his apron in a casual way as if the sight is just part of his day's work. He lets his apron drop, pulls out one of the leaflets come in from Lange Eylandt, and joins in.

'No need to fret yourself, Gerrit. Have a look at this. It means trade for all of us. Let them take over; time will tell whether they have come to stay.'

'No, the Director-General and the Council must resist,' Philipse says when he has glanced down the crumpled page of paper.

Dreper laughs, throaty with tobacco.

'Resist? And where are these resisters, sir? Four frigates and not a single Company warship in sight. It is already too late. If they want to take the city, who is going to stop them? Besides, we will go on here in the same way; the English are already among us, and people from other nations, too.'

As we talk we see a cutter making towards the frigates. The flag of the West India Company ripples out from its mast. Pieter Stuyvesant is putting on a show of nonchalance. He is sailing out to the English as if to offer them dinner. When the cutter arrives by the *Guinea*, a rope ladder unravels itself down the hull like a snake down a log. Two tiny figures scramble up, disappear, then, in a few minutes, clamber down again. The cutter tacks back to the jetty and the men walk into the Fort, where the main gate opens and closes, as if at the end of a play.

Night falls and the mosquito clouds come up. I return home and wait, with the rest of Nieuw Amsterdam. Lysbet asks to stay with me in my house. She is frightened about the English soldiers, she says, and does not wish to sleep in her house alone. I am not in a humour for talking, but give my assent before I take the stairs to my chamber on the first floor. I hear Lysbet opening the doors to the bed in the parlour, the creak of mattress against wood as she settles, and then silence fills the house.

Outside, the crickets have begun their metal trilling. I lie in wait for sleep, hoping that it will catch me softly as it passes. Scenes turn in my mind: Cornelius Vermuyden's nasal voice and his plump hands round my drawings; Jacob Van Hooghten when first I saw him by the jetty at Ely; the Great Level, with its meres floating in the mist; the mud and chaos of the works; and the layers of the road I found, crisp and new as if they had been built yesterday.

In the morning knots of citizens gather at the street corners. Soon the taverns are full. Word spreads of troops gathering by the Breukelen ferry, their numbers swelled by English farmers from Lange Eylandt. At mid-morning, when the tide turns, a tender full of soldiers pushes off from the *Guinea*. Waves in the Nort Rivier slap up against its sides and send puffs of spray into the blue morning air.

Something is happening. Two men disembark, leaving the soldiers on board. It is plain from the way they walk with modesty and without weapons that these are messengers. They are here to hand over something, to tell us something, to open talks. But all this is a matter of form. They know that Nieuw Amsterdam, this little grid of two thousand souls, is open and unguarded. The English can step off their ships and take it.

In the open space in front of the Fort, Pieter Stuyvesant is waiting. The Director-General is surly in his greeting, and despite the impediment of his wooden leg, hurries the visitors into the courtyard. It is plain that he wants them out of sight, yet a group of citizens push in before the gates are closed.

I squeeze in also, and wait with the crowd under the windows of the old Director-General's residence where the councilmen are assembled. For a few minutes nothing comes from the room inside; then I hear an English voice and Stuyvesant's gruff reply, too soft to make out the words. There is a sudden gasp followed by a jumble of raised voices, all in Dutch.

'We must see the terms, Director-General.'

'The Council must decide as well as yourself.'

'You do not have the authority to refuse without consulting us.'

'Show us the paper, sir.'

'Father, please do not tear it up.'

That is a voice I recognise; it is Balthazar Stuyvesant, the Director-General's son, only seventeen years old. Pieter Stuyvesant, it seems, is losing his temper.

Then, unexpectedly, Stuyvesant reappears, banging down the stairs, followed by hurrying Council members. The two Englishmen press against the wall and stand aside for them, as if embarrassed by this display.

Stuyvesant turns first to the crowd and then to the councilmen behind him. He has always been a swaggerer, prosperous and unloved.

'Are none of you with me?' he shouts. 'Am I to let this city – the whole colony, too – go without a fight?'

A woman in the front pulls her child close and puts her arms tight round him. People turn and shuffle, but no one speaks. Stuyvesant's voice comes over to us again. He gobbles his words and they seem to choke him.

'Where is your honour, your duty to the Company? This is Nieuw Amsterdam, your city.'

Stuyvesant is a stranger to honour and duty. Such words do not sit well in him. Besides, such cloudy ideas have never taken precedence here over trade and freedom of life. The Company has ignored Stuyvesant's requests for men and ships. Now he is alone.

Stuyvesant spots the tobacco merchant Pieter Moritz and Clef von Kleist the furrier who stand close by me at the edge of the crowd.

'Are you with me, gentlemen?' he asks.

They incline their heads in a gesture that a man could take either way, but show no resolution to agree.

'You, Jan Brunt; you who stay silent so often. What do you say?'

'I observe that the case is lost.'

Stuyvesant turns away from me. I have not told him what he wanted to hear.

'You all think I should yield,' he says. 'Yet I had rather be carried from here a dead man.'

Not a single citizen of Nieuw Amsterdam comes forward. The silence settles in the dizzy midday heat. Stuyvesant is deserted. No one will help him. I stay still as well. Nausea turns over in my stomach; a feeling of anxiety that arises not from a love of my homeland or a wish to defend the interests of the Company, but from the past rushing through me. Until this moment I have been my own chronicler, sifting and arranging my memories. I have carried my history safe and contained as a sprite in a box. Now England is near and must be acknowledged.

History does not pause for me or for any man, and certainly not for Pieter Stuyvesant, whose face is by turns red and pale. Stuyvesant scrapes his stump across the flagstones. Then he turns away from us to face the two Englishmen.

'Sirs. Go back to your ships. I acknowledge you a too-powerful enemy. I will treat with you, though before I do I demand a letter from Colonel Nicolls signed in the proper form. Come to my house tomorrow; not here, but to my own house. It is just up the street from here at Great Bouwerie; any urchin can point you the way. Come without an escort. There is no need for it.'

And with that he bows and turns back into the old Director-General's house. The little advantage he has wrestled takes the edge off his humiliation. Nonetheless, the end is ignominious. It will be many years before this scene is painted. When it comes to painting history, surrender doesn't sell until it can find a mythic tinge. No painter in his own day can shift a picture of defeat.

And so it is that a few days later the articles of surrender are agreed in Stuyvesant's house at Great Bouwerie. The terms are generous, and printed up for all to read. The Director-General, the Council, and our new masters assure us we will keep our property, liberty of conscience in religion and can trade as we do now.

To mark his victory, Colonel Nicolls wishes the handover to be according to form and for all to see. He demands a ceremony. The officers and soldiers will march out of Fort Amsterdam with drums beating, lighted flares and colours flying. The Dutch will surrender their arms, placing their drawn swords and pikes on the ground in front of them. Then the English will march in.

Stuyvesant signs, and after him the councilmen, one by one. The English sign, leaving off their titles as a mark of respect. It is ten in the morning, everything over in a few minutes. The English bow and take their leave. The Articles lie on Director-General Pieter Stuyvesant's table.

# Chapter 2

*King's Lynn.*
*Summer and autumn, 1651.*

By early summer the prisoners have cleared the path of the new river as far as the site of the sluice and from there all the way to the sea. Warm weather sets in and the shallowest meres disappear. The rivers run low and sink beneath the surface of the fen. Flocks of finches sing in new grasslands, feasting on seeds. In the evenings the skies fill with the rasping cries of geese as they fly to their resting places on the marshes; black nets of starlings shrink and billow from tree to tree.

The prisoners now begin to dig all along the new cut, and to embank the old river on its far side. They labour through the hottest months, controlled by the soldiers. This is devilish work, damp in the marshlands, hot in the listless air. Men languish and die and we do not even know their names. Renswyck orders the prisoners to dig the graves of their dead beyond the camp stockades. I watch the graves fill with water as they dig and see the Irish buried in mud, in unconsecrated ground. The rage of their countrymen grows with each death.

I determine to look out beyond the camps to the new river. I am proud of it, as a father is proud of a child that grows forthright and strong. The cut now runs straight across the landscape, certain and direct. The prisoners dig out the peat, sand and gravel and then line the new cut with clay.

Along the new and the old river, embankments tower up, solid and sturdy, majestic in the flat world they traverse. At their bases they are fully threescore foot wide, narrowing to the top, where a broad sandy path is to be created for the passage of horses and carts as well as those who walk. The washes between the new embankment and the old river are now coming into being, and are a fine sight some hundred and forty feet wide.

A summer storm blows in and rainwater collects in the bottom of the new cut. Standing in the wide trench I look down onto its unsteady surface and see my own trembling face. Inside my cheeks I see my skin ripple. Tiny rills turn over and over on the surface.

'Jacob,' I shout. 'Van Hooghten, come.'

I have forgotten that Van Hooghten is nowhere near; it is Major Wade, out on patrol, who walks up and pushes his neck over the new cut.

'What in heaven are you looking at, Mr Brunt? Why are you in the water?'

The scorn in his voice disperses my happiness.

'Major Wade,' I say, 'you see the ripples here? They tell me that the water is moving. Now I know that the river will flow as I calculated, and take the water away from the land. From this moment, though we may not see it, the whole Level will begin to dry.'

But Major Wade has no interest in the works. His head disappears and he is gone without another word. For a few moments I stand and watch the water falling over itself in the direction of the sea. Elation spreads through me. All my work has led up to this, the moment when my calculations come to life and nature obeys me. Nothing can hold back my joy. Unobserved in the bottom of the cut, I raise my arms to the sky.

Later, in the evening, I ask you if you will come down when it is dark and there is no one about. We walk up the embankment and you stand on the edge in front of me. The water in the new river is stippled in the moonlight. My arms circle you and my chin rests on your hair. You stand very still, and I want you; success is rushing through me.

You appear strongly taken by this, the first fruit of my great labour. I feel you stand straighter as you look down into the cut. After a moment you ask, 'How long will it be until your work is done?'

'In a year this part of the Level will be drained and the new sluice almost complete. Then we must consider where the land needs smaller ditches and dykes. I do not know how long it will be, Eliza;

only that I am happy with the work I have done, since I have never before attempted anything of the size and difficulty.'

You turn round so that the moon shines on me and leaves you in the shadow. I pull you gently towards me.

'When you give it all to the Gentlemen, then it will be finished?'

'For me it will be finished. Other men will make the land ready for dividing into estates, hedging and planting. But no work with water ever ends. In my country we know this and remain always vigilant.'

You are silent. I still cannot see your face, or what thoughts might be running across it.

'Eliza,' I say, my arms still around you, 'will you stay with me tonight?'

'I cannot.'

The disappointment I feel is quickly swept aside by my mood of triumph. If you do not stay tonight, you will come tomorrow. You have never left for long. I no longer allow myself unease.

'Goodbye, Jan.'

'Goodbye, Eliza.'

I feel your lips brush across mine. Then you slip into the dark. You know the ways across the fen; the moon is behind you. In a minute you are gone, deep into the blackness, and I am alone.

I remember that night now, my happiness and the moonlight, but most of all the feel of you leaning against me, your shoulders back against my chest and all of you weighing on me, strong and warm. I can feel my arms around you, hands around your hands, the two of us one being, so it felt to me, standing in the dark on the embankment.

When the autumn rains come the new cut will fill, and as we dig the secondary channels, the expanse of water that has always covered this land in winter will begin to shrink. By next summer the smaller meres will be gone, so water will become land, and this will be a land to make a fortune from, rich with the silt of ages. Where now the sky picks up and reflects back the grey-blue glint of the water, it will then find pasture or the golden ripple of barley in the sun. The colours of this place will change. New forms of life will arrive, inland birds to feed on seedheads, field mice to nest in stalks.

In the summer evenings I sometimes venture out onto the meres, drawn to their shimmering expanses and impelled to present myself, in plain sight, to the hidden watchers. As I glide along I sense them, silent and following, as once I sensed you. Now that my work comes to fruition, my worst fears have faded. I had thought the watchers might menace or attack me, but now they appear less a threat than a simple presence.

Curiosity begins to replace my fear. Gradually I extend my wandering, coming closer to the islands dotted in the meres. One August evening, with the light still in the sky, I come across an island encircled completely by reeds except for an overgrown landing stage half collapsed into the mere. I see no coracles or nets that might give sign of habitation. Perhaps the ague has carried off all those who once lived here, or a better island called them away, and they have not returned.

I tie my coracle up to a rotten post by the jetty and jump out, pushing through the barrier of young reeds into the interior, where I find myself alone, with the red sun slanting in. Before me are several huts, rectangular in form, raised upon stilts to take them away from the island damp. They appear deserted, and I hear nothing except for the sighing of the reeds and, if I stand and listen, the rustle of birds in the reed heads.

I walk round the habitation, stooping as if I expect some attack. No one comes; nothing disturbs me. The huts are built with frames of willow branches covered with mud plaster and roofs that slope up to an apex. Except for the door entrance they have no windows. I bend low and step inside the largest of them. It is quite dry underfoot, the floor of beaten clay with rushes laid upon it. When my eyes are accustomed to the gloom I look up and see that the reeds that form both the walls and the roof are bundled together and tied round and round at intervals so as to form patterns.

Even in the half-dark I am astonished. Grace and harmony fill the space, and light pours through the door to a bright patch on the floor. Rising upwards, the reed bundles have the appearance of the columns and roof beams of our churches and cathedrals. At four points as they rise they are bound round with thinner reed stems, and these circles are found at exactly the same height up each one. Thinner stems are bound back and forth in diagonals across these bands, serving no purpose that I can see except that of joy.

So your people have an idea of the beauty of things. Though they do not paint portraits or landscapes as mine do, yet still they bind the reeds and make patterns with them, taking a pride and a pleasure in their forms. Looking up into the roof and towards the evening sky framed by the chimney hole, I wonder who works these miracles and whether they are held in high esteem, as are the most skilful painters in my country.

Outside again, I walk quickly round in the fading light. Between the houses and the landing stage is a lattice of wooden stakes banged into the ground, some still standing straight, others falling haphazardly. I wonder if these stakes serve as a frame to dry nets or for some other purpose, but have not time to examine them. Fearful of getting lost on the mere, I slide down into my coracle and push off from the jetty, paddling hard to reach a spot known to me before the sun slides beneath the horizon and leaves me lost and in the darkness.

The columns of reed, tied with such exactitude, measured to have an equal circumference, glow in my mind. I remember the church at Sint-Maartensdijk and myself as a small boy who saw the light and grace of God stream through the windows. The men who made the reed columns appear now to me like the stonemasons who built our churches, men who learn from their masters how to take the materials nature offers and fashion them into beauty.

When I get back to my cottage I find it empty. Closed in my parlour, I sit down, then get up, pace across the little room and light the fire, though it is a warm night. I want to talk to you, to touch you, to weave with you our secret world of jokes and habits, to watch you practise your letters while I lay out bread and cheese on the table with beer from the barrel in the corner. I want to talk to you about the island.

Gradually the happiness of the afternoon leaves me. God has gone, and taken his reassurance with him. Now in the cottage I feel darkness and uncertainty press in. I am quite alone, and, by the time I light the candles, I am sure that you will not come. My questions run round the whole rim of the earth and find no answering voice. Where are you now? Are you out on the water with your family? Are you sleeping under such a roof as I saw today? The silence brings me no answers, and I can only push these questions away.

I long for you to open the door and come in briskly, without looking about, as if the cottage has always been your home. Though a man familiar with solitude and formerly settled within it, I am assailed by sadness. Where I want warm flesh there is only air. Where I search for a voice there is a void. I want to touch you, to run my fingers across your lips and feel them pucker and yield. I want to run my mouth over your breast and so learn, as I have learned a hundred times, how smooth it is and how rough at the peak. I want you thus inside me, and myself inside you, possessed and given and gone from myself.

I think for a moment of taking my horse and riding over to King's Lynn. There I could knock on Van Hooghten's door and he would ask me in. But it is too dark. I might miss the path and fall into the river or my horse stumble and throw me off. My only recourse is to walk the way with a lantern, and for that it is too late. Besides, what can I say to Jacob? That I, who chose this cottage out on the fen, am now afraid of emptiness; that I long for you, whose presence I have hidden; that I have seen the beauty of the houses on the fen and wish to tell him of them?

I sit and look at the dinner I have laid out, and do not eat it. Instead I reach for one of the baskets I have hung from the ceiling and find the brandy bottle. It fits easily in my hand and its rough earthenware reassures me. I unstopper it and drink, gulping the gold liquid until the fear in my stomach is quietened.

The brandy soon makes the world swim and myself with it. I forget where I am and seem to see Cornelius Vermuyden in London last winter, praising my progress and promising to report it to my village, a clap on my shoulder as he spoke. How eagerly I drank his words, and allowed them to warm my body. I see my mother on Tholen opening the door to our house. She takes the letter from the postmaster and puts it on the parlour table. It lies there, heavy with Vermuyden's report. My father opens it when he comes home. I see my sisters laugh and chatter, oblivious to my absence.

Then the visions quicken. Lines of prisoners, tied together, flounder across the mere in the dark. A coracle drifts away from its mooring and sinks, listing and full of water. I hear Renswyck's cur bark and lift my head from the table and seem to see Renswyck himself peering in at the parlour window. His eyes are like fires, and blaze through the glass. The brandy has maddened me, I tell myself, as the untethered room begins to turn.

I make myself stand and go to the window. Perhaps you are there, waiting to come in. I can see no one outside, but I open the casement and shout into the darkness. Only silence answers and I turn back to the room. Nausea rises in my stomach and I put out a hand to steady myself by the wall until I can reach the table again. How long I sit there I do not know, only that by the time my head sinks to the rough wooden surface these visions have gone from it. I have banished the foreboding that was settling inside me and shunted it beyond the border of myself. When I wake in the morning I swallow two or three cups of water, take my horse, and ride fast to the site of the works by the sluice. My memories of the night just gone are jumbled and I feel shame that I imagined such terrors.

Day after day, time presses in. The heavy force of it pushes me into the future. By October the sluice near Denver is dug, and the brick placements built. The prisoners are dispersed in groups and camp by the works. I frequently lie in different places, some nights in my cottage, some in King's Lynn, others in the open air. Everything on the Great Level becomes fragmented; the works, scattered across the land; the landscape, scored with new embankments and rivers, ditches and paths; the encampments of soldiers and prisoners; the rhythm of the days and nights, and all our lives.

Then comes another discovery that pulls me up short. It is not of urns or ashes this time, but human forms brought to me by one of the soldiers. He has taken them from a prisoner, he says. They are women, goddesses or witches.

One is baked from clay, the other carved from sparkling rock. Where the first absorbs the light so that her navel and the secret place between her legs are black as caves, the second seems to glow with magic power. I cannot tell if the same hand might have made them, yet they belong together. They are old women, many times mothers. Both are full of ancient art, and once were surely worshipped.

I put both creatures in my pocket, all day feeling the weight of them there and their mysterious force. In the evening I wash them in my copper, wrap them in muslin and conceal them in the strongbox in my cottage. Though they are locked out of sight, their gaze still reaches me through the wood. They add another reason to my wakefulness and another mystery to this place.

One night when sleep eludes me I dress, pull on my boots and greatcoat and step outside. A fire burns in the distance. No sound comes from it, and I cannot make out any figures. With my lantern on the ground I overturn my coracle and let it down onto the water. Thin cloud has come in from the west but there is light enough from the shaded moon to see the banks of reeds and a glistening on the mere.

I paddle softly towards the fire, and gradually I make out several standing figures. They are on the bank in a clearing they have made, and hold poles out over the water. A fire burns on the flattened area between them. Now and again one of the men stoops and feeds it with reeds. They are dressed in jerkins and breeches and have bound their stockings with bands of cloth. They stand still, with no hint of any fear. Yet I know they are watching me.

'Our greetings.'

The voice comes to me in the half-light with no menace or even enquiry in it. It is the man on the left of the group who speaks, inclining a little in my direction as he does. His voice is open and clear, with the rising notes characteristic of the fens people, as if they have added the lapping of water to the ordinary speech of the English. So it seems that I am quite mistaken in my fears. These are men fishing, nothing more. The fire keeps them warm and throws light on the water. Perhaps fish are attracted to it, as moths are to candles.

Smoke drifts between us.

'My greetings to you, sirs.'

I am at a loss now. How can I explain myself? The four men stand impassive, their fishing lines slack. I am disturbing the fish and any fowl they might be after. They say nothing more, though I have come close enough to feel their gaze upon me. Without a word I turn round and make my way back along the reed wall. By the time I reach home the sun has pushed off from the horizon and pulled the cloud up with it. It will be a fine late-summer day, blue and golden.

'I went out on the mere a few nights ago,' I say when you come next to my cottage.

'Why did you do that, Jan? It is treacherous on the water in the dark unless you know the ways of it.'

You stand by the window, looking out. I want to reach out my hand, and bring you close to me. But I do not, for fear you might break away.

'The moon was out and I felt no danger. A fire drew me out. I met four men, out fishing. We exchanged greetings; that was all.'

'No harm was done, then.' You put your arms around me.

'I was frightened. For so long I thought they menaced me; but I was quite mistaken. They did not attempt to question or detain me – seemed only anxious that I be gone so that they might continue.'

'Indeed; fishing and silence go together.'

# Chapter 3

One crisp November morning, I oversee the lowering of the gates into the sluice at Denver, where the tidal river comes up to dominate the fresh one. With the sluice gates in place, all the southern part of the Great Level will be safe from high tides and salt water. It is a moment of joy for us engineers, and Van Hooghten is here to share it with me.

'We are more than halfway done, Jan,' he says, 'and must send word to Mr Vermuyden of this triumph.'

The sluice follows the pattern of those we have in Holland at the mouths of our rivers, built in brick and wood, with doors in the gates that rise to let the water through. The whole gates swing open with the equalisation of the water on either side, so ships can make straight for Ely by the new cut, leaving the old river to wander on its way.

The moment of hazard comes when we close the sluice gates and doors to test them. From the embankment we watch as the tide comes up and is stopped there, rising high above the water level of the new cut, and then, after an hour or so, falling slowly down again. In truth the sluice is no miracle; greater things have been made in Holland. Yet the wild power of the sea has been contained.

Standing up on the embankment by the sluice, I imagine this place when all trace of the prisoners and the works is gone, the scars of the camps healed. The new landscape is smooth and unsullied. Black soil lies flat and obedient, traversed here and there by lines of willow stumps not yet cleared from the paths of old creeks. The reed banks are ploughed into the peat, remembered only in patches of lighter soil. New land stretches away, divided by stakes and young hedges.

Drainage channels glow pink in the evening sun. Russet sails of wind-mills catch the eye as they turn in the wind. In the distance a farmer shepherds his cows towards their shed for milking. It is very quiet without the harsh cries of the geese and the splash of wildfowl as they land on the water, without the shush and murmur of the reeds. On and on, right over to the horizon, the Great Level lies pegged out in perfect order.

A few days later I show you the drawings I have prepared for the next stage of the works. You glance at them quickly, moving the papers from one pile to another.

'Look here,' I say. 'This drawing shows the marsh that pushes out from King's Lynn to the sea, the limit of the land to be drained and made free from salt, and the cuts we will make across it.'

'Now that I can copy and write, I need only learn the workings of drawings such as this to become an engineer.'

There is a fierceness and alertness in you as you say this. I do not say that such has never been, and will never be, work for a woman; nor that it takes years of study and learning with a master to become an engineer. Your stillness makes me anxious.

'I cannot be your master, Eliza. I wish simply to show you how I spend my days.'

'And I wish to look with care.'

'Why?'

The question makes you impatient and you draw away from me.

'Can it not be my study when it is yours?'

'This is my work.'

'I wish to learn about it.'

Laughter and scorn are mixed up together in your voice, and I search to find the tenderness that I long for.

'The idea draws me, that you can make a drawing here, quite flat, and have men bring it to life for you, out there.'

'Your people make new lands also.'

'But not this way. We do as we have always done. We give the water the task, and just help a little.'

I point out to you the figures that show the depths we dig must free the land for pasture. Then I lay out the large piece of paper that has the drawings and plans of the sluice.

'This shows the sluice as if it is cut in half. You see here the height of the walls and the placing of the run-off channels.'

'And this?'

'Those are the wooden gates, with the doors set in them; their widths and heights.'

Full of delight I explain the workings of the sluice, until you move this last page over and stand up.

'I am leaving, Jan.'

'Must you go?'

'Yes, I have work to do tomorrow.'

We kiss then and draw closer, and a warm happiness spreads through me. I am buoyed up by the success of the works and by your touch. I promise myself that soon I will ask you to come with me wherever I may be called next in my profession, and to come as my wife. Whenever I have approached this subject in the last months you have flown away from me. I have told myself that it is thoughtless to take you from everything you know. Underneath that consideration I have been reluctant. To ask the question I must bear the answer, and I have been afraid. Now I have a greater trust in myself.

I am safe asleep under the coverlets when someone bangs on the door. The knock reverberates through the cottage so that I jump out of bed, first upon instinct and then with dread running through me.

'Mr Brunt. Open the door; open the door.'

Instead I open the window and lean out. A figure stands there in the darkness.

'Who is it?'

'Captain Townley.'

'What do you want?'

'Something has happened. Come out.'

'Yes, yes.'

I feel my way in the dark, finding the door of the bedroom with outstretched arms. Cool black air meets me outside. There is no moon, but a faint streak of green on the horizon. Everything is quiet, as it is in the hour before dawn when no birds sing.

Captain Townley holds a lantern. He has been running.

'The bank. The bank; oh, Mr Brunt, it is leaking.'

'How much?'

I am alert immediately, an engineer who knows his work. New embankments, when first tested by a great volume of water, may leak a little. Just as a loose tile in a roof lets rain drip through, so a fissure in a new embankment allows water to trickle out; but just as a drip will not cause a roof to collapse, a trickle will not bring an embankment down.

'I do not know.'

'Where is it coming from?'

'Above the sluice near the camps. Major Wade sent me. He was with the patrol.'

It is a cold November night and there has been rain for days. The new cut and the old river have overflowed their banks and turned the washes into a field of water. This I look upon with Dutch eyes. I have built the embankment to withstand a volume of water that I calculate can never come down from the tributaries that drain into the River Ouse. There is probably nothing untoward.

'Do not worry Major Wade. I shall ride over to check. Can you find Mr Van Hooghten in town if I go on ahead?'

'Yes.'

I ride fast along the path by the river. The sky brightens to the east as I go, the sun sending red shafts of light under the rising cloud. It has almost stopped raining and away to the west I can see the fires of the fishermen. They are burning brightly in the half-light of dawn in greater numbers than I have ever seen them.

My mind is clean and clear, as if it is floating above me. If the bank is still unsettled and water has found a way through, I must deal with it quickly. Rapidly I go over in my mind the tools and materials needed to plug a leak: spades and hatchets, brushwood, turf; even bunches of sedge if things are hard.

After a few minutes sounds come down the path; a confusion of men's voices, shouts and replies. In another few minutes I can hear the words.

'Spades here.'

'No, faster.'

'We are doing it as fast as we can.'

It is evident even before I arrive that Major Wade has summoned help from the camp.

'Over here – over here. More – more!'

'There is another leak – come, come.'

'And over here.'

I ride faster, my horse's hooves kicking up the mud along the path. I can see the camp now, not far up ahead, and, from the top of the embankment, I can see men running out of the huts, pulling on their cloaks, looking this way and that.

The shouting increases.

'It's coming from underneath.'

'Open the sluice gates.'

'Open the doors in the gates first.'

'No, no; then we cannot open the gates.'

'Yes, we must. The water is too high to open the gates.'

I pull up my horse and shout back. 'I am coming. Open the doors.'

'That's Mr Brunt.'

I hope against hope that enough water can flow through the doors to lower the levels upstream and let us stop up the leaks. I can see several groups of men, prisoners and soldiers mixed up together. Some work at the bottom of the embankment, some on the drained land beyond. One group is filling buckets with muddy soil, the other pressing it into the leak, pushing it in with branches pulled from willows nearby. On top of the embankment another man stands anxiously, pointing now here, now there, at the trickles of water – more than one I see now, straight away – two or three, not drips but insistent streams.

I ride up to him, a soldier. 'Here, take my horse. Ride back to my stable.'

He calls out to another soldier standing a little way off. 'Take this horse to the cottage along the embankment there.'

'Yes, sir.'

'And feed him.'

'Yes.'

'Then find Mr Renswyck.'

'Yes, sir.'

The soldier is no longer insolent, as they have been for so long, but quiet with fear. He takes the bridle, swings himself up and urges the horse gingerly back along the path. I turn back to the other man.

'How many leaks – how many?'

'I do not know, sir. There are more down there'. He points along the embankment. 'We are doing everything we can.'

The men begin to shovel earth up at the bottom of the bank, silent now, and desperate. The water is pouring out, bringing mud with it. Are the other leaks as bad? Looking down the bank I see something that makes my heart jump. Four groups of men are working at the bottom of the embankment, spread at intervals – intervals which I know, as an engineer, are more or less equal.

What I feel then, as I stand there, is a shifting of the ground; a settling like a sigh. The weight of water is incalculable; from a trickle to a rush is a moment. It is moving faster now that the sluice doors have been opened.

'Off, off, get off. It is giving way here.'

I run down the embankment and push the men away.

'Go go. Get up on the embankment and run.'

They look up in astonishment. One man shouts, 'I am not getting up there, you mad Dutchman. What if it all goes?'

The others catch his fear and they all plunge into the fen, dropping their spades as they go. I have no time to call them back; I run along to the next group, then the next, shouting.

'Get up, get up.'

None of them obey. I scramble up the steep incline of the embankment and turn to see them running in the direction of the camps. Then I am suddenly tottering. The embankment is trembling, turning to liquid underneath me, taking me with it. Half running, half falling, I manage to stumble along to an area of greater firmness. Everything inside me feels to have disappeared. It seems very quiet, though I can hear a noise like thunder that brings me back again to where I am standing. I turn and see a whole section of the embankment collapse into itself. In a few moments the water has eaten away at its base, taken it under, and surged on through the breach.

All the pent-up water in the washes seethes and boils, a mass of roiling brown that foams grey and white, turning over and over as it is pushed from behind. Rushing through the breach it pulls in more of the embankment from either side, the impacted earth falling in blocks as easily as a child's sandcastle is washed away by a wave.

I run back and look across the roaring water to the other side. There another section of the embankment begins to crumble.

'It's going! It's going!'

'Get out.'

'Go; go!'

All around me men are throwing down their spades. Now we can only stand and watch, feeling under our feet the force of nature no longer denied. The water masses and swells out beyond the breach across land. It hurls itself into the newly dug drainage ditches, impeded by the drop, pushed by the water behind, and comes up in great waves that forge onwards. It smashes new fences and takes them with it as it surges on towards the camps. Only a few minutes have passed since the first breach.

Standing on the embankment, thirty feet above the fen, I strain to see through the spray-filled air. Everything is dim and the outline of the camp is smoky and far away. The air is full with the sound of rushing water and the crack of timber. When the water hurtles up against the stockade there is a crash, a momentary lull, and then down comes the stockade, fragile as a row of matchsticks. The watchtowers, that yesterday seemed so high and strong, fall straight into the flood. In a second the water is loaded with planks of wood and the split trunks of the stockade that swing round in the current like battering rams and smash against the sides of the huts, where the prisoners will just be getting up.

Now the shrieking begins, high above the roar of the water. Through the mist I see the prisoners clambering onto the roofs of their huts. I know there is nothing to be done. I have seen before, as a child, the force of water unconfined; no power on earth can stop it. It will burst open the doors of the warehouses, push aside the stacks of spades, undo the great coils of rope and smash the bags of wooden pegs against the walls. It will rush through the food stores, soaking the piled hessian sacks of potatoes and beans. Everywhere, people will try to climb up out of its way; into the wagons, onto the roofs, up on tables, uselessly. The water will be too strong for them; I have seen this also. Beyond the stockades into the soldiers' quarters and the town it will take down fences and walls, sweep away hen coops and rabbit hutches, and carry its cargo across the fen. There it will spread out, filling the new drainage ditches, merging with the old meres. The water will follow its earlier ways, the channels and rills it knows. The great field of water confined in the washes will empty onto the land and return it to mere and island as it was before.

The sun rises and pushes away the dark night clouds. I am standing on the edge of the embankment looking down into the breach, where the water is still running, knotting and turning over in its hurry to get out. Across the wash the other embankment that runs along the course of the new cut is holding firm. The sounds of the water, the rush of it, and the crack of branches and timber, fill the sky.

For a moment I am in another place: on Tholen, a little boy, standing on the dyke above the Oosterschelde, hearing the roar of the river and hanging onto my father's legs. The river has burst its banks and poured down into the fields beyond. It is winter, and a bitter wind is turning my fingers red and swollen. The whole village of Sint-Maartensdijk is out on the dyke, and as I look a body floats by, twisted and broken. I bury my face in my father's cloak.

Night after night the sight comes back to me. Even as I sleep the pictures gather. How forceful the water is; how helpless a man. And it is not just the dead man who is broken and frail; my father too shrinks and floats away in my mind. Though he is strong, and my father, he cannot stop the flood. He cannot make the world safe.

It was after the flood on Tholen that I determined to become an engineer. I never wanted to see again a battered thing that had lived so soon before. I work to increase prosperity, as I am asked to do, but below that, buried in my mind, is the stronger force. I work never to feel again such fear as I felt that night, and never again to see such misery. Step by step I got there, measuring, planning, taking care. I have been a good engineer, and until now I have never met the flood again.

I look up and see Van Hooghten. He stands on the other side of the breach and gazes down at the swirling water that runs between us. He is shouting but the noise of the flood snatches away his words so that we can only gesture to one another. I want to tell him what I have seen along the embankment; four breaches at regular intervals. Nature does not measure in this way; nature finds a weakness in a structure and concentrates there.

'Jacob. Jacob.'

Van Hooghten does not hear.

'The camps. Get to the camps,' I shout into the noise, gesturing towards them.

Van Hooghten throws his arms into the air. I do not know what he is trying to tell me. Two soldiers are running towards me, covered in spray.

'Go back. Go back,' I say. 'Find Captain Townley and tell him what has happened.'

They are too afraid to listen.

'The rest of the embankment is safe. Go. There will be no more breaches.'

The water has done its worst. I cannot think of the collapse now. I have to concentrate on getting the prisoners and soldiers out of the flooded camps and onto dry land. More soldiers come up along the embankment. Major Wade arrives too, muddied to the waist. To my surprise, when he sees me he doubles over and begins to sob.

'The camps – it is like a battlefield, Mr Brunt. My men caught asleep – hurled against the walls of their huts.'

'Are they dead?'

'Yes, yes, many. Others alive, but with limbs broken. The same for those prisoners who tried to run. The water got them, and the debris too. Tree trunks, bits of the stockade. No man can withstand that.'

I have seen it, I want to say.

Wade is chattering, words falling out of him. 'It is terrible, terrible; I did not think to see such things in this place.'

'Your stores?'

'The powder is lost, many weapons too, or fallen into the wrong hands maybe.'

He looks round and begins to weep again. I keep asking questions to bring him back from the sights in his mind.

'The prisoners?'

'I have given orders for them to be rounded up. Many are on the roofs of the huts. Others trying to get away across the fen.'

'We can do nothing, Major Wade, until the water stops running like this.'

Wade concentrates himself with a great effort. 'How long before the water stops?'

'I cannot say.'

'What happened here? What happened?'

All day the Major's question squats there, and I will not allow it into the light. I am an engineer and a man who measures and orders what I see. What can I say of the day? That no man can outrun water, though some try. Most who tried, or thought to escape with the flood, are swept away. We find their bodies, dozens of them, smashed and broken against tree trunks or walls. Others have been taken out onto the meres where we will find them tomorrow. It is certain that a few have escaped and are hiding on the fen, but they cannot get far, and will be recaptured in time.

Some prisoners who have had the strength have scrambled onto woodpiles sheltered by warehouse walls from the force of the water. Others are lucky and find old banks and islands that still stand above the flood when the water settles. Wade and his men find them there, and the soldiers, without compunction, tie them with ropes and confine them to the higher areas of ground. Until they have cleaned their huts and rebuilt the stockades the prisoners must somehow be contained.

As Wade tells me, the soldiers' encampment, built on the low ground beyond the camps, has been half destroyed and is now encircled by water. The doctor is tending to all the injured, prisoners and soldiers alike, who have gathered by his house. Some sit and clutch at their broken arms, others lie on bunks brought from their huts. Knots of soldiers have managed to clamber to safety on the highest ground, covered in mud. There they clean their weapons with rags, or stand bewildered and silent, more reduced in speech than any battle could make them. All around, amongst the reed stems and the flotsam, and up in the trees, are the chattels of everyday life. High in a leafless willow a white shirt flaps in the wind. In a jumble at my feet I see pipes and tinderboxes, bibles and cooking pots, candles and spoons. Everything is filthy, smashed and torn. A scummy brown film covers what men once treasured or hoarded. A few of the soldiers bend down to pick things up; others simply stand stunned.

Striding from hut to hut is Adriaan Renswyck, his cur at his heels. He is a man possessed by fury, and his russet cloak and the notebooks that he clutches are caked with mud. I watch him lift and drop a pair of soaking breeches, pluck out a wooden cup floating on the water, and set upright a broken looking glass on a smashed and tottering table. When he sees me, he turns abruptly and stops.

'Adriaan.'

He fixes me with his burning eyes and begins immediately to shout, walking towards me until we are close, cocking his face upwards so that his beard juts out.

'You have done this, you fool. You have destroyed the camps, the stockade.'

Coming right up he pulls his fists out from underneath his cloak and I wonder if he is going to hit me. Instead he turns away, delicately draws a cambric shirt out of the sludge and then throws it back with a look of disgust. Finding a chair legs-up in the muddy floor he turns it upright in a single flourish and wipes the seat with his handkerchief, then sits down and pulls a bottle out from underneath his cloak. Oblivious to the other men and to himself, he drinks. Then he begins to shout.

'Everything I built is gone. Everything destroyed.'

'All we can do is clear the camps and start again. It is the force of nature, Adriaan. Sometimes nature is too strong for us.'

'In my experience it is man who is too weak.'

'Adriaan, I cannot talk like this.'

The only thing to do is walk away. I feel Renswyck's anger towards me and towards the whole world; but it is a small thing to set beside a flood. After a few minutes I forget about him completely. With the afternoon, cold sets in. Major Wade orders a detachment of soldiers to round up the scattered animals. Men cannot swim without learning and justly fear the water. Yet animals that we credit with few capacities are endowed with that knowledge, and they swim with ease. So it is that this afternoon I see several cows standing on an elevation in the mere quite serene, having swum from their places of sleep or milking. The smaller animals, taken by the current as it rushed through the camps, are returning. Wading through the soldiers' encampment I see several dogs that have made it back to their haunts. The cats sit on the roofs of huts or in trees. They will find their own ways to the ground. Only the horses, tied up in the stables, have drowned. Their noble bodies, gashed and mangled, now float on the flood.

As I push through the mud and destruction, I watch the water flow in great volume through the breach and spread out across the fen. It has found its old winter habit and will stay, as it has always done, until I can find a way to repair the embankment. Even as I push aside branches and twigs, splintered planks and bottles washed up and left by the flood water, I am calculating and measuring.

It is one task to build an embankment and so to constrain and imprison water. It is quite another to mend one, for now the water is everywhere, pressing in on it equally from both sides. I know that the task is not beyond me; every Dutch engineer is trained to stop up a breach in a dyke. We can clear the camps, repair the stockades and get the prisoners back to work in a few weeks. Though it is a cold, ugly business, we can box in the area of the breach, fill the gap in the embankment and contain the river anew. That much can be done, yet it is beyond my capacity to empty the meres now filled with water. It will be weeks before the sitting water sinks into the ground, and the meres will remain until the spring dries them out.

As the light begins to fade I am standing once again on the embankment by the breach, on the King's Lynn side. Gazing down into the river as it flows through the gap I think again of the four holes set at exact intervals.

There is a tap on my shoulder.

'Jan, it is I.'

It is Van Hooghten, his short hair disordered and mud up above the tops of his boots.

'Ah, Jacob.' I am overcome at seeing him and the sympathy that makes him lean towards me.

'We can mend it, Jan. It is not the end.'

'No, it is not the end.'

I hear my voice, listless and lost to the wind. Van Hooghten takes my shoulders.

'Jan, listen. It is a matter of weeks merely, and then picking up next spring as the meres dry out. It is just a setback. It happens all the time.'

'But, Jacob, the embankment was undermined.'

'That is not possible.'

Van Hooghten is always even-tempered. The misfortunes of others concern him but do not pull him under; their successes are his own. It is his defect to believe too much of his fellow man, or not enough. He cannot see what is plain, or does not wish to. I want to shake him, to throw him in the mud. All the anxiety that I have carried in me through the day, all the dread that I have pushed away, now assumes a shape: yours. Fear boils up in me, rushes through my stomach and grips my heart.

'No, Jacob; there were four tunnels bored into the embankment, each at the same distance from the other. That is not the work of nature.'

'Jan, the disaster has made you imagine things.'

'No. I saw them before the collapse, just as the water began to flow out. I was here. You know that a natural breach is gradual, takes days. This was quick, Jacob.'

'It is always quick, when it falls.'

Again that sudden memory: bitter cold; my father's rough cloak against my face; the body floating past, rushed carelessly along by the flood. Again the roar of the water fills my ears.

'This wasn't the course of nature. The whole section fell like a shelf, all at once.'

Jacob says nothing. I am shouting now. I am covered in mud, exhausted and trembling.

'You take me for a madman.'

'Maddened, Jan. As any man might be.'

I feel then that I must leave this place; must leave Jacob, go away, go away and never return. I picture you suddenly, looking so intently at my drawings.

Van Hooghten pulls me round.

'Come, Jan. Come to my lodgings in Lynn. You should not be out here any longer. There is nothing more to be done today.'

'Listen, Jacob. Someone did this.'

Van Hooghten takes my arm and begins to walk me away from the breach. He is humouring me.

'Who then?'

I clutch at his question. Many men, it is true, have cause to wish the works destroyed.

'Prisoners who have concealed rods and shovels?'

'Jan, they know they cannot escape. You know what Adriaan Renswyck is like; I saw him today prowling the fen beyond the camps, hoping to find runaways to shoot.'

'They are desperate.'

'No; it cannot be the prisoners.'

'Soldiers, then. Many of them want to leave this place and go back to the army.'

'Perhaps. But it's a dangerous business, and they are not acquainted with the habits of water.'

Van Hooghten has his arm round my shoulders now. He is hurrying me along the embankment, past the camps and towards my house. As the sun goes down it casts a red glow to our left across the flooded land. All the way to the horizon is water. I allow Van Hooghten to steer me to my own stable, where we find the horses tied up. The man who brought my horse back has put hay in the mangers; but the cottage itself, when I open the door, is dark and empty.

We take the horses and set off for King's Lynn. I ride like a dead man, letting my horse choose his steps along the muddy embankment. On one side of us the water stretches away into the distance. On the flooded meres a couple of fires are burning, their flames brightening in the fading light. Out towards the western horizon I see a single figure in a coracle, solid and upright, outlined against the falling sun. Though the light is dim I have no doubt that it is you. Your head is raised, your arms are by your sides. You stand like a sentinel, unmoving. The sight of you fills me with longing and, now, with dread.

Darkness takes hold as we arrive in the town. Van Hooghten's landlady calls her son to take the horses. Upstairs in his lodgings, a fire is burning in the grate and the room is warm. Van Hooghten lights the candles, then takes off his cloak, leans his hand out for mine and hangs them both on a hook driven into the wall for the purpose near to the fire. Comfort and a homely ease fill the room.

I sit down without speaking, heavy with the whole day from its beginning.

The close smells of wet wool and tallow mingle in the warm air. I long to fall asleep but tiredness won't come to me, or only its lunatic edge. I stare at the wall, where Van Hooghten has tacked a map of the world, coloured in red and blue. On a small table under the window a bible lies open on a stand, with a notebook and inkstand next to it.

Van Hooghten moves purposefully about, sure-footed and good-natured. First he presses a cup of beer into my hand, then brings out bread and cheese, with apples and a pie on a plate, setting it all between us by the fire.

'Drink, Jan. Eat. There is nothing more we can do today.'

I do as he says, like a child. I want Van Hooghten's warmth to take the chill from my heart. He seems not to wish to dwell on the day's events. He tells me to consider only how quickly we can rebuild the embankment and so finish our work here. He knows better than I how to repair such a breach, being my senior in experience, and we talk quietly in the candlelight about how it will be done. I am grateful, and want to stay by him, fearing my own company; but he urges me to bed and walks me to a small room opening off the parlour.

'Try to sleep, Jan,' he says, and sets the candle down by a narrow bed that is already made up.

Once alone, I stare at the candle flame. It grows and grows as I look at it, until it fills the whole room. Inside me is neither order nor disorder. My mind refuses fear and anxiety. Everything has been swept away. A soundless empty space remains. I sleep as if dead, and wake only when Van Hooghten stands by the door and calls my name.

# Chapter 4

*King's Lynn.*
*The Great Level.*
*Winter and spring, 1651–1652.*

From the top of the battered embankment three days after the flood I can look to the west and see the sun glint across water. If I raise my eyes above the smashed stockade and the mess of the camps, nothing might have changed from my first winter here. Water from the washes has drained out and spread across the land. The whole Great Level seems asleep. Leafless trees shiver over the water and brown reeds ring the islands. Everything is pewter grey, soft and blue in the sunshine. The flocks of ducks and gulls are back, nodding on the shallows.

I stay some nights with Van Hooghten, and then return to my cottage. Van Hooghten rides over each day to the works. He is there to direct the repair of the breach, but also, I know, to keep me steady. I try to maintain the rhythm of life, and the press and hurry helps me. The days are not so hard to pass through, but I fear the evenings. Hope and dread jostle within me each time I open the cottage door, but I am always greeted by damp and darkness. You have gone, and taken my hope with you. Still my body, every particle of it, stretches out to you, wherever you are. I want you now, and with me. I feel in my mind the roughness of your fingertips and the hardness beneath your skin when I lay my head on your breast. I see your sturdy outline and hear the beat of your heart. I do not feel loss, as I expect, but desire. Desire arcs through me so strongly that I understand then that it has no boundaries of time or distance. Even death could not stop it.

This I can never speak. Even if I told Van Hooghten it would do me no good. Speech is no recompense for desire. It cannot assuage it. Even if I could speak there is nothing to say. How can I ask where I might find you when no one knows you are here? How talk, even to Van Hooghten, since he makes no mention of you himself? Silence pools inside me, dark and oily. I fall into it, especially when I am alone, and see myself, a tiny figure, turning into emptiness.

I listen to the rumours about the flood that swirl through the soldiers' quarters. Some blame the prisoners, some the devil, others the spirits out on the fen. The mood amongst the soldiers is skittish at first, but soon returns to the resentment that they showed before. After a few days several dozen escaped prisoners are brought back to the camps. Renswyck puts them to work in the wreckage. One group builds a new stockade, another lays floors in the soldiers' huts, a third digs out the stinking ditches that have filled with mud and refuse. Renswyck prowls past again and again, checking on his charges. He glares at me if we meet, or greets me loftily as if I am far away and he at a great height.

'Ah, Mijnheer Brunt, *goedemorgen.*'

'And to you, Adriaan.'

He looks up. 'You will be getting the prisoners back as soon as the camps are again in order.'

'I thank you, Adriaan. We are ready to make a start.'

I want to know what Renswyck is up to; he is wearing a hooded look and watches me closely.

'Arrests have been made amongst the local people,' he says.

'For helping the prisoners to get away?'

'Worse, Mijnheer Brunt. I am told that some people of the fens were seen near the works in the days before the breach.'

I say nothing.

'Several of them are now in the lock-ups at Ely and King's Lynn. That may make them talk. There are women amongst them, something quite against nature, would you not agree?'

Renswyck does not stay to wait for an answer, and walks away. Although I ask around, discreetly, I can learn nothing about the women in the lock-ups, and wonder if Renswyck has made up the story to unsettle me. I fill the days with labour, and time passes. By the middle of December we have the prisoners back in the camps and a containing wall built round the embankment at the place of the breach. In those first weeks I work like a man spellbound, determined each day to tire myself to sleep.

Then it is that you come to me. In dreams I hear the sound of your voice, low and strong. You talk the language I strain still to untangle, but which in sleep is clear and easy. I feel you moving in the spaces of my mind. When I wake you are still with me. We talk as usual together and I feel you by my side until I leave my cottage. Though my dreams torment me I long for them, since only there do we meet.

Once or twice I am overcome, as if I have been fighting a battle. Then the desire to leave this place begins to worm its way inside me; to leave and never to return. I see myself riding away from the Great Level, as a horseman does in a painting, towards the edge of the picture, then out of sight.

I do not go because somewhere you are here. When I look over the flooded land and see the fires of the watchers I hope that you stand by one of them and watch my cottage at night. That hope pushes away all other questions. It leaves a wide space for your return to me.

I stay too from fondness for Jacob Van Hooghten. His disappointment in me would be more than I can bear. So I go on as I have done since I began my education and my apprenticeship to Mijnheer Van Nes. I rise, and work, and make my calculations before night. When I wake each day I find my arm flung out across the bed, as if it looked for you while I slept. I push off the covers and start again. I am, as I always have been, a man of method and care.

Adriaan Renswyck keeps up his air of feverish command, but he now wears only black, with a white muslin shirt under his jacket. To my Dutch eye, he has the tight look of a preacher. He is never still, and glances round ceaselessly, as if he might miss something. His cur is much fatter, and I wonder what it has found to eat in the flooded camps.

As soon as the prisoners return, Renswyck transfers those who escaped at the time of the flood to the lock-ups at Ely and King's Lynn.

'Surely, Adriaan, you need to put them back to work?'

'To spread rebellion amongst the others?'

'We have need of their labour.'

Renswyck looks triumphant.

'Ah, you are behindhand, Mijnheer Brunt. Occupied with ditches. I am getting more prisoners. New ones. As for these reprobates, they are bound for the colonies. The gaols are to be emptied too; the officer at King's Lynn is entirely of my mind and has everything in hand. General Cromwell himself has sanctioned it. The New World planters will take them all.'

'A man sent to labour thus is a slave.'

'Oh, no, Mr Brunt, he cannot be sold as a slave can; and besides, he has the promise of freedom after seven years.'

Renswyck stands so near me that I can see the red veins marbling the whites of his eyes. I fear to lose control of myself if I do not take a step back, but he seems not to notice, and continues to speak.

'They will do very well on the plantations. The men who contract for them should thank me. As for the fensmen, they won't trouble us in the future, though I doubt they will last long in the colonies. They've no notion of the world.'

'The women that you spoke of?'

Renswyck laughs.

'No need to think about them.'

I do not reply, and he goes on, coming close again, pressing his forefinger into my chest and leaning towards me so that the heavy bottle under his jacket bangs against my thigh.

'Yes, Jan, I have the prisoners back in the camps and more on the way. I have secured an extra detachment of soldiers to keep order. You'll notice the difference. The whole job will be done in a couple of years.'

In my alarm at Renswyck's elation I do not notice until later that he has addressed me in the familiar way. Brandy, not friendliness, has made him drop his guard.

In King's Lynn a few days later I hear a tumult and walk towards it. At the quayside two sea-going ships are tied up. Their gangplanks are out and a few people have gathered, sullen and quiet. Many more are milling about in College Lane, massing where it opens out into the marketplace by the gaol-house. Having no wish to be seen and knowing myself to be conspicuous by my height, I find a doorway and stand there in the shadow.

It is midday, dark and warm for the year's end, with rain on a west wind. I pull my cloak around me. My heart is tight under it. The people gathered here know that something is happening at the gaol. If Renswyck is right, the prisoners will be brought out and driven on board the waiting ships. If there are women amongst the prisoners, one of them might be you. Though I might feel fear or rage, I cannot.

A sliver of happiness glows inside me, because if you come out I shall see you and know you to be alive.

People surge towards the gaol-house doors, which are opening inwards on their great hinges. Into the gloom come soldiers carrying heavy pikes, their metal helmets outlined against the flint-and-lime-stone chequers of the walls.

'Move aside.'

Murmurs rise from the crowd; we can see the first prisoners behind the soldiers. Someone shouts a name.

'Henry.'

'Father, oh, Father, it is me.'

'William, William, come here.'

The names come thick and fast; the prisoners try to turn; they shout and cry. Terror and love mix.

'Stand back.'

The soldiers lower their pikes and the crowd parts. Out walk the prisoners, not singly but in lines, hands tied, with pikemen at intervals. There are many more than I had thought to see. Have they all been crammed into that gaol-house or brought there at night? All wear the same drab clothes, mud-coloured. I cannot tell who might have been a runaway from the camps and who is from this place. Some walk with defiance, but most appear cowering or resigned, as any man might do with a pike in his face. After a little, as they walk down College Lane towards the quay, a few raise their heads and look about.

'Jonah.'

'Richard.'

Soon the first woman comes out, then half a dozen more, their shawls over their heads.

'Mary. Look here.'

A child in the crowd cries out, 'Mother, Mother, oh, Mother. Is it you?'

One of the women staggers and tries to turn to her child's voice, lifting her bound hands as she does so. People run to the line of prisoners, but the pikemen push them back roughly. 'Make way; make way,' says one as he lowers his pike.

Then I see you. Rain is falling and the women have covered themselves as best they can. But I do not need to see your face, though I long for it. It is by your stride that I know you, strong and forceful. You seem to look straight ahead, and I wonder if you can see me through the cloth. No one calls your name.

I have to reach you, and lunge forward, pushing aside two men in front of me as if they were children, oblivious to any harm I might do. My only thought is to touch you, to pull you away, to stop you taking another step towards the ship.

I never get near you. A pikeman bars my way, and he lowers his pike against my chest. I feel the tip of it through my cloak.

'Eliza,' I shout, and again, 'Eliza.'

You do not turn your head and soon you are gone down the road. The pikemen do not move until all the prisoners have filed past, and the gaol-house doors have swung shut. Then they close up to a phalanx, half facing the crowd, half the departing prisoners, and so keep us at bay as they fill the narrow street.

I can hear myself howling now. There is no way down except this one, and though I try to dodge round the pikemen, I cannot get past, and only reach the quay in time to see you marched up the gangplank of one of the ships, your head finally bowed now as if you do not want to look about you.

It is your lowered head, you who always stood so straight, that fills me with sorrow. I push up as close as I can and shout your name again. It joins with the other names on the air in one desperate woven cry: Eliza, Jonah, Richard, Mary, John.

The Irish and Scottish runaways have no one to shout for them. Loss and dispossession carried them here and now push them further round the world. They have no voice to turn to, no mothers or brothers here to leave. In the new place that emptiness will ring loud and turn to rage.

I shout again. Again you do not pause or lift your head. Low murmurs and cries mingle now with the shouts. You walk into the ship and others follow after you till all are swallowed up. The gangplank is withdrawn, the ship closed. Sailors stand on the quay waiting for the word to slip ropes from the bollards and jump aboard.

I cannot stay there with the grey wooden wall of the hull between us, though all around me mothers and sisters, fathers and sons are still calling out the names of the lost. Scarcely knowing what I am doing I walk along to the end of the quay and look down. The water is high and on the turn. As it falls the tide will carry you away; by sundown you will be out at sea.

I wait, with the tumult behind me, until the ships come down. Only sailors stand on the decks. There is not a single prisoner to be seen and no sound comes except the creak of the spars and the gurgle of the water as it is parted by the prow. You are gone.

With the last of my strength I ride back to my cottage and sit out the day by the fire. I stare at the flames, my mind imprisoned. For hours I stay there, immobile. The light goes down and darkness comes in. Still I sit on, sunk into the last of the embers.

Then the fire is out and I stand up. I am restless suddenly, and have to move, leave the room, get out. The rain has stopped and outside the air is damp and salty. I light my lantern, find my coracle by the water, and push off from the bank. For a while I drift, but then strike out across the mere, my way lit by the lantern on its willow pole. Yellow light falls across the water.

The watchers are nowhere to be seen, their fires all gone. I push out into the expanse, until I can see nothing in the trembling light but the surface of the water and the moon streaks in the sky above. The mere murmurs and laps against the coracle; but otherwise there is a silence that lies over the water. The night is warm, and a mist is gathering. This is how the earth might be if the flood of the Bible should come again, and end the world.

I let my coracle go and wonder where upon the sea you are now, and then, not knowing, give up that also. I want to stay like this for ever, without thought, in this nut-shaped craft that tilts and rights itself. Minutes, or hours, pass, with the moonlight coming and going through the clouds and everything glowing moonlit except for the lantern's yellow ring of light.

Then, quite suddenly, I feel the coracle bump and sway. Looking down over the side I see, in the shafts of illumination, a great mass, twisting, slipping and knotting together. Hundreds of eyes and tails catch the lamplight: black and silver eels. Over and over they turn, tails over heads, sides over sides. They move in a jellied ball, slimy and lithe. I balance myself in the coracle and let the eels swarm under and around it, feeling with them that great pulse of life. Leaning over I put my hand down to them. The mass parts, under, over and round, and carries on. The eels swim out with the tide and so obey the mysterious laws that nature has laid down for them. I thrill with it too. I watch the glinting ball as it moves on through the mere and know it is time for me to go also, to begin my own journey to the sea.

# Chapter 5

*Amsterdam, Holland.*
*Spring and summer, 1652.*

This intention, to leave the Great Level and this whole country also, I explain to Van Hooghten as soon as we have successfully repaired the embankment and the flood waters begin to recede. He tries to dissuade me.

'The work here is not yet finished, Jan. Are you not contracted for the term?'

'Contracted, Jacob, yes; but with no term given. Therefore I am free to leave whenever I wish, and now choose to do so.'

'There is still so much to do, and this will be seen as a defeat.'

'I care not how it is seen except by you. I find simply that it is time to go elsewhere.'

To abandon the Great Level with our work incomplete is a blow to Van Hooghten's pride. In his friendship for me he feels my loss as his own; but I do not feel the shame that he fears to voice on my behalf. A change has been made in my mind, as if the flood has swept across it also, and left a new landscape.

As to you, Eliza, you are gone. In the months of days and nights since you walked onto the ship I have pushed the picture of you out of my waking mind, certain that if I allowed it to return too often I would be unable to carry on. You are not dead; of that I am certain. I do not wish to think further, and have pushed an accounting of those days beyond my sight. To look at the time of the flood with open eyes I must be far away from here.

Van Hooghten must have a thought of you still in his mind.

'If it is to do with the girl, Jan, I am sure she lives. Though it is so hard for you now, you will live, too.'

'I thank you, Jacob; and for all your kindnesses to me.'

Van Hooghten hesitates, seeming overcome.

'You are a strange man, Jan; I would have said too hidden for my taste, and yet I feel a fondness for you.'

I bow to him. I cannot talk of you because it will bring the deadness in me up to the surface. I cannot talk of myself, because I am disjointed. So I must talk of other matters. I am happy to leave Jacob in friendship and in a way that will allow him to take credit for his work and mine too. My work here I know to be good; but my reputation, set in the balance with all that I have seen, weighs very light with me.

When I first came to the Great Level the fire of ambition burned high inside me. Van Hooghten and I, late into the night, would talk of the renown surely due to us. Jacob wished to have his maps in the collections of noblemen and city councils, in the libraries of great estates. He wanted them printed, colour-washed and signed with his name. He wished that one might be called *Van Hooghten's Map*, and show a scatter of new Pacific islands. Then, warming to the theme, he declared that as his eminence rose he might move from paper to rock. If he mapped a new-discovered place, and so brought it into being for those who claimed it, it might be named for him by a grateful Estates General. He would choose its name: Van Hooghtensland or Jacobsland.

In late-night, wine-washed seriousness, I, too, wished for some such memorial. I did not like the idea of time closing over me without a trace. New lands, or lands newly improved, might bear my name. Written on a map, copied, printed and sounded out, it would last for ever.

Now all this desire is gone. So much have I seen come up from under the ground that is unknown, so much do I know is lost, that I wish for no memorial to my vanity. Who, in future times, would have a knowledge of the builder of a Bruntsweg, or a Bruntslandt, as it might be? No one, no more than anyone remembers or can name the Roman engineer who built a road here long ago. So what would my name become? A word on the wind, nothing more. Nothing lasts for long, neither improvement nor destruction, only the power of nature which, by fire or flood, can build or break at will.

At the end of March I write to Cornelius Vermuyden with my resignation. Hearing nothing in reply, I buy a passage in a lighter from King's Lynn to the Port of London with the intention of visiting him. Jacob comes to the quayside to bid me goodbye. As I stand at the foot of the gangplank, he hurries up and embraces me. He holds me very close.

'Goodbye, Jan.'

He puts his two hands up to my cheeks. We look at one another and I see that tears stand in his eyes, which prompts me to wipe them away, a gesture that makes them fall the more. I feel a surge of tenderness for him, a return of feeling that gives me hope.

'Goodbye, Jacob. Let us hope that fate brings us together again one day.'

I stand at the stern of the ship as it puts off into the current and breathe the salty mud and the dense vegetable smell of the marshes, then raise my eyes to the expanse of the Great Level as the current takes the ship. Beyond the marshes the Level stretches away to the horizon where a silver band runs all the way round and gives the land a border of light.

I look up Cornelius Vermuyden at his home when I arrive in London; but I do not encounter him. Mijnheer Vermuyden, his wife tells me, is out of town. He is much engaged in business on behalf of the Earl of Bedford. Vermuyden is a man of the world. He has left a letter for me, and my wages, exactly computed until the last day of March.

The letter contains no rebuke, rather a simple distance that is a farewell. Vermuyden thanks me for my work and makes no mention of the flood. He has closed the letter with his seal, upon which his motto is clearly picked out. *Niet Zonder Arbyt*. The words curl prettily through the blood-red wax. *Niet Zonder Arbyt: Nothing Without Work.* I think of the prisoners. I see them in lines on the Great Level, tied one to another, grey and dusty. They thrust their spades in the ground to lift the damp earth as a million prisoners and slaves will do in years to come and millions have done in centuries gone by. For the prisoners who labour on the Great Level these words are a lie. The work they do gives them nothing. Imprisonment and death are their horizon; freedom will be won by a very few.

When I walk out of my lodgings I find London still a haunted city. The murmur of speech and laughter that rises between buildings, that lovely human music that only cities make, is still absent. Instead I hear the sounds of commerce and unease. People crowd the narrow passages: black-clad merchants with beaver hats; women, young and old, in shawls and cloaks. Soldiers walk among the citizens. War is on the march, the great beast waking up for slaughter. Down by the river the wharfs and docks are workshops of destruction. I am careful and silent, the Dutch being unwelcome in this part of town. Soon it is apparent that I cannot stay. My height makes me conspicuous, and though I speak their language, people notice my clogged Dutch sounds and ask me where I am from. Hostility forms the question, and I fear to reply.

I am not welcome in England, and after two weeks I leave without regret. I take a ship for Holland, hoping to feel at home in my own country, but Rotterdam does not bring me the comfort of return. The warm red bricks and gable ends do not soothe me as I expected; and in the cool spaces of the Laurenskerk I feel neither peace nor holiness. I do not travel on to Tholen and my village of Sint-Maartensdijk. I know that my parents will welcome me there, but that they will feel too the failure of my duty to Mijnheer Vermuyden and the whole family. So I write to assure them of my health and my desire to continue in my profession. Having a good deal of ready money by me I send them some as proof of my competence and good intention. Word will reach them soon enough that I have left Vermuyden's employment.

I move about, going from Rotterdam to The Hague, and The Hague to Leiden. There I think of enrolling once more in the university, until I come to understand that I do not wish to sit and learn from a master, but to learn something else and in some other way. I go on to Amsterdam, where I stay for the most part in a room I take on the first floor of a widow's house near Dam Square. I venture out to taverns to eat simply and preserve my savings, and otherwise walk off the daylight hours round and round the half-circles of the canals until I am tired enough to sleep. I preserve an air of purpose, but indeed I have none.

One day in summer I find myself by the office of the Dutch West India Company, and fall into conversation there with an engineer lately returned from the New World. A man in funds, he tells me, will always be welcome in Nieuw Amsterdam, the capital city of Nieuw Nederland, the place being depleted of active citizens. An engineer can pick up work there from the colonists, both Dutch and English, who wish to improve their land. When I ask if the passage is a dangerous one, he tells me he has made the voyage many times. No ships of the West India Company went down in the whole of last year, he says. Boredom and sea sickness may be your companions, but you will soon forget the depth of the sea beneath.

In the next few days I turn this suggestion over. I am a man who has untied himself from his old life and is free to find another. My family will make no objection, the West India Company being well known and respectable. Nieuw Amsterdam is a place of near two thousand people and I am sure to find work where drainage is proposed. There is nothing to keep me here, and, more than that, I am ready to leave.

I write to my father and describe my departure as an opportunity to advance again in my profession. Two weeks later I stow my trunk and box under the narrow bed of my cabin on the *Dolphijn*, a sturdy Company ship bound for Nieuw Nederland. I welcome the change and the new life to come.

As the *Dolphijn* sets sail from Amsterdam to Texel I stand on the foredeck and look back at the Zuider Zee as it streams away under the hull. After the sand dunes of Texel fall over the horizon and the *Dolphijn* steers out towards the English coast, I begin each day looking out to sea, both forward and back. Once past the island of Alderney the open sea is all around us and the ship shrinks to a dot on the water, a tiny vessel on the wide expanse.

I follow the *Dolphijn*'s progress on the map and in the log which the captain writes and shows me. He is an unexcitable man, accustomed to this journey. Day after day the *Dolphijn* rides over the grey sea, groaning with each rise over the swell and exhaling as she comes down. The sun and the stars keep us to our course. The captain navigates calmly, fortified by the forty crossings he has made in his ten years of Company employ.

For many days the past and the future seem suspended. My small cabin is situated just under the main deck, a few feet above the waterline. At night I lie knees up in my short cupboard bed. I listen to the *Dolphijn*'s hull stretch and creak as it parts the ocean. On rougher nights the water froths past my tiny window, black and green. At first the sea invades me. Night after night I dream I am swimming through it and wake into terror, being uncertain in the instant where I am, if not drowned. Then I remember that I took passage from Amsterdam and that I am afloat.

When I stand on the deck I expect to hear your voice in the hum of the wind on the sails, or that I will see you somewhere far off in my mind, and you will speak to me. But for weeks you are not there, either near or far. When I find you in my memory, halfway across the ocean, you do not come towards me. I know that I must decide, since love itself is a decision. How will I be with you, how confront or accept you?

The choice, out on the ocean, is a simple one: to turn away from you or to take you with me. Looking out at the grey sea, where no man I know regards me or even knows that I am here, I understand that the choice is mine alone, the consequence mine alone also. The days gone by still stand before me, all of them, and all that happened on the Great Level also, but I do not have to see or regard them. I can push through them as easily as the prow of the *Dolphijn* parts the waters of the sea. I can forget. I can rub you out, in the way a child rubs chalk off a slate, and I can begin again. No one I meet in Nieuw Amsterdam will ever know about you or the flood. More than that, I can deny you, and the whole Great Level, to the world and to myself.

It is said that the contrary of to forget is to remember, yet that axiom sounds now like something learned at school, a verse recited or a catechism, just a story in language. The contrary of to forget, I see now, is to be a part of, to live with and to share. I watch the ocean disappear behind me and know that a life without a past is a thin one, a life starved of voices and nourishment. I will not forget; I will let memory live, and you, Eliza, live within in it and so, too, within me. You will be a part of me, sharing my new life and my old, and I will stay true to myself and to you.

Two months later I arrive in Nieuw Amsterdam and the colony of Nieuw Nederland, and here I remain, and make my peace with time. On the deck of the *Dolphijn* I decide to remember, and to walk forwards with the past beside me as I have not done before. When we made the Great Level we tried to draw the future on the map and then press it into the earth. We called it a new land. Yet it never truly could come into being without a reckoning with the layers beneath.

# PART FIVE

# Chapter 1

*New Amsterdam.*
*Blossom's Tavern on Beaver Street by the Broad Way.*
*The 20th day of July, 1664.*

I have sat down many times in the evenings since I came to this town to reply to Mr Lee and his proposal. So often I have written out at the top of the paper in an orderly and correct fashion, *Mr Charles Lee, Grace Dieu Plantation, The James River, Virginia Colony* – and each time I have abandoned the task. After that first flourish my pen falters in its comfortable scrape and rasp across the paper long before I sign my name, Eliza.

That's how it is; I must reply to Mr Lee but I am reluctant and impatient. Oh, how briskly his proposal has come, so soon after I have changed my widow's mourning clothes for the bright colours of a new life. He wants one word, he says; just one, sent back to Virginia by the first boat. The first boat has gone, the second and third also. Our friendship, and our close relation as neighbours, demand a reply. There are two words I can write, but only one of them is the one he looks for and expects. And he shall have my word and my reply in good time. Yet, upon examination, I find that first I wish to write something else. I want to explain my decision more amply than in a single word surrounded by politeness.

Being alone in this tavern in the evenings, it comes to me that every story wants a listener to bring it into being, just as every life leans towards others for an acknowledgement; even such a life as mine is, known only to myself. Strange it is that memory, too, inclines towards a listener if we do not check it. I am not a fool. I know that not so far away in my mind there is indeed a listener, a man who long ago suggested to me that I write something of my life, though I had nothing then to say and few words at my command. No matter. I do not write for him now, but for myself, in my own voice.

For so long I was silent, not having the means to speak out, and keeping myself close for preservation of what little I had. Now I have a voice, both in the world and on the paper before me. I have often used the first, especially in the last years; but never yet the second. To write my story – or just so much of it as I wish to write – not for Mr Lee, or any other man, but for myself: how joyful, and how hard, that is. No person but one who has been voiceless herself will understand.

Mr Lee's proposal has drawn my story out, and the evenings are long and hot in this town. I will write down some of it though I shall likely never tell it to another face to face, and may not even preserve it once written.

One thing that Mr Lee cannot know about me, no matter that we dined alone in the last year a dozen times with crystal glass and silver on the table: that this simple act of writing is of great importance to me. I have practised it for fourteen years. When I grasp the pen, dip it in my ink and form the letters, I am filled with pride, and with a happiness that comes from the days when I learned to write, another by my side.

These curling signs, so ordinary, that many read and make without a thought, are to me the marks of a freedom that I won myself. The double half-circles of the E at the beginning of my name, I form expansively, flicking up the tail into a lingering curl. The L strikes strongly down, the I rises up softly; and then the Z, as strong as any letter in the alphabet, snakes down below the line, where I lift the pen off and so conclude with the A. I write my whole name with a flourish that describes me, and with the power that writing and reading have given me.

Had I not been able to pick up a book and read I should never be sitting in New Amsterdam, able to call for wine, send my maid to buy ice for it and settle to writing. These black lines, straight and curled, can tell tales and recount proposals, and more. They make lists and contracts, surveys and accounts, such as I deal in every day; and still they fill me with a pleasure that does not lessen, but rather grows, as the years go by.

So I shall write, but I shall not go back to the beginning. I came from a place where the life was wretched and sickness commonplace.

The ague took my parents and rich men took the whole place. The land was improved and destroyed, as I was. Had it not been destroyed I would not be here in America now, though I played no more of a part than knowing that the time had come, the rest being all the work of nature with a little help such as my people know how to give. Besides, it was in vain and it is now long gone, too far away to be visible. Looking back is a game for fools and not one that I like to play.

So there is no beginning, except the one I made here. My past is just the start of my present, which began some dozen and more years ago, when I stepped up onto the quayside by the Hampton Roads in the Virginia colony. Then I knew not where I was, but not even the hatred in my heart, so hot and flaming that it lit me up, prevented me from seeing the beauty of the country. That quayside, and the voyage that took me there, are as far into my past as I choose to go.

This is America. It is the land of arrival. Those who prosper here are those who do not look back. Besides, no person that I know has ever left America except in failure, and most who fail in this place have no way out, no ship to take them off, just the earth to cover and forget them.

In America, in the Colony of Virginia, I have been translated; changed to something else. Here I came out of the shadows and into the bright light of the New World. All I had was my courage, and it turned out that was all I needed. I made myself a shape to fit the noonday of this new land. Now it lies stretched out in front of me; yes, even here in this tavern where down below me Dutchmen sing songs from Holland and smoke from the pipes comes up through the floor.

It was not like this when I first landed, but already my passage in that stinking ship had shown me that a person in my place, as lowly as it was, might have hope. I met the jetty in Virginia with a strong forward step. I looked into the blinding sun and round about me, to notice how things lay in this new place. First whether I might escape, and that being straight away dismissed, how I might live.

I had been marched aboard that ship with my head covered. I had closed my ears to the call of my name, knowing that if softness stayed in my heart it would eat me from within. I remember little about the start of the voyage, confined in the hold, and do not wish to bring any of that back now. I lost count of the days and nights since they did not matter to me. In the first weeks we sailed south in the cold, and I saw nothing except the damp slope of the hold by my head and those confined with me, women I did not know.

We put in at some islands that I never saw, then turned and sailed into the great ocean towards the New World. This I learned from the sailors who came down to the hold with food and new slop buckets. Two of the women fell sick with fever and died. Their death was my salvation. In the confusion of their sickness I took their shoes, or more particularly, one pair of tolerable shoes and one pair of leather boots, patched but serviceable. These latter I eased off the body of a woman dead less than an hour. She did not need them. I knew that our feet support us, that to walk is to take the first steps towards life. Though I did not know what awaited me, it was never like to be a soft life. The shoes I hid behind a loose plank in the hull. The boots I wore from that time on.

The women's bodies were taken and thrown out to sea. We said nothing, neither fought nor complained. We eased round to fill the space of the dead women; a little more for each of us, more of the miasmic air, food and foul water. My limbs stretched out and helped themselves to extra life.

I lay in the bilges and pretended to the same station as the others; but I already had more, in my boots and shoes. Each morning I checked the shoes, snug behind the planking. Women without chattels, clothes or a single penny between them are near to slaves. I was something different; taking and having these possessions gave me another story to tell myself.

After a long time of sailing we were allowed up on deck, two or three of us women at a time. Some were sick and afraid, not being used to the water, but I had no fear of the bottomless sea. Up in the open air I put my back against the mast and all around was the sun glittering in the water. It was a new sun to me, huge and bright, a fireball to heat up the world. I opened my arms to it, spread them as wide as I could. Each time I came on deck I grabbed another thing, no matter that there seemed no use for it. A nail. A rotted sailor's shirt, hung drying in the rigging, that I pulled down and concealed in my skirt in an instant as I passed. A length of twine. A pair of scissors fallen between the planks of the deck. Down in the hold my hoard grew, and my determination. I set myself a task of accumulation: find something; conceal it; keep it. Each visit into the sunlight grew this purpose, and my spirit with it. Thus do we find ways to trick ourselves to live.

There was little to see off the boat, not a seabird or another ship, just black rafts of seaweed that floated in the ocean. After some weeks porpoises began to accompany us on our way; the same sort of creature as I see now in the Chesapeake River towards the sea. I watched them leap and curve out of the water as if enquiring about the ship, or asking it to join their dance. They played for delight of life and this understanding brought me the first spark of joy since I had gone on board. If such a creature could think to make the filthy ship a playmate, so might I insist that fortune come along with me.

Indeed, I have never been a woman to stand still while life streams by, but what happened to some of us on that ship is not to be written. Though we did not then know why, we were locked in the hold except for the times on deck. The masters we were going to did not want us heavy with child and unfit to work. But the locks turned easy for men with money. A hundred men on that boat, and ten women. The youngest girls had the worst time of it, and it made them mad, and two with child by the time the voyage ended.

I had to give something away to protect against a greater loss. I chose a man by the name of O'Brien, orange-haired and marked with the pox, going indentured to the New World. He was trained in fighting and that was what I liked. O'Brien was an Irishman lately labouring on the works where I had lived. Before that he went for a soldier he told me, though whether for country or king or from starvation I never asked. Caught up a prisoner, he ran away when he had a chance, was taken again and now sent out indentured, shipped out of the way.

I chose O'Brien and he fought off other men for me. It was little to hand over in return for safety. He was a drinking man, and worked to get on the right side of the ship's mate, who kept the list of all the indentures and which planters had bought them. One night the mate lent O'Brien the list and he brought it to me. There was my name, among those of all the women by me. I learned I'd been indentured to a Captain Maybrick. By his name were the words *Norfolk* and *James River*, so that I knew my destination, at least the way it was written.

I followed O'Brien and spoke to the ship's mate, who then allowed me on deck when I wished, the weather continuing hot and fine. I sat by the mast and learned the life of the ship. Though I would never have a use for it, I put that learning into memory and so occupied my mind. I added also to my stock of goods; one day a compass forgotten on the foredeck, another day a glove dropped near the captain's cabin.

The ship's captain walked about the deck or occupied himself in his cabin with his log and charts. The mate took daily charge and treated the ship as if it might be a workshop or manufactory. Their task together was to command it safely across the ocean and with the least loss of life, these two being the greatest hazards a captain faced. Fear of disaster and sickness kept all the sailors and ship's officers at their work. Gunner, carpenter, boatswain, rope maker, caulker, sail maker, cook, cook's mate: all of them had a part to play, none effectual on its own, but all joining to make the ship sail well. I watched what each man did and made notes to the purpose in a book given to me by the mate.

I soon understood that the captain was not in possession of the whole ship, but only in the sailing of it. Another man owned the ship, though I never discovered his name, just that he did not make the voyage. That man's desire was for profit and the captain worked the ship for him just as a labourer works the land for a farmer. He who owns the land or the timbers of the ship itself is he who really commands, though he is rarely seen and never puts himself to hazard. This notion impressed me and I stored it, as the objects I found, for future use.

The captain of the *Hart*, as the ship was named, had with him an apothecary to deal with outbreaks of sickness. He was not a man fit for the job. Many died from fever, their bodies thrown overboard, and recorded by the captain in the log for the purposes of reckoning up with the men who had paid their passage. I learned then from the mate that a man who paid the passage of an indentured servant could claim the land that came with the passage if the servant died.

I did not care how long the voyage took except that I felt curiosity turning inside me to know what was coming, what might be on the other side. Not a man or woman knew me where I was going, or knew what had passed in my former life. I would have charge of my own self in America, there being no person there to tell my story but myself.

Yet I understood that these days at the foot of the mast were the last days of liberty and the life that I knew. My name was all I took with me to the other side of the ocean. Look after yourself, stay alive, O'Brien told me, and after seven years they have to make you free.

The New World came soon enough. A sailor high up the mainmast shouted sight of land after sixty days of sailing. A week later we came into the mouth of a great river to land by the Hampton Roads in the Colony of Virginia. They herded us indentured men and women off the boat straight onto the quay. We stepped into new sunshine that fell bright as knives. I stood there with one thought in my head, to keep the shoes that hung under my shift on a stretch of hemp unwound from ship's rope. Inside the shoes my other things lay packed. I wrapped my arms around my own waist and protected the bulge that they made, and thus in all probability preserved my life, or so it felt then.

A man came with a paper in his hand, and gathered those belonging to Captain Maybrick. He tallied the list with the ship's mate, heads together, and crossed off the two women who had died on the voyage. Then he took us and tied us one to the other. I had seen that in another place and thought to run, but knew myself helpless though anger rose in me at the rope round my ankles.

Straight away I made myself used to the fact of my indenture and opened my eyes to look about me. A river flowed fast past the wharf, so wide that the far bank was a hazy band of green. I knew about water, and saw that the river, though wide and swift, was shallow enough to be a place of plenty.

From the quayside we were set straight away in a smaller boat, the ten of us, and tacked upriver against the wind. In a few hours the river narrowed and I saw rich woods on either side, and places of cultivation between them. The trees stood in water in a way familiar to me, but taller than any I had ever seen, with crevassed trunks and roots that reached out under the surface.

When the moon came up that first night we sailed in its light to the shore. I fell asleep on the deck still tied up, with no thoughts more than the next day, when we set off again and made two turns into smaller rivers and then the man in charge told us we were near. I never saw the Master that had contracted for us when we arrived at the landing stage of Bellevue, though I knew his name and that of the James River that we had sailed up.

They took us off the boat, set our feet on land and untied them. Then past a tidy group of barns to a kind of village with small huts either side of a path and bigger houses at each end. Every window watched another. Gardens stretched out the back of the huts. All of us new arrivals were separated one from another and each taken to a different hut or cabin, except for one man who was marched away to the big house as I learned after, he having the skills of a carpenter. That was that and where this life began.

I had no reason to look back. In the whole world that I left there was only one person I wished for, and I was parted from him. If I turned round then I would see other figures passing back and forth, but they were already dim and seen through gauze. Why pull their spirits to this new place? I was from that first day busy, and kept my eyes on every person that I saw and all that happened. I was not one for being left behind, or tripping over myself, or even thinking of others who ran beside me. From the beginning I preferred things brushed off and clean and everything gathered in my own hands, and to this day I have remained the same.

# Chapter 2

*New Amsterdam.*
*Blossom's Tavern on Beaver Street by the Broad Way.*
*The 21st day of July, 1664.*

I continue the writing of my life having left myself that first morning at Bellevue on the James River, only a day after I set foot in America. Most here remember the boat that rowed them ashore and their first step onto the New World. The stories are recounted over and over for the young. The way they are told hangs on whether a person arrived in hope or in sadness.

I left the old world unwillingly, yet never allowed myself to despair, my situation being little worse than the one I left behind, and in some fashion better. I jumped up onto the wharf at Hampton Roads though my feet were tied the minute after.

Many people here, even of the middling sort, have never entered the dwelling places of the hands on an estate. Everything is left to an overseer, only the profit and not the labour being of concern to all other persons in the colony. I know the cabins from the cramped dark of their insides and the rustle of bugs in their walls. Six women lived in the hut I was led to, three on one side of the door, three on the other. I was put in with Ellen and Tetty, to share one bed, and they explained how things were at Bellevue.

'You just arrived?' That was Ellen, who had no more thought in her head than seeing out her seven years.

'Yes.'

'Your name, then?'

I wondered whether to tell my name, but saw that Ellen offered no threat to me, being frank and open-faced to look upon.

'Eliza; Eliza is my name.'

I took pleasure in sounding it out loud in this new place and found I had no desire to change it, though I might at that moment have taken a new name like a cloak and hidden under it.

'Eliza. And you signed freely?'

'Yes.'

In truth I had not signed, and was little better than a slave; but since Ellen wished it to be so I gave her the lie. Without any telling my history fell behind. I stepped out of it as a person steps from the shade and into the sunlight, there to be seen.

Tetty was a sturdy girl with cropped pale hair and a canvas shift. She asked if I knew the contract for those who come out indentured; the seeds, and the cow and all? 'And the new clothes, Eliza, they are what we long for, with the cow,' she added.

'Tetty came out with me three years ago when just a child,' Ellen said. 'Mr Hawker let me keep her close, though most from the same place are separated.'

'Mind the ague here, Eliza,' Tetty said. 'It carries so many off, especially in the autumn rains. Some take the ague and survive, but it's a fearful thing.'

'I know it,' I said, and then regretted that I spoke.

'Where are you from, then?'

'Nowhere.'

'Nowhere. You want to leave it like that?'

'I do.'

'We don't have secrets here,' Ellen said, 'but maybe you have good reason to keep quiet, Eliza, so I won't ask further.'

They showed me the hut, what there was to show, the mud chimney to serve both rooms, the water tank and privy, and the garden out the back. Such a hut is a hard place for those who have entered servitude willingly and expect better. For me it looked like no hardship, being quite dry and not liable to flood. For such a person as I was, it was the work and not the living that was like to break me. Tobacco is a greedy plant and wears out both land and people.

Soon enough I learned that the terms of indenture confined me to the plantation and the only thing given was the hope of liberty at the end. Many in England had signed on golden promises, and the life of a bound slave soon took them. A few with lucky dispositions swallowed disappointment easy, or had likely left a worse life behind. Some looked at death and the labour and determined to take some fun of it, there being four men for every one woman in the Colony of Virginia. Few men wanted a single life or always to lie with a native woman taken into captivity. Every man was looking for a wife and scrambling over others to get her. A woman could wait and weigh the offers that came her way.

It was not hard to size up the men, being out in the fields every day side by side and seeing the strength of them and their humour, whether they had the disposition to get up each day in the heat, and how their eyes roved. For such as Ellen those things weighed in the balance with the assets a man was like to have at the end of his service.

In this place, as with all others maybe, it is the land that counts most, the acres that come at the end. A man may be of good standing with a boat to ferry goods and people, or be a merchant with goods to sell. Yet without land he is a poor prospect. Land to put your feet upon and title to it, the right of ownership so that it can never be taken away; that is the promise of the New World.

They put me to work right away under the overseer, Mr Hawker, who lived at the top of the village and had charge of all the hands. It was then spring and the job was to take the tobacco plants out of the frames and plant them in lines. Tobacco looks fine from a distance, with its big bold leaves and starry pink flowers. But it is a cruel plant, viscous with sap and tiny hairs. Though I tied rags round my hands the sticky roughness got through and took the skin right off. At night I soothed them in a bucket of water and rubbed them with fat I scraped from the pot.

In time my hands healed brown and calloused; my feet also, that had softened on the voyage. I rejoiced to feel them tough as leather and forced myself to the rhythm of the land and labour. Days passed one after another, no difference between them until Sunday, a day given to prayer and rest. I never took to worship but walked to the church with Ellen and Tetty, sat quiet in the pew and looked about me. The sick prayed; the seven years seemed an age.

Ellen and Tetty had eyes only for one sort of future.

'See there, by Mr Hawker,' Ellen said after a few weeks. 'That's Henry Vine, and a good man he is, I tell you, free next year and knows the ways to get the best from the land and not exhaust it with tobacco every year.'

I looked closely at Henry Vine and said nothing. A month later the ague got into him. He lay in the hut and cried for the mother he had left in England. Many are those who shun the sick, fearing the bad air that hangs about them. I cared not for that, just nothing for Henry Vine, and kept away from indifference. Ellen sat with him till the end, and wept, though his place was soon filled and he forgotten.

After Henry Vine, Ellen took to pointing out another man.

'Over there,' she said, as we lugged wooden pails of water from the river to the fields, two at a time, hung on chains from a yoke across our necks. I was raw and chap-necked. I knew other ways to get water to the fields and raged inside at my imprisonment.

'Put your pails down for a minute, Eliza. Mr Hawker isn't in sight. That there is Jem Kincaid,' said Ellen. 'Arrived a few months ago from Scotland, taken for a soldier, captured, I heard, and shipped out against his will. Works up at the house and mends things in a general way, being a very ingenious man.'

'What is he doing here?' Tetty asked, putting her buckets down next to ours.

'Punishment, I reckon,' said Ellen, shrugging, for punishment was common and used by Captain Maybrick at the time to lengthen the service of his indentured men and women. That was put a stop to later, as making men and women both bad workers.

'Kincaid's run off several times,' Ellen added. 'But there isn't anywhere to run except to the woods or the natives, and then like to be killed. He's been brought back each time, exchanged for something I know not what, liquor maybe. See that mark on his neck? That's the brand as can never be covered. He won't run again, but he's a strong man and will make something of himself if all that anger doesn't burn him up inside before his time is out. You'd be a wise thing to get him, Eliza.'

I stood there with the sun beating on me and the earth eating into my skin and did not even smile. The easy way, so they thought. Find a man and shelter under him till release comes. Seven years. Then you've a few acres somewhere upcountry if he has that coming to him. Add two cows, tools, seeds and corn and what do you have? A lifetime of drudgery like the old country, and a child a year. And that's what Ellen urged, a woman who never used her head.

Well, I took a good look at Mr Kincaid, and a pretty man he was, golden all over from the sun, and with a beauty a woman might lose herself in and forget this life. But though I talked to him, coming up with a quiet I learned long ago, neither my heart nor my head urged me on. I was not yet free of everything I had left behind. I had given myself to a man before, and he was still in me enough that I did not have full possession of myself. That stopped me just as much as my own judgement.

The summer came hot and hard and the tobacco plants grew high as our heads. The hands made a line to the river and passed buckets up and down. Our shoulders ached from the weight of them. In the evenings and on Sundays we tilled our own gardens. Food was the first thing; those who could not get more than the ration fell sick soonest. I made myself mistress of the garden patch and grew green-stuffs to boil over the fire.

At night I hid myself by the shore. The river drew me from the beginning, being a person accustomed to live on water, and to know it. The James River bubbles and swirls more than the sluggish brown channels of the place I come from; but water has its constant habits. It insists where it finds weakness and insinuates where it does not, and these powers that it has are the same here as thousands of miles away. So first I stood in the shallows and listened to the river. I felt fish brush past me and the water grasses turn with the tide.

I learned the composition of the river from the water on my tongue and very soon I set to work. The moon gave me light enough to tie the reeds together in a way I knew and lay an eel trap quite unseen. Soundlessly I lowered it under the water and tied it to a stake. My heart lifted when I returned to find the trap heavy with a catch. I took the eels back to Tetty and made her swear silence so we might share them. From that day I caught fish and lobster in my traps also, but never found a way to snare the birds that slept on shallow water.

In those first months I often sat out the back in the evening after the garden work was done. Time passed drop by drop, warm in the half-light. I'd watch the sun go down and think of the natives who were the only people to live in these parts before men arrived from the old world. I saw them sometimes and knew them to have arms and to be a warlike sort of people though much plagued with disease and like to die easily. I heard they never fought hard for their land, yet, they are such as I was once, in possession of the place. This I cannot think of, it being like to soften me.

The natives have no idea of improvement, though the planters also did little enough, especially those from inland parts. The planters thought only of their lost estates and wanting to make the New World like to the old; setting villages and making fields. Even then I saw differently, and started with the river. Pretty soon I knew the shape and extent of the plantation, the slope up from the water and the river, warm and gentle in the summertime and busy with fish. The fields lay flat and easy along the swampy shore, and the whole was bounded by fine woods behind.

The big house that was forbidden to me, Ellen said, lay a little upriver from our huts with an aspect that looked away from us. I crept there one night, taking care to keep my distance, there being dogs at guard. The house stood upon the grass, raised up and open to the breeze, all made of wood, and white in the darkness. Curtains blew across the windows. After that I went up from the river, kept off the open grass, and sat with my back against the wooden wall of the house as I had against the mast on the journey over.

I longed then to be through the front door and inside, though it was not the house I wanted. On a moonlit night I looked through the windows, and saw fine china and damask on the chairs, I supposed brought from the old country. I did not wish for them, nor the bright night jasmine nor lilies that grew round the house. I saw only a softer life and a step towards liberty.

'Who works out their indenture at the house?' I asked Ellen when we were both bent over in our garden patch, and fit to break after a day topping the tobacco flowers to thicken the plants.

Ellen straightened up.

'None such as us. The better sort as can read or are useful with a needle. Them as talk well or know housework already. Some up there came out with the Captain, from his estate that was taken after the wars.'

'He paid their passage?'

'So I'm told; and wanted them with him as coming from the place he lost.'

Then came the harvest: men and women together cutting, piling; cutting, piling, palms and fingers raw again from the rough and sticky undersides of the leaves. No job harvesting tobacco is a good one; out in the fields or in the barns, laying out the leaves on shelves to dry in the heat of the furnaces. Then tying and packing, hoping for respite, but getting none, with new seeds to plant in trays, fallow land to dig, exhausted land to clear. How many died in the heat I never took a count of. New arrivals filled the gaps.

One evening after the harvest, I slipped away from the huts into the falling light. I had my own way to the house by then, barefoot from tree to tree, then round the edge of the meadow. That evening as I ran silent, I saw her close to me, quite alone. She slept on a bench under a spreading oak, her shawl fallen to the grass and a book beside her. Her hands lay on her lap, white and soft. I looked at them and marvelled. They were hands that never knew the roughness of tobacco stems, the sting of salt water, or twisting willow branches into baskets and traps.

I came up and sat next to her, being sure to keep a little distance. I took the book and began to read it aloud. *Hesperides*, it had written inside the cover, and never having seen a verse then, I did not know it for a book of poems, just read the words one after another until the lady woke up and turned to look at me – and I gathered up her shawl and spread it round her shoulders. Then our eyes met and she spoke to me without fear in her voice or wonder that I was by her side. I have a way to come on a person in silence and it seem nothing strange.

The lady asked how I knew to read, which question I did not answer that a man taught me, but said, 'I learned in the old country.' I could see she was drooping and weak and in a moment she asked me in her soft voice if I could help her to the house. She lived there, she said; Damaris Maybrick was her name.

She was the Mistress and that was my start with her. In a few weeks I was up at the house, at work in her chamber. I straightened sheets and the muslin curtains round the bed and learned to read to her smooth as cream, with no curdling the words.

That was the end of huts and fields, the tobacco plants and burning sun. I had been in the New World half a year and I was away from Ellen and Tetty. Tetty died of the ague soon after I left the hut. Ellen got her freedom and walked out from Bellevue I know not where. I never saw her again.

Damaris, my mistress, was kind and gave me every way to please her. I took pains to find other ways also. By the river I found trees that from their bark and smell I knew to have the properties of a willow. I pulled the brown bark from the trunks, then made an infusion in the way I learned long ago. This liquid lowers fevers and takes away the pain of headaches. I gave it to the housekeeper Mrs Lyle and so earned her friendship. She allowed me then to draw water from the well and heat it in the outhouse copper. Two by two I carried the pails to my mistress's chamber and filled the tub high up. Then I coaxed my mistress out of her tight shift and petticoats to bathe naked, a pleasure quite new to her.

As my mistress sat in the copper tub I warmed her back with water from a sponge and talked of things that I had seen. I told her of the herons' habits, which came familiar to me, and made their creaking sounds for her to smile at. I brought the whole sparkling river inside for her, with the loons that dipped and made their strange cries, the round black eye of the tercel, and the flash of the kingfisher as it skimmed the ruffled surface. And though my duties only took me from there down the back stairs, into the kitchens and up again, I became a precious thing to her, to have by her more than the others who worked in the house.

'Stay by me, Eliza,' the Mistress began to say as the winter came in and the air carried a chill that weakened her. 'I cannot leave the house today. Stay and talk to me.'

And so I did, and bided my time. She must have sent word to Mr Hawker that I was with her, but I knew nothing of that. I stayed all through the winter, rarely going out and living in the house all day with the Mistress. Sometimes I read to her, but more often I listened to her stories and told her of the world beyond the windows when she tired. About the Captain I knew nothing, and hardly ever saw him. My future lay with my mistress, and I stayed in her bedchamber and her upstairs parlour, never attending her to dinner when the Captain was at home.

My skin grew soft and pale as it had never been. When the spring came the Mistress gave me a gown.

'Take it, Eliza,' she said. 'I no longer have any use for it.'

The gown was of dark silk, brought with them from the old country years before, the Mistress told me. I lifted it up from the great cedarwood chest with two arms, like a child, then held it by the shoulders and shook it out.

'Hold it against you, Eliza, so that I may see it.'

I set the dress against my bosom and the Mistress smiled and sighed.

'Take off your shift and put it on.'

So I dropped my shift to the floor and let my mistress see me naked as I laced the gown up and turned my back to her to pull the ties tight.

'Move into the light by the window.'

I did as she asked, and saw as I looked down that the gown was cut low at the bosom and high above the ankle.

'Now, keep it, Eliza. That was how we wore our gowns in the late King's reign.'

I let the gown out to fit me for I was more ample than the Mistress and delighted in it, wearing it constantly and using my old shift only when she and the Master were away. The Mistress gave me a white kerchief to spread over my bosom and shoulders so that I looked like no other of the house servants and might have earned their resentment had I not taken care to do more than my own share of the work.

The sight of the gown upon me brought the Mistress to remember the days in the old country before the Captain had fought for the King, and in her stories everything was easy and beautiful. There was a cool garden and she a young bride, whose head had no room for hatred or war. The estate, she told me, was folded into green hills where sheep grazed. Combe Down was her home, built by the Captain's father, sparkling with glass. Box hedges lined the parterre, bushes were turned into birds by pruning. She and the Captain walked the gravel paths, arm in arm, in the evening. She never saw the sea, and cared not, thinking only of making the estate beautiful and doing her duty as a wife. Twenty servants attended them.

At the thought of Combe Down and her old life my mistress brightened with remembrance. The light came and sat in her eyes. An exile longs to be called back home, to be embraced and returned to familiarity. A person such as I am cannot feel that longing, knows no hope of return and does not want it. My mistress called herself an exile, but after a little, when she spoke of Combe Down and England, her voice turned low and sad. No one called her back. The loss ran through her, and made her weak and sick. Then I saw her for a kind woman and too gentle to last much longer in this new place.

When summer came again, the servants shuttered the house against the sun so it might breathe cool, though it was mighty hot until the river breeze sprang up in the evening and fanned the muslin curtains. In the day the shade collected by the trees in the meadow before the house, where the Captain had built a seat all round the biggest trunk, a thing I never tired of from that day on. Oh, how fine an invention that is, out in the air yet shaded from the sun, raised up from the bad airs that haunt the ground and giving in that way a view of everything round about. From the trees I looked down the grass to the river and across to the far shore, where now I know lie Golden Manor and Tulip Hill, and upriver to Charleville that I could see in the distance, a cluster of houses against the blue of the trees. Captain Maybrick had a boat of his own with two sails and an awning on the deck for shelter from the sun. I sat with the Mistress and watched it come and go from the landing stage. Once when I was alone I observed Captain Maybrick walk up the lawn to the house. A pearl glinted in his ear. I never was at table, nor close up to him that first summer; but I looked about me. No man should think because I am a woman and slighter shaped, that my eyes and my thoughts are smaller than theirs. That is a mistake easy to fall into, as others have done.

# Chapter 3

*New Amsterdam.*
*Mrs Polet's Tavern on Brouwers Street.*
*The 30th day of July, 1664.*

Having moved my person and effects to a more tolerable inn run by a woman of spirit and good sense, I continue my writing in a comfortable situation and with pleasure in the act and in recollecting the time I learned to write. Mrs Polet has brought me tea and water; my maid has brushed my clothes. I have sent her away to the servants' room so that I may sit in my shift unobserved by the window and catch a breath of wind across my bare legs.

I never was a lady like my mistress, yet I fit this place like a silken glove to a hand. I understand that here in America a woman, no less than a man, may draw her own map of the future and bring it into being. Make one mistake and you pay dearly for it, most likely with your life, especially if you arrive with nothing. Life in the New World is a cheap commodity, bought and sold, and sweated away in a fever. There exists no person, whatever their station, that cannot be replaced. This understanding my mistress never got, thinking that in the Colony of Virginia fate would restore her to the serenity of girlhood before war came calling. She wasn't fit to be here, that's the truth of it.

I have had much to transact in this city. My affairs have dragged on for weeks without result. The seamstress I visited today tells me that the English seek to take over this whole colony of New Netherland, though that may be just rumour running round. Whatever the case I find merchants flighty and unwilling to settle to business. Crowds gather at the street corners to talk things over, to no end. Nothing happens, and meanwhile business is lost to useless speculation.

Not wishing to hold too much coin I have sought to discharge it in acquiring goods such as are not made in Virginia, the first an elegant set of chairs in rosewood with ivory inlaid and damask covers for the seats. The maker is skittish and demands a premium in case of war between this colony and the English. He whines that there will then be a shutdown of shipping between the two places. Such nonsense is intolerable and absurd, there being no more powerful force than trade to keep open all pathways and oceans. Upon my saying I would take my custom elsewhere he has of course relented, but at the cost of inaction and difficulty in this wretched place.

The commissions for myself I have completed with a fine Dutch chronometer, an article impossible to find in Norfolk County, where goods of necessity come from London, and several gowns that are now being sewn for me. The seamstress presses upon me the latest styles, and except for one gown made to my own preference, I have kept to the fashion. In that one, I have refused a long skirt, and instead ordered a simple fine skirt that falls short of my ankles, the better to walk in.

In these small tasks I pass the hours; otherwise in the cool of the morning sometimes I have walked unobserved to the shore and there stood in the shallows, as I like to do. The days drag, but two more weighty matters still detain me. The first is the need for more secure labour than that of indentured servants, and that better suited to the heat of summer. The second I have held close, it being a delicate transaction: the purchase of the woods above my estate. This opportunity I heard of sometime since, and have quietly taken.

I have kept my counsel about woods. Had others heard that Mr Smallbone's son was selling, they would have wanted them also, all land being now scarce in the environs of the James River. I should have had them in the end, but the interest of my neighbours, Mr Lee especially, would have raised the price, and I am unwilling to pay a premium for another's desire. The fact is, the streams that rise in those woods run through my estate to the river and now all these watercourses belong to me. This pleases me, and will preserve them. I know well that though water may get on without land, the contrary is not the case. The planters here lust for land, but to my mind their desire is a paltry thing and incomplete. Without water, land is lifeless and barren. Wish then for the two together. A few woods may not seem to have great value beyond the timber, and little if the trees remain. Yet the water that falls upon the wooded hills satisfies the needs of the land, and this is the value of the woods I have bought.

The business I have undertaken in the name of water brings to mind a man I knew in another place. Even on a paper for myself I shall not write his name. I learned some years ago that this man came from Amsterdam and lives here in a house built by himself that looks over the canal. He makes his living in his old profession. I enquired about him when I first arrived some weeks ago and thought to go in search of him immediately.

He is well known here, it seems, as a man of unusual character, yet one much trusted by his acquaintance and preferred to all others in the practice of his profession. It is reported that he is apt to fall silent in company, yet has several friends in the city. He shuns gatherings of more than a few, preferring to meet acquaintances singly in his house, where he keeps a large collection of objects never before seen in these parts. He is not married, but has a housekeeper who attends to him daily.

This man, I am further told, seldom goes to church and is suspected of a laxity of belief, even in this city famed for its indulgence in matters of observance. Upon my saying – by way of explanation – that I might have known him in the land I came from, all here roundly deny that possibility. Many declare they have heard him say that he never was in England, so much as to make me doubt for a moment that this is indeed the man. His name is common enough.

But I know it to be him. Reports of his person leave no doubt and catch at my throat, so that even as I write this, my breath sticks there. His tall stooping manner; the habit he has of standing a little way off from the door when it is opened to him, as if he might at any moment flee; his dark hair thrown back from his forehead and now streaked with white.

Long ago I left him behind. I pushed my memories away until I had thought they were dissolved. I lived well without the thought of him, and it is only being in this city of Dutchmen, and knowing him to have come here, that I faltered. I allowed the past to push open the door that I had closed. Now these reports and the thought of his person weaken me. That is why I cannot write his name. When I write my own name I feel that its letters form me; but the writing of his might make for my dissolution.

I long now to touch his sleeve and pass a finger down his cheek; or to come quietly upon him and surprise him into desire. Oh, how I wish for that. That was my power; and may be still. With him it was my pleasure, too. All this I want, and also to hear his voice, dense and low, with layers in it like the rills of a stream; to have him turn to me with surprise in his curious eyes. I want to run my hands to where his back curves in and out, and rest there for a moment before I pull him towards me and feel his body heavy against mine, his arms round me, and know the rest, quick or slow. And then to laugh and tease him and hear him reply with his slow wit – to lie with him, limbs under and over.

These thoughts come with the sense of him as strong as if we were together, and take the ground from beneath my feet. Thinking of his person I am become conscious of my own self. I feel suddenly alone here, with too much air around me; I who am at ease with my own solitariness and can do without another person by my side.

Yet though he may be close, I will not go to him. I cannot meet him, though I long to. I am not ready. I had closed and sealed myself tight, like a casket. My heart, once shut up, I counted as deaf to that sort of call. But now I find that that is not so. Hearing of him, my heart stirs. Under the skin it is still alive, ready to quicken. Wakened by itself it began to beat loud when I heard these accounts of him, and a great wave passed through me, a longing that came unbidden. I was ready to go to him, to give up everything and go to him. Writing these words, seeing him again, feeling his hands upon me, I am ready now.

Ah, that heart. It still remembers, long after the rest of me has forgotten, or has decided to forget. Memories drag us back like thorns. The heart is subtle; it does not deal with us even-handedly. Give yourself to it and you will give your wit and reason too. In this New World I have built myself to survive. To see him, to touch him: with that I should risk losing all I have got. Nothing is worth that; certainly not a man I loved once, who once loved me.

My own wits tell me that two people who have loved, and love each other still, may long always, and feel their hearts stretching towards one another. They may even meet again and still it come to nothing, fate having set them different paths. One may have gone one way, one another, so that though love remains, they cannot reach it. Too much sits between them.

I do remember. I remember him each day in the things that I do. Memory for me is an action, full to the brim with purpose. I do not turn back. I have taken the love that lies there unused and I have made it into something else.

Eleven years ago, in the summer of the year 1653, the Master first took notice of me. A blazing day enclosed us in its heat, and the Mistress sat in the shade of the trees with her fine hands wound round a cup of sassafras. This drink, which the natives call *winauk*, the Mistress declared to have healthful properties. She took it very often, only changing it for wild mint leaves boiled in water when she needed variety.

The Mistress was losing ground even then, though perhaps she did not feel it, giving the climate of the place as the cause of her weakness. Still, she was beautiful, pale as the moon when it rises in twilight. Her long dark hair fell across her neck and throat, her thin arms hidden in blue silk. I was with her when I saw the figure of Captain Maybrick appear up on the meadow from the landing stage. He crossed the grass and in two bounds came up to the seat and sat down beside her, throwing off his hat and stretching out his legs.

At the Master's arrival I withdrew into the shade a little way off, never having been in his company or being made known to him.

'What is this stuff, Damaris?' Captain Maybrick said, picking up the silver drinking cup and glancing at his wife.

'You know, James, my dear, I take it for my health.'

Captain Maybrick lifted the cup to his nose and put it back on the table.

'It will make you ill, Damaris. Stick to wine and water.' He looked about with impatience and added, 'Where is your bonnet, besides, in this heat?'

I saw the mistress close up a little and become agitated.

'I will run and get it, my lady,' I said from the shadow.

When I came back I walked to the bench and at my mistress's nod I tied the bonnet under her chin, lifting her hair to pass the strings under it. As I straightened up I felt the Master's eyes upon me. His look was alive and greedy and I saw he was a man accustomed to take what he wanted.

My mistress noticing nothing, I withdrew again, near enough to hear but far enough for them to feel alone. The making myself unseen is a skill I learned a long time ago.

'Very good, Damaris,' the Captain said. 'I shall leave you. What is the name of that girl?'

'Eliza.'

'When did she arrive?'

'Last year, I believe. She was put to fieldwork but somehow I came upon her and found that she can read. I took her into the house to work upstairs. She is a comfort to me, James.'

I watched Captain Maybrick shift in his chair, lean towards his wife and put his hand upon her arm. He let it rest there a moment, light enough to take up again. I saw in that gesture that he had decided already to go, to get on with his business.

'Good; then let her be about you often.'

With that the Captain stood, smoothed out the lines of his fine shirt and left. It was then I understood, when I looked at the Mistress again, that she was no more than thirty years old.

I saw nothing more of the Captain that summer, and tended to the Mistress as well as I could. Fever hung about her, especially in the evenings. Sometimes she was simply weak and stayed resting upstairs while I read to her. I sat on a stool by her bed, watched her sleep and cooled her with a fan of palmetto leaves. Sometimes I slipped my hand into hers as she slept, feeling the bones in her fingers and the faint beat of her heart.

It must have been the Captain who summoned Dr McBride from Norfolk one hot evening. I watched the sweat run off the doctor when he arrived panting up from the landing stage. An outside servant brought him up the steps to where I waited at the door and then I followed him up to the Mistress, behind his thighs that rubbed together under the heavy cloth of his breeches.

The doctor bowed to the Mistress, came up to her chair and looked at her. Sweat glistened on his bald head as he bent over.

'Bring Dr McBride wine and water, Eliza,' the Mistress said to me, and I went to fetch it, walking back with the bottles and glasses on the finest silver tray. The doctor was looking into the chamber pot when I returned, wiping his hands on his muslin handkerchief.

'I see nothing dangerous here, Mrs Maybrick. No black bile or blood. You must rest and sleep. Let fever do its work of casting out the bad humours brought on by this poor climate. You will be well in a few months.'

The doctor leaned over and whispered loud in the Mistress's ear, 'A child would bring you fast to health. The Captain needs an heir.'

I knew better than the doctor and I fancy the Mistress did too, though she never said a word. When Dr McBride had left the room she pulled herself up in the bed and smiled.

'A child, Eliza? What was Dr McBride thinking of?'

'I do not know, my lady. Of your happiness, perhaps.'

'Ah, Eliza, that's the strangest thing. I have found a contentment in my illness that I have never had since arriving in this place. The Captain is kindness itself.'

Being ill in her body made my mistress well in her heart. Who was I to say a thing against it? I helped her out of the high bed and she gave me her arm to come down the stairs. At the front door we watched the doctor walk away with his guinea. The Mistress never called for him again. We managed alone, with the herbs of the country. Mrs Lyle, the housekeeper, who had been with my mistress from her childhood, helped me. I stood in the kitchen by the open door to catch a breath of air with Dorcas the cook as Mrs Lyle herself boiled water for the Mistress's sassafras and mint. I praised the kitchen and asked Dorcas to tell me about the bunches of herbs she hung to dry in the sun outside.

'You are quick to take the meaning of things, Eliza,' Mrs Lyle said.

'I wish to learn,' I replied, and that was no more than the truth.

I wanted to know everything about Bellevue and the land it sat on; the times of rain and flood, the places upriver, the crops that might grow, the character of the country. Standing there in the doorway, looking out to the yard and up at the trees in the woods on the hill, I felt the future, all the time that was to come, and wished to open my arms to it, no matter that my mistress was ill and the days uncertain.

In the summer storms that bring floods and destruction, Damaris Maybrick and I stayed upstairs. I held her arm and walked her from the bed or settle to a chair by the windows where we might see the great oaks as they bent in the wind and hear the whole wood groan on the slope above the house. That is another reason why I had to buy those woods now, to have them for myself.

After such a storm the cypresses in the swamps stand heavy and silent. But when the clouds part they lift their branches to the light and the sun comes down to the water. Then everything sparkles and even in the house I could catch the sound of the trees dancing. Once, when a storm passed over, I said to my mistress, 'Can I go, my lady?'

and ran across the meadow to the swamp. I stood there between the trees, knee deep in water.

Just out of the swamp, I saw a snake curled on the stump of a fallen tree, white stripes down its body. It looked lazy, or half asleep. I kept a good distance away and watched when it raised its head off its body as if it knew that at that moment its skin would break near its mouth, neatly as a bean breaks when it is ripe. Did the snake help its old skin off, rubbing against the stump, or did the skin perform that action for itself, with the knowledge that it was no use any more, and only impeded the new life underneath? The old translucent scales peeled themselves back as I watched, and the snake drew itself out from the opening, bright in its young skin. For a second it darted its head in my direction and I saw its eyes; then it slid into the green water and swam away in brisk undulations. The old skin lay on the stump, grey and lifeless. I pushed it off with my hand and waited for its papery length to fill with water. In a few moments it had sunk out of sight onto the muddy swamp floor.

I turned away then and walked into the lightest part of the swamp where the sun was shining. Then I began to sing, the first time I had filled my voice and sung since I arrived in the New World. First I sang old songs that I knew. My voice grew in strength with each one that I sang, and the words I sent out came back to me from the folded trunks of the cypresses, softened and changed. I sang those old songs to bring myself alive, and when I tired of them I made a new song, light and strong. It mixed with the bright voice of the river, and belonged to the place.

When I returned to Bellevue, Damaris Maybrick looked me over. Sand and swamp mud stuck to my clothes.

'Where have you been, Eliza?'

'Just a step away, my lady, to look upon the water and the trees.'

As the days shortened the Captain began to visit the Mistress when he returned from his business, which pleased her as attentive to her state. As he straightened from brushing her cheek with his lips I saw something in his movements that the Mistress, so soft and uncomplaining, never did. The Captain was greedy, to be sure; but he was also anxious, a man hiding worry inside his air of command. I watched him more closely, met his eyes as he came in the door of her upstairs parlour. He soon came every day, which made my mistress more content and less like to stir herself to get better.

'Eliza,' he said to me one evening, 'go down to the hall and pick up the papers I have left there. Bring them to me.'

'Yes, sir.'

I looked at those papers on the way back up. Of course I did. I saw at a glance that they held accounts and that the sums were not in the Captain's favour. Beside one set of figures he had scribbled another and some hasty writing. I peered at his notes as I walked slowly up the stairs, taking my time. One read, *Bellevue near 1200 acres*, with a figure next to it. Down the page the Captain had written, *Monies in*, and underneath that, *Years of indenture*. The figures were large, large enough for me to see that though Captain Maybrick might be in debt, he was also a rich man.

I walked quietly back into the parlour and handed him the papers. He set them down on the table as if they were heavy as lead, and every now and then he glanced at them. When the Mistress fell asleep he opened them, and then rolled them up quickly.

One evening, meeting me outside the door to the Mistress's parlour, his eyes roved over me and he said, 'Eliza, why are you here?'

'I attend the Mistress, sir.'

He laughed at that. His eyes were black and sparkling.

'You are a woman of spirit to give me such a reply. You know what I mean.'

'Sir?'

'Were you one of those forced into indenture or did you come of your own accord?'

I stayed silent, knowing that the Captain might ask the overseer about me and though there were dozens of us there in the fields, Mr Hawker knew well the ones who'd come from jail, who'd only get a set of clothes with their freedom, nothing else.

But the Master only laughed softly.

'No matter. You have found your way to the house, and to Damaris too.'

I said nothing in reply, but stood back so that he had to pass and enter the room. I came in behind him and saw him already seated on the bed lifting the Mistress's hand to his lips. The last months of my mistress's life were made happy by her husband's devotion to her.

That winter of 1653 Damaris Maybrick, my mistress, faded away without complaint. Day by day she grew weaker, as if everything within her was slowing and could not be started up again. Oh, I tried, for I had no wish to see her die. When the spring came, and she would no longer leave the house even to sit upon the bench in the shade, I told her how bright the new grass was in the meadow, and how lively the birds were at their nesting.

'Talk to me, Eliza,' she said. She lay in her bed all day now, the coverlet over her thin legs and her voice smaller than before the winter. I spoke to her of all the flowers of this place, though I then knew no names for them, but could only speak of the trails of hanging flowers in the meadow, scarlet and yellow; the great white cups on the trees at the swamp edge; the starry orange carpet in the marshes.

Damaris my mistress put her head down on the pillow and closed her eyes. Her voice was so small I had to lay my head by hers to hear of the cowslips on the bank at Combe Down; their tiny buds. Rough encircling leaves uncurled as the flowers came out, slowly offering their treasure, she said. She had picked great bunches of them, filling silver tankards with mounds of yellow.

My mistress never felt herself graced by fate. How fine her life was; how easy. Yet she was sick, and only pined for the gentle green world she had lost. She died quietly one morning in May, the Master kneeling by the bed, myself in the shadows ready to close her eyes. A week later she lay under the earth, in the burial ground beyond the meadow. The Captain carried purple lilies to the sandy grave; the pastor alone attended him. Later I learned that two little children were buried there already, but I did not know that then.

In the weeks after my mistress's death I was watchful and quiet, and took care to stay hidden when I was outside the house. I feared to catch in the thoughts of Mr Hawker the overseer, for now that Damaris my mistress was dead I might be sent back to the fields. When the Master was in the house I made sure to be round about but not too near. Mrs Lyle gave me indoor tasks. I polished the silver and slept under the eaves as I had always done, having long before found a cupboard there that I had for my private use and shared with no one. From its small window, high up, I watched the Master come and go.

One evening in the autumn he called for me.

'Captain Maybrick is asking for you to attend him,' Mrs Lyle said.

There was no choice about the summons. An indentured servant may not run away or refuse. The overseer walks the lines in the fields and can pick out women at will. A woman with a man and a family might be left alone; but that depends on the desires of the overseer and the temper of the place. Captain Maybrick was spoken of as a man more interested in luxury than women, yet I had felt his eyes upon me in the months my mistress was ill.

I went into the parlour by the servants' door that was cut from the panelling in the back of the room. I came up to the Master, in this way, from behind, as he sat before the fire and looked for me at the main door.

'Captain Maybrick, sir. You called for me?'

Then he turned, still sitting.

'Eliza. Come here.'

I went towards him, stopping a little way off. We looked at one another. I saw a gentleman, dressed in green velvet with a white lace collar and silver buckles on his shoes. A Cavalier, with a high sense of himself. A man, too, I knew from those accounts I had seen, whose plantation was not as profitable an enterprise as he would like, who owed money. From the open doors to the meadow came a cool evening breeze. He held out a hand. I did not take it, but moved to the chair opposite his.

'Yes, sit down. No, close the doors first.'

I drew the doors together and slipped the arm of the catch over to hold them. Captain Maybrick and I were then shut in together, quite private.

'You are a fine woman, Eliza; the sort of woman I wish for.'

'You are a widower, sir. Your wife lately dead.'

'I will ever honour the memory of Damaris, Eliza, but come, every man needs a woman, especially here. Do you not feel the emptiness of this place, the emptiness out there and nothing to hold it at bay?'

To me, all America is brim full. It hums with life. The great beyond, that the Captain felt as emptiness, vibrates with the unknown, which thrills me. What might be discovered there? Creatures unknown to us, sights never witnessed by us. All such things, even those that might be monstrous, I want to see. Those that bring danger I wish still to read of. Why draw a boundary there, between the known and the unknown world? More discovery is certain, and I long to know of it. This desire was always there from the moment of my arrival, and will never fade.

*

I did not tell the Captain any of that, but only nodded. He desired me to come to him, to preserve his dignity, to ease his fear. I had a choice only in the manner of my agreement. I said yes, and willingly, though I did not speak of love. I became the companion of his evenings. I entertained him. As time went on I gathered small privileges, beginning with a room to myself on the first floor, away from the house servants.

Mrs Lyle, who had loved the Mistress, watched my advancement and became my ally. The housemaids and men who worked about Bellevue kept a distance from me, and what they said I never learned. Dorcas the cook, softened by my admiration, arranged the matter so that when the Captain demanded that I alone carried his food from the kitchen and set it by him at dinner, no word of dissent reached me.

Soon I had a seat at the table, if the Captain asked me to sit. He softened under my attention and took to calling my name when he came back from the estate, so that it rang through the house, wishing me to sit by him as he worked on the accounts and letters to the merchants who supplied him and bought the produce of the plantation.

'Write this for me, Eliza,' he said. 'Copy this letter into the letter book. Settle this account.'

Little by little I took over the tasks that were irksome to the Captain's sense of himself as a gentleman and soldier. I soon knew which merchants and boat owners he dealt with in Jamestown and along the James River and the Chesapeake, and learned how he might save money here, or get a better price there. At night he asked me to his chamber, and I went, returning to my own room at daylight; still a servant, still not free.

By the summer, ten years ago, when I was in my twenty-ninth year, I saw how a compact might be made. Captain Maybrick liked my company. He wished for me in the evenings, to talk business. He wanted me at night, when I sat naked over him on the bed and showed myself to him; all the parts I wished to show. Captain Maybrick believed me to be wanton, or a woman unschooled, though I am not. Yet neither am I niggardly in matters of the heart. I had a gift to give that might bring a kind of peace and I lay willingly with Captain Maybrick and with pleasure. I watched his face soften as I lowered myself onto him, or drew him into me.

When the Captain murmured kindness and told me that I had captured his heart, I found a way to say something that was yet nothing. I gave him what I could, in gratitude for the life I got in return, yet however much I gave him, I did not give him all. I kept something back, something insoluble that stayed inside me, reserved. The line was always fixed; I never let Captain Maybrick overstep the boundary of my soul.

This boundary can be breached all at once, or slowly dissolved, but once gone the thing it protects is lost. A person may start off giving little and find too late that she has given all; or give everything and then find that she has taken it back. Man or woman, it makes no difference. I did not change; I patrolled that line and kept it in good order, its watchtowers all in place. Captain Maybrick never noticed. He delighted in my form, though it is a rough and ready thing, and eased himself happily into his old way of being a gentleman.

So a year passed. I trained up a servant girl, Annie, to wait on us, and gave her my attic cupboard to make her loyal. The Captain and I then sat across from one another at table. We slept side by side. One by one the unmarried men of the neighbourhood, some of whom kept women also, were invited to our table, and I presided as the hostess at those evenings. That is how Mr Lee and I first became acquainted, the plantation of Grace Dieu, then belonging to his father, being next upriver to Bellevue and sharing with it the transportation of tobacco to the wharfs at Hampton Roads and other conveniences.

There being so few women in the southern colonies gives us weight in the scales of fate, which most often fall so heavily on the side of men. Though it is a puzzle, yet it is the case that for free women, and such as myself, our small numbers make us heavier and bring the scales closer to the place of balance. It delighted me to see how conduct slipped and the scales rose on one side and fell on the other, for what was being weighed was not persons, but power.

I watched and rejoiced. I saw that the lowliest free woman could choose a man she liked the look of, just like that. Even those inden-tured, if spared the overseer's attention, might cast about for what they wanted. Men of property took all sorts to their beds and still worshipped in their churches on a Sunday.

Discretion forbade my entrance into the society of married planters. Word of me got abroad, and since I was not a native, as was common for young men to take to their bed, many men, and some of their wives also, treated me even-handedly when we met, and did not remark on the state of affairs. No children were born to us who might be looked upon as bastards. Nothing outward in the Captain's life changed from the days of Damaris's sickness. Death sucks away so many here, even amongst the richest, that after a few years in the Colony of Virginia neither men nor women are as scrupulous about life as in the old country.

The Captain and I took the boat to Jamestown where I chose muslins and silks for my clothes; gold silk that held the sun and muslin the colour of mist. The seamstress carried the finished gowns up from the landing stage in her arms with the delicate care of a midwife. Captain Maybrick stood and watched as she dressed me and sewed the hems. His eyes glinted when I showed my ankles underneath the skirts. That evening he ran his foot up my calf and on, all the while with his eyes on mine and one hand on the stem of his wine goblet. But though he said one morning, 'Will you call me James?' and I began with some reluctance to use that name, he did not speak of the future. I did not ask, but preferred to keep my thoughts to myself.

Though I might sit at Captain Maybrick's table in certain company and share his bed, I was still a servant, and bound to work every hour and every day if he wished it. I was then approaching my thirtieth year. Life streamed past me. I could not hold it. I had four years and more to work out. In that time what might I miss; and after that, what then?

Captain Maybrick stayed quiet on the subject of my freedom, so I took matters into my own hands. From the very first I had seen the beauties of the place. The James River rises and falls with the tides and overflows into its swamps at storm time. Bellevue Plantation fronted the river and possessed many swamps that the Maybricks deemed useless, but were to me an opportunity. To have arrived in a watery place was my great good fortune. How I knew about marsh-lands and the draining of them I did not say, but one evening, Captain Maybrick was talking of his monies in a general way. His complaint was the expense of new land, there being a constant increase in the settlers of the region which made the prices rise.

'Rather than buy far afield, you might bring more land into cultiva-tion, James.'

'How so? I am using every acre I possess. Stop talking nonsense, Eliza. Come here; come, come.'

The Captain held out his arms for me, unsteady on his chair.

'I beg you, listen.'

'Very well; very well, but then, I expect you'll come to bed.'

'You have a great deal of land at present lying idle that we might turn to use.'

He looked at me then in frank disbelief.

'What land, Eliza? Tell me what land, when here I am asking Hawker to push out the edges of the fields to the utter limit? You are thinking of the land that lies fallow? That is tired land, madam, tobacco exhausts it.'

'I am speaking of new land.'

'I have no new land, except if I purchase more at a distance from this place, and that I lack the money for.'

'The swamps, sir, may be drained.'

'It has never been done.'

'Then you may be the first to do it.'

He threw his head back at that and laughed, a laugh that was full and hearty and with a thread of scorn twisted in it. The Captain had a fine deep voice that drew me to him, but yet he was as unfitted to this country as Damaris his wife had been. In this place it is more use to understand mud and water than swordplay and fine language, but the Captain had no sense of that, thinking, if he did think at all, merely of his crops.

When we lay on the bed with the moon coming in, the Captain liked to talk about his life. The truth is that he had never been a farmer, or planned for any sort of life but an idle one in the army or at the King's court. He had inherited his estate at a young age and had always had a man to look after it and many men who worked there. He loved Combe Down, as Damaris his wife did, and as a child does the home where he has always slept in the same bed.

Like the Mistress he wished to talk of what he had lost, but with more anger in his voice; like her, he was foolish. He called England home, and carried that corpse over his shoulder every day.

'Damaris spoke to you of Combe Down?'

'Yes,' I said. 'It must have been a place of beauty.'

'Yes, yes, I see it still when I close my eyes.'

He spoke as if possessed by the spirits of that place, dragged back by them. I wanted to shake him, but I said nothing. I wished to know how I might serve the Captain and myself together.

'My estate was laid waste in '44; the house burned to the ground, the sheep and horses taken by the Roundhead soldiers, the farmyards and hayricks set alight as they passed through. I wasn't there, serving as I was and straggling home defeated. I came back to the ruin, and Damaris fled to her father's house. My regiment being stood down at the end of the fighting, I had no funds to build it up.'

'And so you came here with the Mistress.'

'My uncle Henry took possession here in the year '30, a younger son without prospects, like many who first came out. He prospered with tobacco, and offered us a refuge. I thought to sit it out until the war ended and then return.'

'Yet you never did.'

'The Parliament sequestered Combe Down, gave it to the commander of a regiment in their army. They killed the King and I was abandoned to this place. My uncle died suddenly in the year '50. He left me his heir. There was nothing to go back to; I had no choice but to stay.'

He paused and then said, 'We had two boys, Eliza, that both sickened and died here.'

'I am sorry for it, sir.'

The Captain's voice trembled as he spoke, and he dipped his head before bringing it up again and gazing away to the corner of the room. I felt his sadness, yet knew that he did not wish for comfort or more acknowledgement. Our Virginia colony is a graveyard for all ages. It is a common lot to lose children here. Up in the north, and even in this city of New Amsterdam, I'm told that the climate, though extreme hot and cold, is more favourable to life.

The Captain dropped his head into his hands and stayed a moment quiet; that was all. Then he said quietly, 'John was two years old; Samuel died later, being born here in the year '48. I buried Damaris by them, as she wished.'

After a moment I said, 'Damaris said nothing to me about them, James.'

'She considered this place their death; wished for another child and then sickened herself.'

The Captain never spoke of the children again. I went to the graves a little later when he was away upriver, not saying anything to a soul but wishing to see for myself. A flat stone marked the place where my mistress lay. It was in the middle of the plot in front of two small ones for the boys. There was another large stone, upon which was carved the name of Henry Maybrick, uncle to the Captain, with the date of his death, *20th September 1650*. The Captain told me later that all the stones came out in ships from England, there being in the Virginia colony no skill in carving them, and that he wished a piece of England to stay with them.

I tend to the plot myself now, though I would choose for myself a grave in water. A wall surrounds the place, with a gate to get in by and flowers of the country growing in the square meadow. Along the end wall grows a line of oaks and to one side stands a circle of trees whose flowers open to wax-white cups.

These days my hands are soft, as Damaris's were, but I do not heed any damage to them. With a kitchen knife and a strong brush I scrape the moss off the stones myself each spring, kneeling on the grass and tracing the letters of all the words with my fingers, as once I learned to read. I go early in the morning, not wishing to be seen.

Here lies the body of Damaris Maybrick and here cowslips flower. I sent to England for the seeds, demanding in particular that they come from the middle of the country, that a bit of it might live and mingle here with my mistress. Thus I honour the dead. The plants take well to the dampness that gathers at the base of the stones, and in the shade of the trees. I make sure they are watered in hot weather.

# Chapter 4

*New Amsterdam.*
*Mrs Polet's Tavern on Brouwers Street.*
*The 27th day of August, 1664.*

There being a tumult in this town today, I stay indoors with my pens and paper. Another letter has arrived from Mr Lee, which repeats his proposal and adds a request that I come home, life being dull and flat in my absence, which has now stretched to many weeks. He has ridden past my door; Bellevue is empty and melancholy without me. That is his flattery. Bellevue is not empty, or only of my presence. A dozen servants now work in and about the house, six inside with Dorcas the cook and John Campbell my steward, and six others outside in the park and kitchen garden. Mrs Lyle is my housekeeper, and I have long taken her into my confidence. On the plantation Hawker and his men keep the hands at work and he has all the business of the planting and harvest. I leave that task to him, but keep an eye upon him. Hawker hopes for advancement from me and may get it.

But then – home. What a word, what a word. There is nothing for me inside it. It is a round O, scarcely held in by the weak letters either side. It is like an empty box or a stringless viol. Home is a false promise. Long ago I had something, but I left it and can never return. For several years I had no thought of home, or any new place, my mind being fixed upon survival only. Now a place has come to me, but I maintain my hold upon it in certain circumstances only.

Mr Lee has often sailed down from Grace Dieu to dine at Bellevue, and I have often been his guest since his father died. The house there sits right at the confluence of the Jones Creek with the James River.

Ripples on the water come reflected into the dining room when the sun shines low. The woods (the same woods after many weeks of wrangling and legal business are now mine) being further away from the house than those at Bellevue, he does not hear the trees thrash in the storms and sigh in the breeze. So much is fine at Grace Dieu; the tablecloths, woven with a pattern of leaves and flowers; crystal glasses from Waterford carried from Ireland on straw beds in wooden boxes; the steady tick of the long-case clock, made in London; the portraits of the family mounted on the wall.

I do not believe, when Mr Lee asks me to come home, that he sees me alone in his mind's eye, but rather sees me framed by my estate and made desirable by it. This is what his request and his proposal mean to a woman in my situation. If he married me I would be his, a part of his property. What then of my estate? I would no longer have one; Bellevue would be his.

Mr Lee is a fine man who knows the country and that propriety matters less in a place where death cuts so many down than it does in the old country. We have much to discuss over wine when we have thrown our napkins down and pushed back our chairs from the table. We talk business, with other thoughts woven in. Mr Lee desires me and Bellevue together and expects from me a return of the feeling.

While I might perhaps return Mr Lee's desire, being a woman like any other, I do not wish to pay the price attached to it. Besides that, I cannot touch the idea of home. It flies away from me and I have given up the pursuit. Land, and the possession of it; these are the words I can grasp. The land I own is warm to the touch after a long summer day; the river runs gently over my hands; the tree roots move constantly in search of a foothold. Underneath lies the rock that is anchored to the centre of the earth. This is solidity and I have title to it.

Captain Maybrick began to understand the value of his idle land only when I drew for him my first maps of his estate. Until that time, he knew the extent of Bellevue only by what Hawker told him of acreage and yield, and had little understanding of its elevation or the creeks that ran down to the river. He could not join my enthusiasm, but he could be a gentle man to those he considered lived within the boundary of his power, and I was one of them. So he allowed me to tour the whole plantation on foot and use one of the small boats as I needed it. He could not know the joy I felt to glide away from the jetty alone and row myself up a narrow creek, or paddle with a single oar in the green shade of the swamps with frogs for company.

Yet I never stayed longer on the water than my business demanded. A few weeks later I presented Captain Maybrick with a map of Bellevue, having begun with the sketches I found at the house, which showed the extent of the Captain's holdings and the boundaries of the whole estate. This I supplemented with a better drawing of the shorelines and swamps made from my own observations of the river and creeks.

I wished to give the Captain something as beautiful as others I saw long ago, made with the help of a chronometer and plumb line and a training in trigonometry and drawing. Though I lacked the tools and skills for that work, I nonetheless painted the edges of the tobacco fields with a brush dipped in saffron yellow, filled the James River and the creeks with blue and washed the swamps with spinach water. The map, once unrolled across the parlour table, showed a full third of the estate to be green swampland, that the Captain could see immediately.

'You wish that I drain these swamps? How is that to be done?'

I told him how sea walls would prevent the high tides getting to the swamps, and sluices on the creeks would regulate the flow of water to irrigate the fields. Then a variety of new crops might be grown. The Captain objected to that idea, saying he had never seen it and wished only to continue with tobacco, but added that I might draw him a plan of a sluice to explain its workings. This I did, along with a plan to show where I intended for the sluices to go. Though I presented both to him, he took them away and said nothing, and for some months things went on as usual, with no more said about my scheme.

In the summer of the year '55 Captain Maybrick left to undertake business in New Amsterdam. I roamed the house in his absence and allowed myself to study such accounts as he had left to lie about. I never found the map of Bellevue and the plans I had made with the drawings of the sluices I proposed.

The Captain returned early one morning a month later. I came down the steps when I heard the boats arrive at the jetty, and stood waiting in the hot sunshine.

'Ah, Eliza, Eliza, here I am.'

He took me in his arms then and looked at me quizzically, saying nothing. A few days later he remarked while we lay side by side in the great bed, my hand upon his thigh, 'I think we may begin the works.'

'You have given it some consideration.'

He turned towards me with a smile.

'I enquired in New Amsterdam for an engineer. I was directed to a Dutchman reckoned skilled in that work, who has built the canal there, and has worked on many farms around the city and up in the English colonies to the north.'

'A man of experience.'

'You would not have believed it, dressed as poorly as he was.'

'His name?'

'Name? I do not remember, Eliza. It matters not. He believed that I wanted to hire him.'

'And do you?'

'It seems I have no need of him.'

At that moment my heart turned inside me. Blood flooded my cheeks. The Captain noticed my agitation.

'You are distressed, Eliza; angry that I consulted another? Come, come. How could I do otherwise, you being a woman?'

I pulled away from him, and hoped he had not felt my heart beat through my skin. If he had looked into my eyes he might have seen that I felt not anger, but joy.

'What was he like, this Dutchman?'

'Oh, nothing much,' the Captain said, 'though he spoke English well. A large man, much taller than most Dutch. I was warned that he was abrupt in manner and without civility. He was not the sort of person I should have chosen had he not been spoken of as the best in the city.'

I knew then that it might be the man that I had known, and something passed through me, half shadow and half bright light. I wanted him, not just the solid form of him; no, much more. I wanted to settle with him of an evening and talk over my plans and everything that had passed while he stood at the fire and turned the dinner in the pot, or lifted the peat so a shower of sparks fell in the hearth. For a moment I wanted to go back, fit myself against his shoulder and fold myself into the past.

'Is he to come down to Bellevue?' I wished that the Captain had demanded it.

'No, no. That is not possible, Eliza. You know that, and, besides, he assured me the plans are sound. I paid him for his services and left.'

I looked past the curls on the Captain's head. They had turned to grey and gave his face a softer frame than a few years before. Through the window I saw thousands of bright stars in the black sky, and the moon travelling across it. Into its light I took myself, until the Captain and the bed we lay on disappeared. The moon was alone, yet it shone brightly, lit by the sun that burned so far away. Closer and closer I came, until my soul touched the moon's surface. It hung there in the moon's white light, quite free.

That moment was a balm and returned me to myself. The man I knew was in the New World, in New Amsterdam, I was quite certain. That must now be enough for me. I had my present life with the Captain, and would close up the weak place in my heart. It would not break. I would tell the Captain nothing, and nothing would put in jeopardy the small freedoms that I had.

'You are smiling, Eliza. You are happy that I took those plans to New Amsterdam.'

'Yes, James, I am happy.'

'It seems I have found myself a good engineer.'

He laughed then, a full laugh, pulled me close and kissed my breasts, one after the other.

'This way I may clear my debts without having to buy any more land. Who would have believed, Eliza, that you had any knowledge of such things? You have hid your light under a bushel, madam.'

That night the Captain took me as if he owned me. He pushed himself on me, into me. He was triumphant in possession. I was the path to his prosperity and he desired me all the more for it.

The next day we began. That is to say, I began. I talked first to Mr Hawker, explained to him the need for more land and appealed to him as a man in charge of many others. More land, I said, would mean more hands. When the draining was finished my first task would be to build a bigger house for the overseer. He leaned towards me at that, resting on his staff, and it seemed to me that we came to an agreement. He would forget that I had been indentured and picked tobacco until my hands bled. I would give his position the importance that he wished for. His new house would be the biggest built for any overseer in the county. I asked him to look out for a site that might suit him, and promised that it should be two storeys high.

To the Captain I explained the need for more hands.

'I wish to select and hire men to carry out the works.'

'So you may, Eliza.'

'A person who is indentured has not the right to conduct business freely. My dignity demands my freedom, James.'

The tussle between keeping me indentured and having the works proceed was soon settled and forgotten as if it had never been. I became a free woman. The Captain signed each contract as the owner of Bellevue, and I insisted on ceremony; that they be written on the finest linen paper, laid before him, and stamped with his seal. He never felt his authority weakened, though I took the whole project into my hands.

In truth the works were not as hard or long as some I have seen in another place. I selected those men fittest for the task, and found ways to reward them if their labour was good. I had the women make new smocks for all the hands so that they were uniformly dressed, which delighted the Captain, giving them the appearance, he said, of servants in the old country.

After a year or so the biggest of the swamps was drained, surrounded with defensive pilings against the overflows from the river. Three new sluices controlled the creeks. By my new maps I reckoned that Bellevue was the larger by a fifth, the outlay only that of labour, wood and bricks. Marshes and reeds still stretched along the James River, but the prospect from higher by the house was more open and airy. The Captain remarked that the view from Bellevue resembled more and more that of Combe Down, there being now meadows that stretched away from the house on all sides.

Only one thing grieved me. I had to fell the cypresses, which groaned as they came down into the swamps. I did not stay to watch the hands cut them into planks after the felling, though they made fine floors. Whole trunks were used to make pilings for new wharfs along the riverbank. Yet I am pained by the loss. Away from the immediate surroundings of the house I have maintained several swamps. There the trees still grow proud. After storms I wade into the water and lean my whole body against their rough trunks. When I know I am quite alone and out of sight I sing and listen to their speech.

From the day that I began the works, Captain Maybrick became happy in his fashion, which was the fashion of a gentleman. I saw that he disliked the business of the fields and, even more, the sale of tobacco, and, one by one, I took these tasks away from him. I made myself the mistress of the accounts; first those of the works, then those of the house, and finally those of the whole estate. Captain Maybrick, having money with his banker, and time to do as he pleased, did not complain. Perhaps he scarcely noticed, except for the lightening of his mood. His content spread like silk between us. As time went on he began to ride a fine pony from house to house and visit his neighbours. He built new offices at Bellevue and supervised the putting-up of Mr Hawker's big house.

After the first harvests I suggested a new occupation for the Captain.

'It would delight me, and be worthy of you, if you undertook to make a fine garden and bring renown to your estate.'

Formally laid out in the meadow to one side of the house, surrounded by a low brick wall, the Captain's garden soon engrossed him. He divided the ground into squares and other shapes within them, all picked out by borders of box and divided by walks of sandy gravel taken from the river bed. Flowers filled the box shapes: lilies, irises and glossy peonies. Roses, most of all, were the Captain's favourites, their roots brought bare from England in wooden boxes in the holds of ships. White and cream and pink, they threw their scent across the garden in the evening, as we walked between the little hedges of the parterre and, like a proud parent, the Captain bent and knelt to see the beauty of his creation.

He called the garden his other Eden, and by making it he came to mind less the place he had left behind. I forbore to say that though he lost one thing he gained another, but watched as he dragged the weight more easily. One day in autumn he picked a bunch of purple-red flowers, Sweet William he told me was their name, and, offering them to me, asked for my hand.

'We are used to one another, Eliza. I am past forty years old, and see no impediment, despite the difference in our station. What do you say?'

'I say yes, sir.'

The fact was that the Captain had grown dependent upon me for the running of the plantation, and had no wish to learn that trade again as he must have done had he married another woman. His pride was hurt at the thought of my lowliness, but it was vanquished by his need, as may happen in the New World though it never could in the old one. I was a free woman and had more than once hinted at that, usually as we lay in bed.

So it was that seven years ago I became the Captain's wife, and mistress of the whole estate of Bellevue. We married at Jamestown, and our names were entered in the register there for all to read. I might, at last, sit at the table as his wife, and all the planters and their wives visit me from round about. We soon enlarged the house to match the garden and all sorts and conditions of men and women took pleasure in their visits to Bellevue. From the beginning with the Captain I kept a fine table and freely poured his wines. I mixed my guests according to rank and habit.

Gentleman planters came for dinner or to sit under the trees and talk business. Land, and the getting of it, was their great subject; that and the shortage of labour and women. Their families came also. I kept two ponies, and had Hawker's men build me a small cart with wooden seats to pull behind them for the children. I sat and listened. With the tea or dinner I handed round questions and heard stories. Of myself I spoke little.

There were one or two gentlemen coming to Bellevue who called themselves antiquarians or botanists, given to collecting objects. They wrote letters back to England about what they found here, and waited months for the replies. Some drew fine pictures of river creatures or plants with medicinal use, others sent narratives of the new-discovered land.

Talk sometimes turned from the curiosities of the natural world to the natives of this place. Mr Turner, a merchant of the neighbourhood, made a study of their habits and life. Of these people I pretended to know nothing, but I had sometimes come across them in the swamps and observed them closely. I had seen that they were ingenious in the matter of trapping and growing, and at home on the water. Though not able to make coracles, they fashioned bark into canoes and got about in a manner familiar to me that I longed to try. I saw the natives and forbore to call them savage, since they were savage in a way I know.

There has been a struggle between those newly settled and those who once lived here, who once owned this land. We who have arrived are already the victors. The natives are everywhere in decline and on the move. This is the way of the world that I have seen before. It is the operation of strength and skill and money, all of which the colonists possess in greater quantity than those who were content to let nature put a sufficiency in their hands. This I learned in another place and I applied the lesson to the New World; there is no more to be said of it.

When the guests went away the Captain and I walked in the garden. James Maybrick, a slender man of more than forty years and curly-haired; myself by him, a woman of the same height. The Captain wore his soft boots. He took his ease, the strings of his white muslin shirt untied, his velvet breeches loosened. I liked to loop my right arm under his left, a silk shawl over my gown, my ankles neat beneath my skirts. I wore silk slippers with turned heels that the Captain especially liked. Behind the house the oaks begin their rise up the hill; in front the ground falls away to the river where the pinnace and rowboat lie in the boathouse.

I doubled Captain Maybrick's patrimony, and year by year his prosperity grew. He and I were happy together in our fashion, though no children were born to us. This lack saddened my husband, it seeming that he had a barren wife. He never gave up hope that we might have a child, being still young enough in years. I had that hope also, but learned to content myself with being fertile in ideas and in carrying them out. Bellevue stood proxy for our progeny. With purchase and drainage I enlarged it to an estate of two thousand acres. Had I been able to find more labour I should have bought more land. The Captain took more of the meadow for his garden until it became the wonder of the place.

When Captain Maybrick died suddenly of a seizure in his forty-eighth year, I found myself a widow and the mistress of Bellevue. More than once the Captain talked of his own death and, upon my asking what his wishes might be, he answered that he preferred to be buried with his wife Damaris and near to his two sons. Whatever his wish had been I should have honoured it, the dead being not so much gone as all around us, wherever their souls may have taken flight.

So when my husband died, I had my mistress's headstone lifted out and the grave dug open. I saw her bones there, the winding sheet fallen away into the sandy soil, eaten by termites. The sight of my mistress's white bones, arranged as if she slept, did not make me afraid. I greeted them and spoke also to her spirit, which I know to be in the air here, like a soft arm around my shoulder. I laid the Captain's coffin next to her bones, added his name to hers on the stone and set it back into the sandy ground.

After I had buried the Captain the visits of condolence began. Single men from miles around stopped to pay me a call, and, stooping over my hand to kiss it, turned their glances to the fittings of the house. They remarked upon the fineness of the situation and I agreed as to its beauty. Yet I took care to make it plain that I intended to observe the strictest mourning, and so I did the whole year after until now.

Then it was that I took passage on a boat coming up here to New Amsterdam for I had business to transact, thinking once more of the expansion of my estate. And I have found much to interest me, besides the usual duties of commerce. This morning, out on the street to learn the source of the tumults here, I talked to a merchant just arrived from Santa Domingue. It is a fertile place, he says, and many crops may be grown there. In the middle of the island lies a great marsh that collects rainwater from the mountains. Here they grow rice in standing water and with great success. This we spoke of for some time, he having made a tour of these rice fields and seen the ease of cultivation. I have further invited him to visit Bellevue and explain to Mr Hawker how it might be done there.

The thoughts of my return to Bellevue, and the Virginia colony, bring me to Mr Lee's proposal. I have not replied to it, but my answer is a blunt one, and I do not wish to clothe it in sweet words. No, is the answer that I will give; no and never. These words must do; they must be enough to forestall any new approach. As to my reasons, I have already written that I have closed my heart enough to keep myself safe. And then, what have I been, until lately, but a possession? I have had no title to myself. I have been a part of men's estate, a parcel of property, with no claim upon what I am or what I might be. From time immemorial this has been the case for women. That old country that the Captain mourned, how could I feel for it as he did? I could not, even if my station had been higher, because I am a woman. The country that he loved was not my possession, neither as a woman, nor as a person coming from the place I did.

No country can be mine while I am a woman and the property of men. I have been a daughter, a servant and a wife. I have not had possession of myself. Only a widow such as I am, an inheritor, may feel that sense of ownership. And now I do feel it, and the freedom and joy of it. Bellevue is my plantation. It is mine in law and to improve, enjoy and bequeath as I wish. Whom I shall bequeath it to, I do not know, but I have many decades to make my choice. I know the value of my land, of all kinds of land here in this place where land is everything.

There was a place that once I inhabited, though I did not own it. The loss I suffered was not of possession, but of use. I do not look back at it now, and feel no grief for it. If any person enquires where I am from I always reply that I am from Virginia. Such is the truth. In Virginia, in America, I arrived, and made myself as I wish to be.

I shall never allow loss to befall me again. My land and my heart are my possessions, never to be relinquished until I die. Bellevue is my safety and my solidity. Owning it, and owning my own heart, I own myself and will never be the property of any man. Sometimes I sing for the joy of it, as I did here in New Amsterdam a few weeks ago, calf-deep in the water by the island's edge.

At Bellevue, by the river, the summer air is dense and the heat sits heavy. Snakes come up the riverbank and slide towards the house. At night the crickets rub their noisy legs together, and pause, and begin again. Bellevue, inside, smells of wood in the summer, when the floors grow warm and release the close presence of the woods that grow on the hills behind. To come into the house and feel the heat wrap around me, thick as an unwanted blanket; that is a mark of this new world. There at the water's edge the night is alive, the velvet air is full of sound.

No, I shall never marry again. If I need a person for my days or my nights I shall find one. I am content. I have no fear of this vastness, of the forests that stretch beyond the horizon, of the moths bigger than my hand, of my own tomb. Sometimes I lie awake at night and through the windows see the stars that shine and shine in the great dome of heaven, and feel a joy to be in this place. My soul takes flight over the lands we inhabit and the mountains we know. It travels into unknown spaces that are more huge than any we have imagined. It hovers there with the moon, and looks; it sees the unexplored wilderness in all its plenitude. America. My spirit feasts here. This is the fruitful place; this the fertile land.

# PART SIX

# Chapter 1

*Nieuw Amsterdam and New York.*
*My house by the Heere Gracht.*
*The 28th day of August to the 8th of September, 1664.*
*Hot every day.*

Our Director-General, Pieter Stuyvesant, having been forced by his own citizens to hand over the city, Nieuw Amsterdam is dissolving. It will disappear and return, with the same streets but another name, New York. The British agree to stay on their boats at night; but one afternoon I see a pair of soldiers strolling past my house. They look about them with an air of possession already. In this way the handover approaches, but Nieuw Amsterdam seems not to notice or to care. The city lives its last days in the usual way; at work, and with gossip, brandy and tobacco in the evenings.

Not wanting to idle through the time, and uneasy in crowds, I take a boat to Lange Eylandt and make my way to Quawanckwick. This place was inhabited by wildmen and is still known by the name of those people, though now in the possession of Oloff Van Cortlandt, a wealthy citizen who has called me there.

Van Cortlandt has removed the fallen remains of the old dwelling place and built a clapboard farmhouse in its place. It stands square on a grass meadow surrounded by neat new fields. He now wishes to bring into use the expanse of marshland between his farm and the shore. This is Dutch work, a simple matter of drainage, dykes and windmills at intervals to take away the water that lies on the fields after rain and snowmelt. Yet I have let it hang about me in a way contrary to my usual habits. For the last three months I have been reluctant to go far from the city. I have been waiting, not as Nieuw

Amsterdam now waits, with resignation or indifference, but with a hope that has lined my days with golden light. The note I received, a half-glimpse in the street and the sound of a song across the water, kept it alive; but its glimmer is no longer enough. Mijnheer Van Cortlandt is impatient, and I am here in answer to his summons.

I find, when I begin my work, that I am settled by its familiar demands. I start by the shore, walking the tideline. I see where the water streams in rills across the sands and the places where the sea pushes vigorously inland up deep-scored creeks with sandy bottoms and muddy sides. The tide is out, the sun high and the sea is quiet. On the beach the departing waves have deposited sparkling undulations, silver arabesques curled across the sand. On the mud above the sand line the dry purple flowers of sea lavender rustle in the breeze. Flies and beetles, egrets knee deep in mud and black cormorants standing sentinel on outcrops: nature is busy at work.

I stay several days in comfort at Van Cortlandt's farm, and make a simple map of the place with which to draw up a plan of works. Perhaps I will leave a little more of the marsh in the plans than the containment of nature demands. I will preserve the edge, where the creeks begin to narrow, though it might with ease be turned to pasture. Here reeds grow in abundance, and shake their feathered heads.

One evening I sit on the meadow and watch the sun sink red through the reed beds. The light fades and the wind drops. An interval of silence falls over the marsh. Everything is quiet and beautiful. Then, as darkness falls, night herons start their nocturnal song.

There is no need to destroy all this. Oloff Van Cortlandt will never miss the extra *guildern* that cutting the reed beds will bring him. I will explain how sedge and reeds can halt the tide surge across his fields in the spring and break the fury of the wind. But the truth is that I wish it this way. It suits me now to let the unimproved land and the new cultivated land exist here together. Both are beautiful, and side by side will help one another.

Two days later when I get back to Nieuw Amsterdam, the shadow that falls from the Fort onto the stones of Het Marckvelt is sharp in the morning. The time has come: there is no room for equivocation in the brightness, no merging of lines in mist or marsh. Under this sun, in this place now, everything is definite and defined. People have had to make a choice, one thing or the other; and the citizens have chosen England over the Company, a king over the republic. The choice, it is true, has been made in the presence of a gun, but still it is made. Commerce and convenience have swept away old loyalties. So now it is all over. The world has turned and new rulers hold sway over us.

What is left to perform is the ceremony, the acknowledgement. The English soldiers stand in the sun, lined up and alert, with Colonel Nicolls at their head. Their weapons gleam clean and sharp. At a distance we citizens wait. The walls of Fort Amsterdam rise above us, slanted inwards. The mortar is crumbling. Valerian grows in the spaces between the red bricks. Taking a few steps back I can see the noses of the cannon that stand on the four corners. They point down, unmanned.

After a few minutes Colonel Nicolls looks up and the crowd follows his gaze. I sense a shifting, a shuffle towards the English. Out of the rustle comes a murmur, the sound of acceptance. The Company flag, a ripple of blue, white and red, drops slowly down the flagpole and disappears. Drums roll inside the fortress and the great doors swing open. For a moment time seems suspended, then the drummers come, sounding the march; and then the standard-bearers with the flags of the Company. Then, at last, in the hush, two by two the men of the garrison cross the shadow of the gateway and step into the sunlight.

Colonel Nicolls bows. His soldiers turn and bang their pikestaffs on the ground. Out onto the forecourt the Dutch march. Two by two they lay their swords on the ground, straighten up and swing left into Het Marckvelt. A Company ship, the *Gideon*, is waiting to take any soldiers and others who wish to go. Director-General Stuyvesant is holed up at the Great Bouwerie. He declines to leave, preferring to be a subject of King Charles like the rest of us.

When the Company soldiers have rounded the corner out of sight, Nicolls turns towards all of us standing there. A trumpeter sounds a triumphant call and then Nicolls declares, speaking in the English language, that from this day the city will have a new name, given us by His Majesty in honour of his brother the Duke of York and Albany. Nieuw Amsterdam will become New York; Fort Orange in the north will be named Albany.

In the crowd his words are passed along in Dutch by those who understand; people bend towards the news. There is a murmur, then silence as the trumpet sounds again. The English soldiers are moving into the Fort, their flags held high and drums rolling. They go two by two into the shade, until only the sentries are left by the open gates. A few minutes later the red and white of the English flag rises up and unfurls.

That's it. Something has come to an end; something else begun. We stand and look up at the flag. Its scarlet cross ripples out over the city. The crowds break up; people drift off to their labour, into their houses, back to the day. How easy it has been.

I fall in with Mr Sharp who jokes that I am now a subject of the English King. Have I ever seen the King? he asks, though he knows I have not.

'You resemble him,' he says. 'King Charles is a tall man, I'm told; swarthy and secretive like yourself.'

I run along with the joke.

'With the difference that I'm a Dutchman, still, Mr Sharp.'

'Ah, so is he, perhaps; become one in The Hague.'

He laughs and claps me on the shoulder, a way of telling me who governs here now, though being from New England he has no love for the King, only amusement in so far as it will help a joke. For myself it matters little. Am I a Dutchman still? In truth I do not think so. I am just a man, no more changed inside than the stream that runs beneath the wall at the top of the city, flowing one moment under Manatus Eylandt, the next under Nieuw Amsterdam or New York as it now is named. That stream has a Dutch name, and will soon have an English one. The water in it has the same composition. Besides, the wildmen have another name for it, a name that few of the citizens of this town will ever know.

In the ground one kind of plant grows next to another. They jostle for space but push their roots down together in the soil. Columbine curls round the straight grass stem; one flowers in spring, the other in the summer. I have watched bees on hot summer days. They do not live in one hive, but many, and fly from portal to portal laden with pollen.

Then, that wall; what good did it do in the end? The Company built it to keep the wildmen from our city. Soldiers patrolled its length in pairs, looking north for danger. But danger came from a power too far away to be seen. The English arrived by ship and sailed to Lange Eylandt, advancing on us from the east. The wall did not save us; we looked in the wrong place. The wildmen are so little a menace. We made a story that did not fit the turn of history and so were unprepared.

Sometimes history leaves us forms, conceived in the imagination of man, that are wonders. Such are the figures on my hearth, left in the mud and brought across the sea. They seem as emissaries from one world to another, yet I know not what message they carry, only that the world that made them is no more. Such history as they tell is not what chroniclers write, of nations past or the spreading fame of men, but is the history of all things, of the whole earth as it heaves and wrinkles down the ages. It is all the lives of women and men that seem long gone and mingled with the sky, yet still remain around us. The people who made these forms may be forgotten, but still once lived, and now add to the strangeness of the world.

Every day I look at the figures, and the mystery they hold inside themselves, and know that though so much is unclear to me, yet everything beneath and beyond the heavens happens according to nature's laws. The English boast of uniting all their possessions in one line from New England down to Carolina, but under the surface everything is already joined. Beneath the rivers and streams lies the clay bed, and under that the old hard rock. Who knows how far the deep rock stretches; under the sea, all the way to the old world, and, further south, to Africa.

West India Company map makers of my acquaintance, indeed the great Hessel Gerritsz himself, who have surveyed and drawn the wild coasts of Africa and our colonies of Suriname and the south, say that the curved shore of Brazil that finds its easternmost point at Cape Augustine fits snugly into the indent of the coast of Africa. The two lands, they say, must therefore have been broken apart by some great unknown force. It may be that the wildmen and the men of Maroc are thus one and the same people, though of distinct language and custom.

This notion pleases me, that the two lands once fit to one another as a baby to its mother's breast, and that one moved away from the other, as a child learns to do without its mother. If the lands were joined, so must have been the people. The same earth fashioned us, and once, perhaps, we all stood side by side.

Understanding this notion is not difficult, yet everywhere I see men set themselves one against another. Whether this is the result of ignorance or desire I cannot determine. I am a man who witnesses and records. So I conceive my purpose here, and the small conclusions that I have made from this my life are enough, though many men will make note of how little I have accrued to myself: neither estate, nor family, nor worldly office of any kind. My understanding, in all these years, has come to this: the whole universe just is. It just is.

A man who looks at me might conceive this task to be a lonely one. But I am not alone. The surgeon Abraham Lucena also carries and records his story, and the story of his people, who have been moved across the world by fate. Ten years ago they came to this place from Recife, far to the south, and so we met, began to converse, and found a friendship. Long before their exile from Recife, he told me, the Israelites were hurled about the world by hostile powers. They have, for centuries, been used to moving from place to place and carrying their histories on their backs, and this way preserve themselves for ever.

None of this I say to Mr Sharp as we stroll across the city. At my house by the Heere Gracht we say goodbye and I open my door with the sense of contentment that comes across me when I return. Lysbet comes hurrying out of the back parlour, disturbing the air.

'There is someone to see you, Mijnheer Brunt.'

She uses my formal name, as if the occasion warrants it. By this I know that the caller is not Abraham or any friend known to me.

'In the front parlour,' Lysbet says, and I feel my chest tighten with hope.

Opening the door it is not you, who I have been longing for and thinking of. It is a man, who turns towards me as I step in. My heart first drops, then picks up and leaps like a young fish hurtling out of water. Unmistakably, joyfully, it is Jacob Van Hooghten, grey-haired and smiling.

'Jacob; oh, Jacob.'

'Jan. It is you.'

He comes towards me and I look down into his eyes again, familiar and deep-set among the wrinkles.

'Jan.'

I am staggered and unable to speak. All this time I have been expecting you, and instead Van Hooghten has come. Two worlds that were once joined and then seemed parted for ever have come together again.

Van Hooghten puts his arms round me and draws me to him. He is still thickset and solid. Comfort spreads through me like cream. He pushes me back, looks at me, and pulls me close again.

'It has been – too long.'

'Yes, yes – too long,' I say, my voice almost failing me.

'Thirteen years, Jan – fourteen almost. We are old men.'

'Jacob, you are in the prime of life. What are you doing here? You sent a boy to me to say you would be coming.'

'Jan – Jan. One thing at a time. It is not like you to be disordered.'

'Forgive me; forgive me. I am delighted to see you. You can stay a little?'

'Yes, yes. I've come on Company business, Jan. But I sent no boy. I am only just arrived. It is easy to find you. I heard a rumour in Amsterdam that you had come here and once arrived I merely asked and was directed here.'

'Forgive me, again. I received a message some time ago announcing a visitor; of course, too long ago. No matter. I will ask Lysbet – you have met her – for coffee and you must tell me all your news.'

I hurry out into the hall. There is nothing more to think; you sent a note and have not come. Instead, here is Van Hooghten, a man I love, who did me great kindness long ago and whom I welcome now. For a few moments I walk up and down to calm myself. Now, no more than then, do I wish to let out my rawness and disappointment. Besides the indignity to myself, what an unkindness that would be to Jacob who has shown himself in every way my friend.

'Lysbet. Lysbet,' I call as a distraction, and ask her to make coffee. By the time I return to Van Hooghten in the parlour I have sealed over my agitation and determine to show him only my happiness and gratitude. You are not here, but he is. If I believed in miracles, this might be described as such.

Lysbet brings almond biscuits in a Delft bowl with the coffee, setting them down with a flourish. As I pour the coffee I accustom myself to seeing Van Hooghten in my house, with the rug on the oak table, and bright blades of sunlight glancing through the half-open shutters.

The colours of my parlour are golden and red, deep with the life I live here. I think of Van Hooghten the last time I saw him, on the quay in King's Lynn, the viscous grey mud glistening with salt water, the sky low and the air heavy with rain, and feel a sudden lightening. After all these years when I have kept him in mind, my past has come out of memory, looped around and is here to meet me. Life, suddenly, shines bright and rich.

Silence falls as we look at one another. Van Hooghten is smiling and I know that I am also.

'Jacob,' I say finally, 'tell me how fortune treats you.'

'She treats me fairly, Jan. I am grown old and prosperous. I work for the Company and came here on regular business on the warship *Gideon*. Then this happened; this takeover.'

Here Jacob throws his arms wide and laughs.

'And so what now?' I ask.

'Now they ask me to stay, there being few Company officials in this town. I will oversee the Company's departure from this place – accounts, files, any other property they demand back home.'

'A great responsibility.'

'Not so, Jan; just a sudden one. The Company has lost interest in Nieuw Nederland, seeing more profit in sugar and spices than in furs. A mistake, I believe.'

'It is of little importance,' I say. 'The world turns and empires come and go.'

In my mind I see a picture of the wildmen of this place in a line of canoes and then suddenly, as if Van Hooghten's presence has conjured it, another picture, of the prisoners by the embankment so long ago, one tied to another, their spades rising and falling in arc after arc.

I hesitate then, not wanting to turn our talk to the Great Level, but Van Hooghten goes on.

'Our work on the Great Level is done, Jan; long done, and well. The Level is drained, just as we planned and foresaw; though...'

'Though?'

'Well, Jan, we are Dutchmen, accustomed to gravels and clays, and I have reports that we overlooked the nature of the place.'

'It is flooding?'

'No, no. Not that. Those are Dutchmen's fears you voice. It is a matter of land, not water, or at least land drained of water, separated from the element that it had lived in. It seems the peat is shrinking.'

He laughs and shrugs.

'Nature is a demanding partner, is she not, Jan? The men there will have to treat with her, find a truce.'

'Renswyck – did he stay on for that task?'

Jacob looks at me keenly then.

'Renswyck – ah, no. Reason left him, Jan, after the work was done. He refused to leave the camps and drank his way through the day. His clothes turned to rags, his mind slackened and the only thing that was left was his rage. He sought my company, sometimes, in the evenings.'

'And you listened to him.'

'For some months. He railed against the world and all the people in it, until his mind was overthrown completely.'

'And then?'

'Then he left the Level, and I never saw him again.'

Sadness passes over Jacob's face like a gust of wind; then it rights itself and comes back to me.

'And you, Jan, have you made a truce with nature here, or is it even wilder than in that place?'

I am not ready to begin.

'We have much to talk over, Jacob,' I say. 'The work will keep you awhile in the city?'

'Some weeks, certainly.'

'And you will stay here as my guest?'

'With great pleasure, Jan. You have done well for yourself.'

'Well enough.'

I can see that Jacob wants to learn more, he wants my story, pat as I can tell it; but there is little I can really tell him, in truth, and nothing of the sort he might like to hear.

'Tell me more of yourself, Jacob,' I go on. 'You are married to Maria?'

'Yes, indeed; we married as soon as the Great Level was drained and I had returned home. I was set up well for the world then, and earned the approbation of her family. We live in Amsterdam with our children – four of them, Jan – but spend much time on my estate.'

'You are become a man of property.'

'Yes; I have a small estate. It is near Muiden up on the edge of the polders. I've built an elegant little country house; everything well ordered and modest. I am improving the lands there; planting also.'

'And you work still as an engineer?'

'Ah, Jan, that's a labour for a younger man. I no longer set my feet in the mud these days.'

Van Hooghten places the delicate coffee cup on the table with care, and looks around. He seems to be searching for something to indicate success and wealth to balance his own.

'You have a fine parlour here, Jan. And a wife yourself?'

'No; I am content as I am.'

I see him hesitate.

'Yet you had a woman in England?'

'A long time ago.'

'She was sent as indentured labour along with the prisoners, was she not?'

'I saw her go, Jacob, at least I believe so.'

'You said nothing of that to me.'

'No. There was nothing to say, or know. She was gone.'

'And is?'

'And is.'

'In truth, Jan, there were rumours about the breach. Renswyck insisted on the guilt of the fensmen.'

'Ah, he did.'

'Yes.'

Van Hooghten leans back and looks straight at me.

'Did you notice nothing, Jan? Did you see nothing?'

'See? What did any of us see, Jacob? So little, either near or far; either above ground or below it. Now I am in the New World, I observe that it is the same here. We all of us see just what we want to and no more.'

Van Hooghten shrugs.

'You are probably right, Jan. Besides, the flood was forgotten soon enough, though for your sake I kept an ear open to news. After some months I heard that your woman was taken indentured by a Captain Maybrick, a planter on the Chesapeake.'

'Maybrick?'

'Yes, I am sure of it. Captain Maybrick. The harbourmaster at Lynn had the lists and told me the name.'

'Ah.'

Then the world recedes; Van Hooghten disappears and I am with Captain Maybrick in the Ship Tavern. Captain Maybrick. When was it that he sought me out with those drawings? Eight or nine years ago, at least; and I sat there and looked at them, the drawing of the sluice especially, made of brick with wooden gates in the Dutch style. They were good drawings: precise and simple.

Oh, Eliza, you made those drawings. Of course you made them. You missed no detail of the sluice, and there it was on the paper, taking into account the tides in the particular place where you now live. Why did I not recognise the movement of your hand across the paper, not understand Maybrick's reluctance that I should go down there? Bellevue; it is a plantation on the James River that flows into the Chesapeake.

Maybrick was ashamed that his engineer was a woman. He came to me not knowing who I was and am. He did not want my services, since he had yours. He wished merely to know if your work was sound.

'Jan?'

I glance up to see Van Hooghten looking anxiously at me.

'I have brought back something you prefer not to remember.'

'No, indeed not, Jacob. It is a thing far away.'

'Is it of importance to you now, Jan?'

'Yes, and, no; something close and yet long gone.'

Van Hooghten laughs.

'You are still the same, Jan.'

He stands up and I stand too.

'May I return tonight, and send a boy with my things from the inn?'

'Of course, you need not ask. I will be very happy to have your company, Jacob.'

We move into the hall and I open the door for him. He pulls me to him and kisses me again, three times, in our manner.

'I have to hurry, but I look forward to the renewal of our friendship, Jan.'

'It was not lost. Nothing is ever lost, Jacob.'


When Van Hooghten has turned the corner into Begijn Gracht I climb the stairs to my garret and sit at the window. Gradually the sun goes down outside, while inside it seems to grow lighter. I am coming to the end of my history, or this relation of my past. You have not come, though you may, perhaps, on another visit. Instead Van Hooghten has come. He will be my guest and I his host as long as he stays here.

Long ago I came to understand that nature does not divide us up so simply, for we are all present in the other. Van Hooghten my guest is also my host, for he listens to me and brings forth from me much that has lain dormant for many years, and so carries that within him henceforth. No stranger then need be an enemy as many here have it. Every stranger may one day be my host and I his, each thus to carry the other through life. I am here, if anyone wants to find me: Jan Brunt, engineer.

Jan Brunt: but today I have another name in this new-city of New York. In English I am John Brown, and I like my simple name in that language, it being the name of any man. I am a man reluctant to obey and unwilling to command; neither a man of achievement nor one who seeks obscurity. I live with doubt and questions, observe the world and seek to understand it. I am its citizen.

Here I live, and here live Karl Carstensen, a Norwegian; Congo, once a slave; Thomas Fransen, a quarrelsome Hamburg merchant; Maria Jans, who sells liquor without a licence; the musician, Albert Pieterson, and his son Claes who runs about the streets barefoot; Asser Levy, a trader in cotton and silks; Lysbet Thyssen my house-keeper, widow of Maryn Andiessen; Abraham Lucena, a surgeon and my friend; William Sharp, a furrier. Here live two thousand others, in all conditions and states of content. Because they are here, it is a city, and a place where I feel safe.

I thought, until Jacob came, that here on Manatus Eylandt I had cast my anchor for the last time. I was secured to the bedrock, and found no need to go further than my work might take me, no need to sail the seas again. But this evening, as I look round my garret, at the note that still lies on my table and the figures on my hearth, I sense that another air has nosed its way into the house, and brought disturbance and possibility.

Jacob has come here, full of life, and rearranged the layers of the past. I told him no more than the truth when I said you were here and yet long gone. Wherever you are, dearest Eliza, in this city, or already travelled beyond its borders, you are always here within me, and I in you. Some day we must stand side by side and reckon with one another. Already my wings are opening, to the south.

# Acknowledgements

I have been incredibly fortunate to have had Chatto & Windus as my publisher for over twenty-five years, and to have had Jenny Uglow as my editor. Chatto has been a haven for me, a beacon of fine publishing and a place of encouragement and safety. Many years ago I met Jenny, perched in a tiny office, looking at the world with a wise and beady eye. I decided then and there that I wanted to work with her. How lucky I have been; always encouraging, astringent when necessary and a wonderful writer herself, Jenny has been my literary midwife, and constant friend.

Over the years Jenny has been helped by successive heads of Chatto; Carmen Callil, Jonathan Burnham, Alison Samuel and Clara Farmer. All of them have been at my side, none more than Clara Farmer, who has shown me a kindness and humanity that has gone way beyond any professional obligation. I am profoundly grateful to her.

In the wider Chatto and Random House family I would like to thank Parisa Ebrahimi, Juliet Brooke and Charlotte Humphery, who edited my manuscript with insight, generosity and flair. Mary Chamberlain copy-edited the finished book with immense patience and skill, Sarah-Jane Forder proofread the whole with admirable tolerance for my poor spelling, Stephen Parker designed the sumptuous cover, Graeme Hall guided the book through production and Lucie Cuthbertson-Twiggs took it into the world; many thanks to them all.

I'd like to thank my agents Gill Coleridge and, now, Clare Alexander. Over many years Gill has been my mainstay. As reader, friend and tenacious spirit she gave me the courage to carry on. Clare has read several drafts of this book, shepherded it towards its conclusion and helped me make it much, much better.

Simon Schama heard the whole story, was the first to read it and has been a fount of love, humanity and knowledge of all things seventeenth-century Dutch. Arthur Legger helped with Dutch words and Joel Carbonel accompanied me to the fens and shared with me his knowledge of plants and his great love of the natural world. Kind friends Nicholas Berwin, Deborah Cohen, Malcolm Gaskill, Lucy Heller, Claire L'Enfant, Elizabeth Locke, Romilly Saumarez Smith and Rachel Watson read the manuscript and suggested ways to improve it. I have also benefitted hugely from the discussions between historical novelists and historians at the Novel/History Salon; to Sarah Dunant, Juliet Gardiner, Philippa Gregory, Richard Davenport-Hines, Eva Hoffman, Alice Hunt, David Kynaston, Diane Purkiss, Rebecca Stott, Kate Summerscale and Anna Whitelock, my thanks.

To my friends from many countries and my children Grace and Lori, my love. This book is for Bob Schuck, who will always live in my heart.